Rules for Werewolves

Rules for Werewolves

A Novel

Kirk Lynn

MELVILLE HOUSE
BROOKLYN · LONDON

Rules for Werewolves

Copyright © 2015 by Kirk Lynn

First Melville House Printing: October 2015

Melville House Publishing   8 Blackstock Mews
46 John Street   and   Islington
Brooklyn, NY 11201   London N4 2BT

mhpbooks.com   facebook.com/mhpbooks   @melvillehouse

Library of Congress Cataloging-in-Publication Data
Lynn, Kirk.
    Rules for werewolves / Kirk Lynn. — First edition.
        pages ; cm
        ISBN 978-1-61219-476-9 (hardcover)
        ISBN 978-1-61219-477-6 (ebook)
        I. Title.
    PS3612.Y549R85 2015
    813'.6—dc23
                                        2015013933

Printed in the United States of America
10 9 8 7 6 5 4 3 2 1

For Carrie

Those who wanted milk scratched at the soil with bare fingers
and the white milk came welling up. Pure honey spurted,
streaming, from their wands. If you had been there and seen
these wonders for yourself, you would have gone
down on your knees and prayed to the god you now deny.

—*The Bacchae of Euripides*,
    translated by William Arrowsmith

Part One
BECOMING

1

Susan tells Bobert how to become a part of the pack.

—Hey, it's cool. I'm not gonna hurt you. I just wanna let you know you can't sleep there.

—Why not?

—It's gonna get cold tonight.

—I'll be all right.

—Yeah, but you could do a lot better.

—Says who?

—My name's Susan.

—All right. So?

—It's cool if you don't wanna tell me your name.

—All right.

—But you should also know there's a security guard who comes around.

—I'm not scared of rent-a-cops. They don't have any real power.

—You figured that out on your own, huh? How long you been out here?

—About a week. But I've been here before. You?

—Shit. I dunno. It's been months.

—My name's Bobert.

—What kind of name is Bobert?

—It's a nickname, I guess. I hate it.

—Then why tell people that's your name?

—I got so used to being called Bobert, I guess that's who I've become.

—You know, you could use this running away to become something else.

—I'm doing all right.

—You're in the parking lot huddled up between a Dumpster and the walls of a Speedy Stop. Without a roof. You're not doing as good as you think.

—I'm trying.

—I know, Bobert. It's cool.

—Do you have some kind deal with the Speedy Stop where they give you a free burrito for every homeless kid you scare away from the Dumpsters?

—I should ask 'em about that.

—Hey, you're not really helping. You're just doing the rent-a-cop's job for him. Telling me to move along. He might not even see me.

—He saw me when I tried to sleep there.

—I just. I don't. I don't. I don't know what to do. I . . .

—All right. All right. It's cool. Don't cry.

—I don't—

—All right. It's cool.

—I don't wanna get inside the Dumpster.

—Let me get to what I'm trying to say, Bobert.

—This sucks.

—Why don't you come with me.

—Why?

—Because.

—Where are we gonna go?

—I have some friends. They have a house. Not a house they own, but just a place where we can stay. There's about twenty of us sleeping there, maybe. Look, it's not legal. They don't own the house. But it's warm. It's warmer than this. And it smells better. You just have to go along with what they say.

—Like what?

—Nothing really. They just like to fight, some of 'em. Mostly it's

4

bickering. But if someone catches us in this house we have to be ready to run. And if one of my friends tells you to do something you have to do it. Or be sure you could win a fight against that person.

—What do you mean?

—You'll see.

—I don't want to come.

—It smells like shit inside that Dumpster, Bobert. And when I was in there, I thought it was the lowest I could go. But it's not. I'm not gonna tell you what lowest is. You wouldn't even look at me if you knew. But if you come with me then maybe this can be the worst for you and everything'll just get better from here.

—What kinds of things do people tell you to do at your friends' house?

—It's not like that. It's weirder than I can really explain. But you don't have to do anything you don't want to do. In fact, it could help you become someone who never does.

—Okay. All right.

—Don't cry.

—I know. I don't want to . . . Just let me get my bag. I'll get my bag, and then we can go, and I'll get myself behind a door and get warm.

—All right. You're gonna like these guys. It's like a family. Everybody sleeping in the living room. Watching out for one another. It's safe. And it's warm. And it's all ours until somebody finds out.

2

Don't answer the door.

—What's that sound?

—What?

—Something just woke me up.

—Did it sound like some asshole calling out, "What's that sound?" 'Cause I just heard it, too.

—Stop it. You guys are freaking me out.

—It was probably just the new kid, Bobert, trying to find his way around.

—He doesn't sleep in the den with the rest of us. Bobert sleeps in the pantry.

—How do you know, Susan? Did you go looking for some sugar?

—Shut the fuck up. I think someone knocked on the door.

—You sure?

—The sun's not even up yet.

—How would you know when the sun comes up?

—It leaks in around the edges of the curtains, like over there, by the stereo.

—There's the sound again. It *is* someone at the door.

—What should we do?

—Be quiet. Maybe they'll go away.

—Shhh. It's cool. It's cool. It's cool.

—I don't want to get caught squatting in these people's house and get sent to jail.

—I don't wanna get sent home.

—How many of us do you think there are right now?

—I dunno. Maybe twenty. Maybe more.

—Who cares?

—'Cause we can probably take 'em, unless they have twenty on their side, too.

—Who do you think it is?

—How should I know?

—Let's just be quiet and wait and eventually they'll go away.

—The house is empty.

—Except for us.

—Why would anyone knock on the door?

—It could be the paperboy . . . or a girl . . . selling Girl Scout Cookies.

—It's too early.

—Or it could be a neighbor with a gun who wants to protect his home from an infestation of us.

—Go up and look through the peephole.

—Fuck you. You go do it.

—Both of you—shhhhh!

—It's probably the cops 'cause you were screaming so loud last night.

—Malcolm started it.

—Let's go out the back door and over the fence and disappear forever.

—If it was the police and they knew this wasn't our house they would've shouted at us by now.

—And then kicked the door in.

—If it's not the police, then it's probably not anybody who knows we don't really belong.

—So?

—Go answer it and say you're the Baxters' cousin. Say they asked you to house-sit while the place was on the market.

—The Baxters' was the last place.

—Find a piece of mail or something that says whose house this is.

—Say you're the niece on summer break from Wesleyan and you needed a place to stay for a couple of days with a few friends and Uncle Baxter told you it was all right.

—Some of us are a little too old to be on summer break.

—You can be a grad student.

—And what am I?

—There's too many types of us to all be from the same lie.

—Whoever it is isn't going away.

—'Cause they can hear you talking.

—This isn't what I wanted.

—You don't even know what it is.

—I wanted to live with my friends.

—We're your friends.

—In a different way. I thought we'd have more to offer. To one another. I thought we could be an example of how to live without working by being more in tune with the earth.

—Take off your clothes.

—Why?

—That's why you couldn't answer the door right away—you just got out of the shower.

—I wish Doug was here.

—Don't move.

—I'm gonna go look through the peephole.

—Angel, don't.

—Don't be such a quivering shit.

—Angel—

—It's Malcolm. It's just Malcolm—

—I thought Malcolm was upstairs in the master bedroom with Tanya.

—Now he's out on the porch. Should I open it?

—What's he doing out there?

—Bleeding. From his face.

3

Malcolm, Tanya, Bobert, Anquille, Angel, and five or six more are talking.

—What happened to you?

 —Does it look bad?

 —Your face is bleeding.

 —Let me see.

 —Ow.

 —Shhh.

 —Go in the kitchen so everybody else can keep sleeping.

 —What happened?

 —I got hit by a car.

 —We've gotta get out of this neighborhood.

 —Not yet.

 —Someone musta seen it.

 —A dog, maybe.

 —They know we're here and everyone in the neighborhood hates us.

 —What were you doing out so early?

 —I felt like it was getting time to move so I thought I would do us all a favor and go scout a new area. It wasn't in my plans to get run over.

 —What kind of car was it?

 —A slow car. So I guess I'm lucky. It was at a corner. I was crossing the street and this car rolled up, real slow, as if it was gonna stop and wait for me to cross. 'Cept it didn't stop. It surprised me. I never expected to get hit by a car. And it just kept hitting me, almost gently, shoving me out into the intersection. You know how people say some accidents seem to happen in slow motion. Well, me, too. For real. It's like this car was fucking with me. Just pushing me and shoving me around. The same way a big kid would pick on a little kid at school. Except it was a rich person with a fancy car picking on me 'cause I was walking around so early—there was no one around to see the two of us. I was afraid it was a set up—like this car was gonna push me out into the intersection and then some other car was gonna come along and wipe me out. I started banging on the hood with one hand. Harder and harder and harder. Then the car finally accelerated and I fell down and that's when I got scratched up on my face like this. I guess my face hit the pavement, and my arm a little.

—Let me see you in the light.

—You smell weird.

—I'm sweaty.

—I'm worried we're all gonna be fucked by this one little mistake.

—I was just crossing the road.

—And now we're all fucked.

—We're not fucked.

—I wasn't doing anything wrong.

—I didn't say it was your mistake.

—We need to clean this out.

—There's still gravel in there.

—Jesus Christ, that's disgusting.

—There's, like, a flap.

—Somebody needs to turn into a doctor.

—I'll do it.

—Wait.

—Shut up in there! We're trying to sleep.

—Come with me to the bathroom.

—Wait! Jesus fucking Christ! Everybody wait for one second!

—

—I wanna show you something. Even though I got scratched on my face and my arm, I got this . . .

—What is that?

—Is that a hood ornament?

—It's a lion.

—What kind of car is it from?

—That's a Peugeot.

—What's a Peugeot?

—It's a French car.

—How do you know it's a Peugeot?

—I used to work at a mechanic's.

—You never worked at any mechanic's.

—I did.

—Like a job?

—They gave me money and I worked.

—You might've got paid by a mechanic, but I seriously doubt you've done a day's work in your life. You probably rolled yourself up under the car, rubbed oil all over your face, slept for two hours, then rolled back out and said, "I can't find anything wrong with this *Peugeot*."

—You're supposed to tell someone when you go out, Malcolm. And you're not supposed to go out alone.

—Last time I went out alone I found this place, didn't I?

—What are you gonna do with a hood ornament?

—I'm gonna put it on a chain and wear it around my neck.

—You're gonna look like some kind of ooga-booga tribe leader.

—Then, after the sun goes down, I'm gonna walk around the whole neighborhood and I'm gonna look for a car that doesn't have a hood or-nament and I'm gonna match up my hood ornament–necklace to their mistake.

—*Then* what are you gonna do?

—You know what I'm gonna do then.

—No, I don't.

—You're not gonna do anything stupid are you? I like this place. I don't want to have to move out.

—We have to move out, anyway.

—We should start being smart about it.

—You all know exactly what I'm gonna do when I find that Peugeot.

—No, we don't.

—We should have plans for getting out of a house the same way we do for getting in.

—If you really have no idea what I'm gonna do when I find that Peugeot, then just keep watching. 'Cause you will. 'Cause you're all gonna come with me.

—This is gonna be awesome.

—Oh shit.

—I'm gonna sharpen my hammer.

—First, one of you come with me to the bathroom and clean me up so I don't get infected. That's all y'all need is an infected tribal leader.

—Who says you're the tribal leader?

—I'll do it.

—Come on.

4

Malcolm wants to move.

I like walking through neighborhoods and looking at all the houses. I like comparing the lawns. I want the grass to be bright green and thick even while the rest of the world is in the middle of a drought or whatever. I want a tall fence.

I've never trusted the idea of neighbors. When I take a walk through a new neighborhood I'm thinking about moving into, I can see 'em looking at me through the cracks in their curtains. I don't know if it's me or them that's "suspicious." I don't know in which direction that word works best, given the situation. "The neighbors are suspicious of me." "I am a suspicious person." Maybe some words should come with arrows so you can tell which direction they're meant in.

Sometimes I steal a dog so it looks like I belong. Actually, I'm not sure if "steal" is the right word. I open the gate and let the dog come out if it wants. I take off my belt and use it as a leash. Not to control the dog and drag it toward dead ends and cul-de-sacs, but to protect it from dickweeds in Peugeots who refuse to stop for people they consider suspicious.

For that one motherfucker in that one Peugeot I'm willing to move out of "suspicious" into whatever word lives next door. If suspicious means you think I *might* be so dangerous that you need to run me over, I'm gonna move into a place where you know for sure, where you're gonna regret not doing a better job of keeping me down. If suspicious means I think I might be *capable* of doing something rotten, I'm gonna go ahead and become talented at some really awful skills. Bumping me with your car like I don't exist? Like I haven't been put on this earth to prosper, motherfucker?

I like walking through a neighborhood with a newly loosed dog as my scout. I like comparing the colors of paint the different husbands and wives have picked out. The colors tell you so much they practically sing. I can hear in the tones which colors were picked by compromise and which colors caused fights. I can hear the pigheaded husbands insisting on off-white or green or whatever. I can hear 'em saying, "If I'm gonna be doing the painting, I'm gonna be picking the color." I like to guess which reds and purples were picked by wives who wouldn't even listen to suggestions. "You can't even choose a tie to go with your fifteen-year-old blazer when we go out to eat once a month. Why would I let you pick the color of a house we have to wear every day?" Then there are the compromise colors: pale yellow, pale blue, slate gray. There's gay colors, too. And lonely, old single colors. And widowers. And brick.

If the dog likes a house I take note. I want to live in a house where a whole pack of us will feel comfortable. I want a big backyard. I wanna have cookouts and grill, and a pool would be nice. We haven't found a pool yet. I'm gonna tell everybody the Peugeot hood ornament is a good omen because "Peugeot" means "pool" in French.

That's a lie. Maybe. I don't know. I don't know what "Peugeot" means. It sounds like it could be a foreign word for "pool." It's probably just some normal Frenchfuck's name. But I still think it's a good omen. I was walking with a sweet dog when I got hit, like a little chocolate pit bull. The dog didn't get hit. While I got hit I was pounding on the hood with one hand and with the other I was pulling the dog out of the way. I musta dropped the leash when my face hit the pavement and the dog got away. That means I'm out a good belt. I gotta get another one before anyone starts to change on me. A good belt is a big part of everything we do. But when I let go of the dog—I caught a lion. So, maybe, in a way, the dog still helped me pick a good house. Because when we find the Peugeot, that's gonna be the house the dog picked out.

I like walking through a new neighborhood with a dog and imagining what the inside of each house looks like. In the morning when a mom or a dad leaves for work, or when one of the kids runs out to catch the bus, the door is open and you can take a quick peek down the front hallway. The morning is the time when the doors are opened the widest, in my experience. But in the early evening you can see through all the windows of the houses when the lights are on. Usually about 9:00 or 10:00 p.m. there might be nothing down a whole block but the lights of the TVs shining out the windows. If you go out on a big TV night, like when there's a premiere of a long-running action drama or the finale of a reality show, then all the TVs are in sync and you get a kind of light show—all the windows down the block turning the same colors in unison. GREEN, then RED, then YELLOW: that's the field and then the helmet and then the decal on the helmet of some fucker during the Super Bowl. On those nights the whole neighborhood glows in isolated unity. Except maybe that one house on the corner. That one house that has to be different from everybody else. That one house that wants to watch some news show. That one house that likes to read. That's always the house we pick. Because that house has the least contact with its neighbors. Or it's the house that's empty. The abandoned house. The house that wouldn't sell. We live in a lot of for-sale houses. In this market, that's a safe place to live for a long time. Usually we can stay a week or more until some Realtor shows up and calls the cops. Then we grab what we can carry and go over the back fence and run. Once we get busted in a neighborhood, that's it for that neighborhood, and we go off looking for a new house. I'm trying to stay one step ahead of that. You can lose people when you get busted and everyone scatters.

The best way to get into a house is to ring the doorbell. Ninety percent of the time they open the door. If it's a for-sale house there's a little blue box on the doorknob with a key in it you're supposed to only be able to get into if you know the combination. You can break that box pretty easily with a sharp hammer. Or a lot of times we just look under the obvious rocks in the garden where the old owner has left his or her extra key. But even if you get a for-sale house, you still need supplies, and the best place to get those is at a regular house. The way I think about it is: we'd hafta rob a bunch of different stores to get what we need to live, and why should we have to go to a bunch of different places and risk getting caught over and over again? So instead we just go to a regular person's house, a person with a regular family, because that family has already been to all those stores for us. The more regular the better. Loners and gay houses, widowers, for-sale houses and just-builts—that's where we wanna live. But average America is where the plenty is hidden. We pick someone from the neighborhood who can afford to water the lawn. We pick someone who has a minivan or a station wagon, who can carry a lot of stuff back from the stores in a single trip. We pick someone with a nice dog that hasn't been trained to bark at strangers.

We're misfits, a group of all ages, mostly younger than thirty, most of us able to pass like we're selling magazine subscriptions to earn points toward paying for a vacation to help us just say no to drugs. Sometimes we pretend we're Jehovah's Witnesses. We pick up a stack of *Watchtower*s at the Laundromat. Then we ring the doorbell. We divide up the rooms and someone does the garage for gas and tools, and two or three people do the kitchen for food and beer, and one person does the bedrooms for clothes and money, and one person is on "fun duty," just running through the house looking for movies and comics and music. And just recently we started to put one person on the bathroom for pills and first aid. We learned that one the hard way. Sorry, Doug. Sorry, Val. Y'all needed a lot more first aid than we thought. I need some, too, now that I got hit by that Peugeot.

5

Tanya takes Malcolm into the bathroom to have a good look at his face.

—Ouch.

—Hold still, baby. Your face is full of street. Or do you not want me to clean it good?

—My blood tastes like metal.

—Open this bottle for me.

—You wanna taste my blood?

—No way.

—Shit. What's in this bottle? It smells weird. Is that hydrogen peroxide or alcohol?

—I wanna surprise you.

—Give me something to bite.

—Like what?

—Like Vicodin.

—Sorry, baby. Somebody snuck in the kit and ate those a while ago. I think you're gonna have to settle for a washcloth.

—No thanks.

—You afraid one of us already used it?

—I'm afraid about six of us already used it.

—But it mighta been the ones who ate the Vicodin. They coulda used this washcloth to wipe off that Vicodin sweat. You could get a secondary buzz.

—Give me your shirt.

—Then what'll I wear?

—Come on. I'll be able to taste you. And smell you. That'll take my mind off all the pain you're about to inflict on me.

—All right. Fine. Here.

—You look good without your shirt. You should go around like this all the time.

—Do I look good enough to distract you from this?

—Jesus. Fuck. That stings.

—It's supposed to. That's how you know it's cleaning.

—Still . . .

—Bite the shirt and shut up.

—Owwwww.

—Don't bite a hole in it.

—Whoa.

—Just let the air hit it and dry it out.

—I'm gonna have a nice scar.

—You got blood all over their pretty yellow tile work.

—Don't clean it up. We're moving out soon enough.

—Give me back my shirt.

—I will. Hang on.

—Do you think they'll all come with you tonight to look for that car?

—You mean come with *us*. 'Cause I think *you'll* come with me. And yes. I think most of 'em will.

—I think Bobert will come with us. And Anquille.

—Angel's the one I'm worried about.

—You should tell whoever won't come with us to find a new house.

—We'll just leave 'em behind. We're gonna take over Monsieur Peugeot's house and anybody who isn't with us isn't gonna get the forwarding address.

—I hope this guy who hit you really is French and totally into French stuff.

—Like wine?

—Sure. But also like movies, and magazines, and music.

—You don't speak French.

—And I never will if I don't get exposed to it.

—You look funny saying that with your shirt off.

—Give it back.

—I will. Hang on.

—I never got to go anywhere before all this, and we're never gonna get to go overseas. If we really do get a French guy's house it would be like a weird vacation. To get to listen to his CDs and watch his movies. Maybe he'll have a couple of French kids and we can lock 'em in the basement and spend weekends with 'em, asking 'em questions and bringing 'em things we find and asking them the word for it.

—French-kiss me.

—You're a dork, Malcolm.

—So?

—All right, baby. Come 'ere.

Kiss. Kiss. Kiss. Kiss. Kiss.

—Ow. Even kissing hurts.

—You're right.

—What?

—Your blood does taste like metal.

—See? You can believe what I say.

—You goin' back to your tribe already?

—I don't want 'em getting any ideas while we're in here.

—They know we're an *us*.

—I don't want them getting the idea that I need a lot of doctoring.

—Give me my shirt.

—Here, take mine.

—It's all tore up.

—It'll look good on you.

—It's sweaty.

—You can get a secondary buzz . . . I'm the one that took the Vicodin. I took it with Bobert and Anquille.

—Where was I?

—You were watching *Snow Dogs* with Susan and Angel in the basement.

—Why didn't you come get me?

—I needed to bond with 'em. To keep 'em close to me.

—That's bullshit. You need to tell me straight.

—Maybe it's bullshit, maybe it isn't. You said they'll come with us tonight. Maybe it was 'cause I included them in the Vicodin?

—Next time include me, too.

—I will. If I can.

6

Bobert, Angel, Tom, Susan, and two or three others try to guess what's goin' on in there. Malcolm and Tanya come out when they least expect it.

—What the fuck do you think they're doing in there?

—He's turning into a werewolf and she's trying to stop him from doing it.

—The moon's not full.

—It doesn't have to be if you get hurt bad or if your life's in danger or if your soul mate's dying.

—You think the two of them are soul mates?!

—It'd be cool if they were.

—The only way to find out is to try and kill him and see if she changes.

—I'll volunteer to keep my eyes on Tanya if someone else will volunteer to try and kill Malcolm.

—I'd fucking love to.

—Why do you hate him, Angel?

—I don't hate Malcolm. I just wanna see how strong I am.

—If he's a werewolf, why didn't he change when the car ran over him?

—Who says he didn't?

—He survived being run over by a car, didn't he?

—He got hit. He didn't get run over.

—What's the worst thing you think you could survive?

—Out of what? Like the worst thing out of all possible things that could ever happen?

—That's a lot of things.

—I sometimes go without food for two or three days.

—I don't see what the big deal is about that.

—Then *you* do it.

—I could, but why would I?

—I go without food for two or three days because it gives me a special kind of strength. If I know there's food inside a house, I can punch my hand through a window and just not care that I'm gonna get cut. Or if I don't eat for a while, my fear of stealing goes away. I'll steal any kind of food, no matter what kind of assistant manager is watching me at the Safeway.

—If you have food why would you need to stop eating it to steal more of it?

—Because we have shitty food. We eat shit. We sometimes try to eat dog food. I have. That's shit. So sometimes I stop eating. You should have noticed that by now. Then, when I'm hungry enough I sneak off to a good food store and I steal whatever I want. And I've never been caught at it. When you get a real serious look in your eyes, which is what happens after two or three days, assistant managers won't say shit to you. They get scared.

—That's werewolf.

—What is?

—Oh, hey. Your face looks good.

—So does your shirt.

—Oh. I guess we got confused.

—I guess.

—What's "werewolf"? I heard you saying something was "werewolf."

—Yeah.

—Well, what? I want to know what's "werewolf."

—She is.

—You think?

—I do.

—How is Angel a werewolf?

—She says she doesn't eat sometimes for a long time to make herself hungry enough to steal. She doesn't eat the shitty food we have so she can steal real expensive food.

—You never brought any expensive food back to the house.

—I fucking eat it all right there.

—In the store you're stealing from?

—Sometimes. Or in the alley. Or in the bushes.

—You should bring it back to share. That's what I would do.

—Well, let's do it.

—What?

—Let's both not eat a few days and see who brings back the better food.

—All right. But not tonight. We both need our strength tonight. Tonight we're gonna go looking for that car.

—When was this decided?

—It was decided in the house meeting I'm calling right now. Wake everybody up and let's meet in the living room in five minutes.

—All right. But starting tomorrow neither one of us eats.

—Fine.

7

Angel is thirsty.

I started to not eat because I like to drink. The less you eat, the more bang for your buck you get per bottle. I started hanging out with these guys, these squatters who I'm living with now, at a party. I was shit-faced. I was walking home from a bar, and I was alone, I think because I pissed off the rest of my girlfriends. To be honest, I don't remember. All of a sudden in the middle of a pitch-black night, there was a door lit up full blast and all these guys were in it. It was open, so I went in.

I like drinking. I would pay to drink—even now. Even after I've sworn off money forever. If I ever get any money I'm gonna take one or two of these guys, the ones I think I can trust, and I'm gonna take 'em to a bar and buy 'em the time of their lives.

I think that's the only thing money's good for: determining what you really love. Because money's like a gem you have to mine for in the pits of hate. No one would go to work at a Walmart if there wasn't something else out in the world that she loved. Most people love security more than anything, so they spend most of their money on a house or an apartment. A lot of people love other people, so they spend their money on them. Everybody says they love nature but it's very rare to find somebody who actually loves horses or birds or something like that, at least loves them in any real way.

Take for instance what we find when we break into a house. We find house stuff. We find clothes and DVDs and shit like that. What I would love would be to break into a house and find it lined, wall to wall, with little statues of all the breeds of horses. Every little statue on its own little shelf with a label on the wall explaining the Latin name and the things this horse was bred to achieve for mankind. Every room just filled with kinds of horses. A connoisseur's house. I don't know if there are that many kinds of horses. But they could be grouped thematically. Plow horses and agricultural horses in the kitchen. Dray horses and cart horses in the garage. Quarter horses and Thoroughbreds and entertainment horses grouped around the walls of the living room, facing a TV they keep on 24/7 that'd play the greatest horse movies of all time. Maybe we're not squatting in the right neighborhoods for that sort of thing. But I want to find some house where someone has just given her life over to something. Any one thing. Something one degree from ordinary—only one. It could be first editions of mystery novels with all the clues underlined in red. I don't care. But we need to find a new, awesome house, because all the ones we've been finding have way too much in common.

I don't know how long I'll be here. We find beer every once in a while. Or we break into some stupid family's house and clean 'em out while they're down mining in the pits of hate. There's a lot of talk about what to do when we take over a family. What to do with the dad and mom. How to take the kids into another room. How to use the mom against the dad and vice versa. But it's all bullshit. We never break into a house when the family is home. I think we *should* take a house with a family—then we'd have cable. Malcolm says they do sometimes take a house with a family. When I say, "When?" he says, "Before your time." But when I ask around it must have been before everybody's time 'cause nobody remembers it, ever. Malcolm's been around the longest. That's why he's the leader. But when I'm the leader we're gonna use some of my ideas.

Sometimes I go out on the weekends and wander around looking for a party. If I find a party I just go in and say, "I'm a friend of John's." Everybody knows a John. My name is Angel but if somebody at the party asks my name, I tell them, *Tanya*. That's Malcolm's girlfriend's name. I don't tell 'em that because I want to be her, but because if word gets out that some crusty-punk girl is crashing parties in the neighborhood and it gets back to us, I don't want it to be me that gets in trouble.

I used to make whole sets of rules before I walked into a party. *I'm just gonna drink beer. I'm not gonna stay for more than twenty minutes. I'm gonna let my body be my clock and make myself leave as soon as I have to pee.* But it didn't matter how many fucking rules I made. If I step foot into a party I'm gonna go all the way through it. I'd rather be a woman who's true to her word than one that lives by wishing.

Maybe a party is a mine shaft, too. I feel like I can find a vein of fun and dig it out of anybody. Everybody. I'm the one that gets a gang of four or five boys doing shots. Or I can find the girl who wants to dance but is just waiting for somebody else to start dancing. I like slamming some baggy-jeaned fuck's beer on the table and yelling "SUCK IT!" so he has to if he doesn't want to get covered in foam. I have a talent for flipping through the bullshit CDs on the rack and finding the one song that's perfect for that moment on earth. That sort of thing. It'd be my calling if the world really rewarded that kind of talent. But above all, I love to drink and I can find the liquor. If we're squatting in a new house I can tell which baseboard the sixteen-year-old hid his Southern Comfort behind. I can tell which high cabinet Mom keeps the sherry in. I can think in the mind of the member of the household who hides the hooch. Every time.

Back to this one party, the party where I met these guys I squat with. This was a few months ago. I'd broken away from who I was with before and drifted off alone into the night. I wandered into this party and just got loose. I was wild on some sangria they were letting us scoop out of a huge bowl with a huge clear plastic dipping spoon. The spoon had a really odd long curve to it and it rattled nicely in the bowl when you dropped it back in. I don't think the sangria was on the up-and-up. I think there might have been some Everclear in it, or some sappy-sweet Boone's Farm or some fortified bullshit. I don't remember the taste. It got me totally unhinged, though. I remember deciding to take that spoon and use it to break every wine glass in this big china cabinet. A couple of guys thought that was funny and started throwing beer cans in support of my effort. Full cans of beer were whizzing past me and breaking shit in the china cabinet all around me and I was swinging that spoon like a sword. A couple of full beer cans hit me in the back and somebody nailed me in the back of the head and eventually I realized I was just holding the handle of the spoon. The bowl of the spoon and most of its curve had broken off.

Later I remember falling down into the open fridge and laughing my ass off about it on the kitchen floor. I remember the owner of the house, some dude in a white polo golf shirt, yelling at me and slapping me. I told him I didn't care and he slapped me harder. And I remember pretty clearly this moment in which he realized I *really* didn't care and he could slap me as hard as he wanted. It became a sort of science experiment. I have a crystal clear memory of it. This young man who wasn't even angry anymore in a white polo shirt and tan shorts who had been given permission by a certain amount of wicked sangria and broken glass and the chanting of the crowd to hit a woman as hard as he wanted. He got into it in a way that was a lot more dangerous than anger. And then I remember some other big bear of a partygoer coming in and just flattening the polo shirt in one punch and pulling me out of there.

I woke up on the lawn. This giant bear on top of me. I knew he had at least *tried* to fuck me. I had a little bit of hope he had passed out before he could manage to come. I started wiggling out from under him and I was almost away when he grabbed me by the ankle. He grabbed me by the ankle and pulled me back. It was six in the morning. We were on some really soft-grassed suburban lawn. I kicked the bearman who had saved me and now wouldn't let me go with one of my bare feet, but he just grabbed me more tightly. The more I kicked him the more he woke up and the tighter he held onto me. He rolled over so I could see his face and he was fucked-up. He had a big scab on the corner off his mouth. I don't know if it was some sort of cold sore gone wrong or an actual injury he maybe got at the party that was starting to go bad. But it wasn't the sort of face you want on somebody who you're pretty sure has fucked you. He started pulling me back by the ankle and then put his other arm around my hip and he had a good hold on me. So I stabbed him with the handle of the spoon. I still had the plastic handle. That was a major lesson for me. Hold on to your weapons. I stabbed him over and over again until he let go. And then I ran. I ran until I couldn't run and then I walked. My feet were fucked-up. And all of a sudden somebody called out to me. It was someone standing in the living room of a house with a FOR SALE sign in the front yard. All the windows were open and he was saying, "Hey come 'ere." He recognized me from the party. There were about eight or nine of them in there. One of the girls noticed I was leaving bloody footprints on the carpet. They had a kit with first aid in it. The guy said he was just telling a story about me, about how wild I got last night at that party. He was telling them about all the stuff I broke with that spoon. I held up the handle to show him that I still had it. Then I asked him if I could borrow his pillow. He was holding a black nylon cylinder that looked like some kind of couch cushion. He said it was a sleeping bag. I said, "That's fine." He said, "Let me ask Malcolm." I didn't have anywhere else to go. And that's it. That's that story.

8

Bobert, Anquille, Susan, Angel, and Tom decide the hat is a god.

—You guys'll do anything he tells you to, won't you. That wasn't even a meeting. It was just Malcolm fucking bossing us around.

—You cuss too much, Angel.

—Fuck you.

—I don't wanna have any more meetings.

—Then how are we gonna decide what to do?

—Do whatever you want.

—We should elect a leader.

—Fuck voting. Voting is just a fist the majority uses to beat up on minorities.

—Yeah, fuck voting.

—Then what are we gonna do?

—I say we write down every single thing we can think of to do, forever, and we put all those ideas in a hat and then every morning we pull an idea out of the hat and then do whatever it says.

—What if we write "Go lie in the sun" and it's raining outside?

—First of all, who's gonna write "Go lie in the sun," Susan? Why not write "Live inside a fucking Chevrolet commercial." And second of all, fuck the weather. If we do write "Go lie in the sun," I'm not gonna ask the weather if it's all right if I live my life. I'm gonna go lie in the sun no matter what it's like outside.

—This is perfect. This is totally perfect.

—What if I write "Fuck the hat system, let's vote on shit."

—Then that's what we do for that day.

—This is perfect. I'm gonna write "Go home and go back to the way you used to live."

—Shut up. Listen. Fucking idiot. I wanna go home sometimes. But the hat is perfect because I don't want to go back permanently. I just wanna go see my little brother. Just for one day. Make sure he's all right.

—If you go back home, Bobert, your mom is gonna tie you to your bed and bring in a psychologist to ask you why you want to live like an animal.

—I got away once. I can get away again. My family isn't a kind of trap that can keep me locked up forever.

—Leave him alone.

—What are you two, Susan? A fucking "mated pair"?

—Leave 'em both alone.

—This is cool. I say let's do it. The hat. Just for one day.

—All in favor, raise your hand.

—Ow. What was that for?

—Fucking raising your hand. We're not voting. We're just doing it. Don't do it if you don't want to.

—All right.

Scribble. Scribble. Scribble. Scribble. Scribble.

—All right. Now someone pick one.

—This is so cool. I'll pick one.

—What's it say?

—"Go steal a bunch of beer from the Speedy Stop and get drunk!"

—The hat is a god!

—Let's do it.

—I don't know if this a good idea.

—Don't be a fucking coward, Bobert.

—You're just as bad as Malcolm, Angel.

—You're just as bad as a soap opera, Susan. Mooning over your little boyfriend. Staying behind to protect him.

—I'm not staying behind. It sounds cool. But if Bobert wants to stay then let him.

—Bobert?

—I'm staying here.

—Suit yourself. But the hat is a god. It's going to punish you if you don't do what it says.

—I think I'll be all right.

—We'll see.

9

Malcolm and Bobert talk about games. Later, the others come home.

—Where is everybody?

　—You don't want to know.

　—If you know, Bobert, tell me.

　—Don't get all bossy on me.

　—You don't mind me getting all bossy on you when I find a new house. When I find a stack of video games. When I find you a TV.

　—I was playing that.

　—Sorry. I accidentally turned your game off. But I wanted to have a conversation. I wanted to know if you knew where everybody was. Don't answer. The reason why I ask is because I know where everybody is and I want to know if it upsets you that they left you behind.

　—No, I told 'em I didn't wanna do it.

　—Didn't wanna do what?

　—I thought you knew.

　—I do. I'm just trying to make conversation.

　—You have no idea where everybody is and you're trying to get me to tell you.

　—Everybody else is out in the fresh air. Everybody else is getting their exercise. While you sit and rot playing these infernal games.

　—Stop fucking with me. My whole life is people fucking with me.

—This is a baseball bat.

—So?

—I'm trying to put your behavior in context.

—Leave me alone.

—This baseball bat—this simple, stupid piece of wood—is what games used to look like. A lot of people call the baseball bat the first Nintendo. They do. It used to be that if people wanted to play a game they had to pick up one of these.

—They woulda called it the first Atari or the first Nimrod. Nintendo wasn't the most ancient video gaming system.

—You know a lot about this stuff.

—It's what I'm into.

—It's good to have a hobby. I do.

—Fine. We both have hobbies. Now, let me get back to mine.

—You didn't ask what my hobby is—

—Get out of here.

—You know, I bet that's where everybody is. They're all at the park and they're playing "catch" with their "mitts" and "caps" and other bullshit words from the 1830s. They're probably having a "tourney." That's the way things were in the good ol' days. And people say our generation never gets any exercise?! They say all we do is hide in the dark and play—what is this? Legend of Zelda! Is it good?

—Stop.

—I just want to know if it's good.

—You know I like it.

—I know.

—Then let me have it back.

—Tell me about it.

—No.

—I'm not going to let you alone until you tell me about it.

—Fine. Zelda is a princess who's been captured by Ganon, that's the bad guy's name. Zelda is beautiful and good and Ganon is manipulative and bad. And the person playing the game is named Link. I think it's because you're the "link" between this world and Hyrule, which is Zelda's world. Basically, the whole game is just wandering through the forest looking for the Triforce pieces, which are courage, wisdom, and power.

These pieces give you the strength to turn Hyrule into a good place and get Zelda back and make her happy. And that's it, basically. But there's like seven different versions of the game so far. So little stuff changes in each version. Like sometimes Link has a partner.

—And because of this game they think you're such a dork that they didn't invite you to the park to take part in their "three-legged races"?

—I just want to stay here and play this.

—You know why they call them "three-legged" races?

—When you guys move on. I'm not going with you. I think I'm gonna go back home for a while.

—You're not gonna be invited to go with us when we move on, Bobert.

—They practically begged me to go with them. They said if I didn't go I would be disrespecting their god.

—Who's their god?

—That hat.

—That's my hat. I've been looking for that hat.

—It's Susan's hat.

—Are you in love with Susan?

—Just leave it alone.

—Fine. I won't touch it. But I do wanna explain to you the reason they call it a "three-legged" race. The way it works is they release one person, like you, and that person is known as "it," and then everybody else chases that person, trying to get him, and while everybody is running, trying to catch you, they're all getting sweaty and worked up, and sometimes, one or two of the dudes will get an erection from the excitement and that's why they call it a three-legged race.

—They're at the Speedy Stop.

—No. They're at the park. I know it. That's why there's no ball. There's no gloves. Just this bat.

—They're gonna try to lift some beer and get drunk.

—I don't know how to bridge the divide between you and them. How can I get some sort of conversation going between a bunch of old-world, conservative, fuddy-duddies who want to play baseball in the park and a cutting-edge, cyberpunk kind of guy like you who wants to stay home and play video games? How can I get this bat to interact with your TV? The TV that I found for you? Maybe I should try something like this—

Smash. Smash. Smash. Smash. Smash.

—What are you doing?!

—Oh hey, you're back. Bobert and I were just talking about you guys.

—This is why everybody thinks you're a dick, Malcolm.

—Everybody thinks I'm a dick because that's my hobby.

—You're good at it.

—I'm just glad you got home safe.

—And we brought beer.

—For the whole house.

—Give me one.

—Fuck off, Malcolm.

—No. Give him one.

—This is good. What kind is it?

—Read the label.

—I can't. I'm too busy looking after all of you.

—We're the ones that got beer.

—What did you pay for it?

—We didn't pay anything.

—We don't have any money.

—Then I guess you have to pay in Zeldas and TVs. That's what it cost you. But that's cheap. It could have cost you this whole house.

—We didn't get caught.

—Yet. But you know they have video cameras in those stores.

—So?

—So now they've got a picture of you. They can send out those pictures to all the cops in this patch zone. That's how our cops split up the city, into "patch zones"— the zone into which a call is patched. You get it? Now they can start looking for you. It gives the cops something to do while they drive around. They can look out the window and look at the kids in the park playing ball until they get a match. That's the game the cops play.

—We'll lay low.

—Nothing helps you lay low like beer, huh?

—We'll stay in.

—So now you're too scared to go out looking for that Peugeot with me, huh?

—We're not scared.

—Good.

—Isn't it just as dangerous to go after Peugeots and to squat in houses and live off the shit we steal from other houses?

—There's no video cameras in houses. And when we break in a place to scavenge I never give us more than five minutes. If you follow my instructions and take everything you get your hands on there's no fingerprints that way. And when we leave a house and find a new place I go back in the middle of the night to the old place and burn it down.

—You do not.

—I always tell the truth. For instance: this is really, really good beer.

—Fuck off.

—I think you should all have some. It'll put you all in a good mood. It'll get you all a little wild. That way, when we go out tonight, maybe we can find that Peugeot. We can put your good moods and your extra energy to use. After the sun goes down. So let's have some fun until then.

10

What's the worst thing you could survive?

—Living here. Getting bossed around all the time.

   —Living in an apartment and going to work at IBM.

   —I think being held in a cage, being watched, no matter what I did.

   —Finding out that I'd been watched and videotaped the whole time I was in college after it was over.

   —You mean like videos of you online doing everything you did in college?

   —Oh god, that's a nightmare.

   —It's not what you can't stand. It's what's the edge of what you could survive.

   —Living here.

   —I think I could survive being shocked. I don't like it. But I've survived it from electrical outlets and stuff.

   —I think I could survive being in solitary confinement for a long time. Not forever, but I think I could do years.

   —I guess I know I can survive being raped. Or I can go on. Whatever. Shit, that was dumb to say. I thought I could just say it. But I guess I don't want to talk about it.

   —I think I could survive on eating the same thing every day for the rest of my life.

   —Oh, that's good. What's the worst food you could survive on?

—I think if I was hungry enough I could eat anything.

—You think you could kill a neighborhood cat and eat it?

—I think I could.

—Imagine you have to hunt dogs and cats for food.

—Can I use a weapon?

—You can only use a fork.

—That's gross.

—I would hunt from the roofs. I would climb up there and just crouch and wait. Then when a dog or a cat came under me I would jump down on them and crush their backs with my feet.

—Have you thought about this before?

—I just made it up.

—You think you could go totally wild and eat a cat raw?

—If I had to I could.

—I don't think we know half of what we would do if we had to. Human beings have a lot of untapped potential. We're smart enough in five seconds to think up a roof advantage over dogs to break their backs but we never have to use that part of our brain. It just sits there, waiting and waiting for the opportunity.

—Until something comes along that wakes us up and all of a sudden we start thinking and doing things we never could do.

—That's what this is. Living like this. We're waking up that part of brains on purpose instead of waiting for the plague or whatever happens next in history. That's what makes us werewolves.

—What else?

—I think I could survive never going out into the world again. I think I could live in a box and just get food slipped in under the door.

—All right. Imagine you live in a room with nothing to do. No TV. No anything.

—Is there a toilet?

—Sure.

—Because otherwise where does all my shit go? It would just pile up.

—There's a toilet.

—But that's it. Nothing on the walls. No books. You get fed once a day through a slot in the wall.

—Give me a beer.

—Go slow. We're running low.

—The sun's coming down.

—And the moon is rising.

—What would you do in this imaginary room if there was nothing to do?

—I would do push-ups and sit-ups. I would pace.

—I would make up stories. A different story every day. I would make up stories about why I was there. And who was keeping me.

—I would just assume I was in some sort of zoo and I was being watched and I would try to act normal.

—What does that mean?

—Just normal.

—Show me.

—Okay. Watch.

—

—You're a fucking dork.

—It's a little bit scary.

—Watch.

—

11

Everybody goes out hunting through the neighborhood for a Peugeot.

—I want everybody to meet back here. No matter what. At midnight.

    —It's dark.

    —It's a new moon. You can't see it but it's up there.

    —Shouldn't we make a plan, baby?

    —Like what?

    —Divide up into four groups and each pick a different direction.

    —Just use your instincts. You don't have to cover a certain number of blocks or anything. Don't try to run through the whole neighborhood. You're just out for a walk. You can go whichever way you want.

    —Then why are you talking to us like a coach?

    —Cover as much ground as you can. You can go in whatever teams you want to. Go alone or in pairs. I mean obviously we don't want to all walk down the street together in the same direction. Some go some way and some another. If you find the Peugeot missing its hood ornament come back here.

    —So we're all just supposed to wander through a pitch-black neighborhood and keep our eyes peeled for something that's not there.

    —Pay attention. If you see the cops, don't automatically run. They'll chase you if you run. Just wait and see if the cops are even interested in you. If they question you, tell 'em you're looking for a party. If they ask where, tell them 732 Glenwood Springs. That's on the other side of River Oaks. That's important. If they turn on their lights or get out of the car— then you run. If you have to run from the cops go into backyards, start jumping fences. Cops can't jump fences. And don't stop running. Don't ever think you can hide. They want you to hide so they can catch up. That's how you get away from the cops.

—How do we know when it's midnight?

—Who wears a watch?

—Not me.

—Not me.

—Fuck.

—We can look in through people's windows at their clocks.

—Like that won't attract the attention of the cops.

—Why are you so obsessed with the cops, Malcolm?

—Because you fucking stole beer from the corner convenience store four hours ago, you dumb fucks. It only takes one little mistake for this whole thing to be over. You only have to get the cops just a little interested in us. Or the neighborhood association. Or the fucking dogcatcher.

—All right. Chill out.

—We're squatting in houses. This isn't gonna last forever. Some of us get to go back home and some of us will go to the settlement house. But we only have as long as we're smart. We only have as long as we can get along.

—How about we just use our best judgment about midnight and we look for watches in the future?

—And I'm not obsessed with cops. I'm just trying to be careful.

—All right. All right.

—But if you do get any attention from the cops, if you do have to run and hop fences and all that, do it in the opposite direction. Run away from this house. All right. We can't all meet up back here if there's a bunch of cop cars here. All right?

—You're totally obsessed.

—Fuck off.

—Stop it.

—You're messing up my fucking hair.

—Your hair?!

—Fuck off.

—We're looking for a psychopath who runs over people like us!

—I'm not. I'm fucking out of here.

—What do you think we're gonna do to this Peugeot guy when we find him? It's gonna mess up more than your hair. This is our first hunt. And you're walking away like a fucking kid.

—Leave him alone.

—He'll come back.

—He'll probably be the one who finds the Peugeot guy.

—So we're really gonna do it? We're really gonna fuck this Peugeot guy up?

—Just come back here when you find him. Don't try to be a hero and check out his house or disable his security system or anything you see from the movies. Don't do anything to tip him off. Just come back here and we'll all go after him as a pack.

12

Bobert, Tom, and Anquille go around to the other side of the school.

—Do you think it's midnight yet?

　—I think it's like nine p.m. I think we've only been walking for five minutes.

　—Jesus, we'll cover the whole city by midnight.

　—I think that's the idea.

　—Let's head up to the school. We can sit on the swings or something.

　—Like little pendulums on a clock to pass the time.

　—I don't even wanna find the thing we're looking for.

　—Yeah.

　—I had what I wanted.

　—Yeah.

　—Legend of Zelda could have kept me going for weeks.

　—I liked playing it, too.

　—I like to get high and make myself believe that video games and movies are real.

　—That's a good idea.

　—My house, my living situation, was always shit. You're older, it's different.

　—Not always, Bobert.

—I have a stepdad.

—Yeah, I guess you get rid of those when you move out.

—But if I have to go back home that's what's waiting for me.

—What's his deal?

—Typical shit.

—What?

—You know.

—I don't.

—He's just an asshole.

—What? Does he beat you up? Or make you suck his dick?

—Neither.

—Why won't you tell us?

—He doesn't make me touch it. He just jacks off while he looks at me. He makes me stand there and watch him. And I'm not allowed to move or say anything. He likes to come in my bedroom at night. But he'll also do it if he catches me on the toilet or just sitting there watching TV.

—What if he catches you sharpening your machete? I bet that would make him think twice.

—I never told anybody.

—You have to tell people.

—I know. I just can't.

—You told us.

—Yeah. I guess.

—It wasn't so bad, Bobert, was it?

—I survived.

—And we don't think you're disgusting, or a freak, or a pussy. We're glad you're here with us. We're glad you got out of that shit.

—I have a little brother.

—Is he still at home?

—For another six years.

—Unless he becomes a werewolf.

—I guess he gets by the same way I used to.

—How's that?

—Whenever I got my hands on a comic book I heard this little voice in my head, like a carnival barker, saying, "Step inside. Step inside."

—So you pretend the TV or the movie screen is just like a portal through which we can watch what's happening in this other world?

—I don't pretend it. I try to make myself believe it. I want it so bad. I can almost do it without getting high.

—Then you would be crazy.

—But if you could control your craziness, wouldn't it be a good thing? If you could adapt your reality to the situation, you'd be the perfect animal—unstoppable.

—But that's impossible—*controlling your craziness*. The whole point of craziness is being out of control of your thoughts.

—My mother and father are the King and Queen of America. It's a secret. Not even I know it—or I'm not supposed to. But when they die, I'm gonna inherit the whole earth. They were so worried about how I would rule, they were so uptight about how they should raise me, they went a little overboard on the discipline. So I ran off. But when we get caught, or however it ends, you all are gonna go to jail, but I'm gonna be taken back to the White House—

—Caesars Palace. Or Trump Tower. The King and Queen of America would live somewhere fancier than the White House.

—and my mom and dad will reveal to me their true nature and apologize for how shitty they were to me.

—Then you can give us pardons.

—Maybe. Some of you. And even if I don't go back to the White House—even if they put me in jail with the riffraff to teach me a lesson, I can just make myself believe I'm in paradise and the food is perfect and I'm secret royalty.

—It's kind of like a total "Fuck You" to the whole world. You can say to the cops, "Put me in my chariot and take me to my palace." And if you said it over and over again, eventually they would.

—The only thing you have to give up to be perfectly happy is hope. Any hopes you have that you really could be the president, or that you could be the ruler of your own video game empire you invented—you would have to give that up.

—Believing in yourself is the only thing that stands between you and paradise.

—Can you keep a secret?

—I'm not gonna tell anybody.

—Not about that. I want you to promise. If we find the Peugeot, can we please ignore it and say we didn't?

—We would get in so much trouble.

—Not if no one ever found out.

—Well, no one would ever find out from me.

—Then look right there.

—What?

—Up in that driveway. The house right across the street from the elementary school. What kind of car is that?

—Holy shit.

—That's a Peugeot, isn't it?

—It's hard to tell because it doesn't have a hood ornament.

—But look at the dents in the hood. He must have been banging it pretty hard.

—Banging what pretty hard?

—The hood of that car.

—I don't see any car.

—Me, neither.

—All I see is a like a portal to hell. A portal that drags people into a big fight and puts some of us in jail and some of us back with our families and just destroys everything.

—We're gonna wanna stay away from that.

—Yeah. Let's go back around to the other side of the school and take a left this time and keep looking.

13

Angel and Susan make a drink for a new recruit.

—Look, it's a party. Look at all the people. All the fucking clothes and hair.

—I wish we had cool friends.

—We do. We are cool. You wanna go in and get a drink?

—We shouldn't.

—If we lived by "we shouldn't," we'd still be single-cell slime balls. Let's climb up out of "we shouldn't" and start walking around on the two legs of "why not?"

—This is a bad idea.

—No. Fuck. Just follow me in. We're not even gonna ring the doorbell. Just act like you belong. Look, there's people all over this house. There's more out in the backyard. There's no guest list. I always figure at any party like this there's three or four people like me who don't belong.

—What if somebody talks to you?

—We'll talk to them first. Like this. Watch— Hey, excuse me. Excuse me! I'm looking for a guy named John? John told me to meet him here.

—I think he's in back.

—You want me to make you a drink from some of this?

—Sure.

—I'm making you something of my own design. You, me, and my friend Rachelle. Rachelle, meet . . .

—Craig.

—Hi, Craig. We can only stay for a little while.

—We can only stay for one drink. But what a drink it's going to be! Do you have a bottle opener?

—Here. There's one on my key chain. But you're not putting beer in that, are you?

—Oh, nice key chain, Craig.

—What's *your* name?

—Tanya.

—What do you call this drink, Tanya?

—It's a drink I like to call the werewolf.

—You gonna make me howl at the moon?

—Is that a come-on?

—No.

—It's a shitty come-on, if it is.

—You take it how you want to.

—And you take this and drink it all up and you'll be a changed man.

—One who doesn't make shitty come-ons?

—You too, Rachel.

—Rachelle.

—We'll pound ours with you and then we'll be changed into women who don't care.

—You want us to drink the whole thing at once?

—What do you think? Now: go!

Drink. Drink. Drink. Drink. Drink.

—Oh, god, that's awful.

—The second one tastes better. Give me your cup.

—I'm like a time bomb now. I still feel sober, but I've got a pint of alcohol in my gut waiting to get into my bloodstream!

—I'll make us one more round.

—No. You said we could go after one.

—Come on.

—I can't drink like you can, Angel.

—I thought you were Tanya?

—The drink changed me into an Angel, and I came down to earth to give you a kiss.

—Now who's making shitty come-ons?

—Tanya, let's go find John, like we said we would.

—What time is it, Craig?

—It's ten thirty.

—That's a nice watch.

—Thanks.

—All right. Let me make these drinks and then we'll go find John and then we'll go before it gets too late. We've got plenty of time until midnight.

—What happens at midnight?

—Sorry, Craig, but Tanya and I have another party to go to.

—Maybe we'll take Craig along?

—No. You said this would be simple. You said we could have one drink and go.

—The one drink made me change my mind.

14

Bobert likes to be alone

I like to be alone. When we get a new house I like to find a walk-in closet or pantry I can claim for my room. I've been with them for three houses but they still call me the new kid. No one else we've picked up has really stuck. In the first house I just slept in the living room with everybody else. Almost everybody sleeps in the living room together. If there's beds, we drag all the mattresses out and push them side by side. If there's not we just put our sleeping bags on the floor. We leave the TV on all the time. Malcolm and Tanya take a room together. Sometimes another couple will form and drift off into the house somewhere. Every once in a while you wake up and a couple is forming right there on the living room floor. It's a kind of weather that passes through the group. Susan took me upstairs in the last house. The next day the storm passed and she treated me like any other guy. She went back to the living room and I went back to the pantry.

I like to have a door. I believe in doors. Doors are the greatest invention known to man. Before doors there were no families. A caveman could walk into your cave in the middle of the night and take your wife. Or he could come in and take your whole family. He could carry your son out to the forest and hold him down by the neck and if the boy made a sound it would only attract the dinosaurs who would eat the both of them. No one loved anyone before the invention of the door, because what was the point in loving something that could be taken away at any moment? You might as well fall in love with a single moment from a single day.

When I lived at home no one was allowed to lock any doors. That's a rule that Donald made. And he walks around the house and checks. It doesn't matter whether you are going to the bathroom or trying to have a private phone call or if you want to try to talk to Mom again about what Donald has done. You can't lock the door. And if you do, if Donald tries the bathroom door and it's locked, he will start banging and he won't stop until you open it. If he finds your bedroom door locked in the middle of the night he will start banging on it even if it wakes up everyone in the house. He wants to know what you've got to hide. And Mom believes him. She said, "If you've got nothing to be ashamed of then you don't need to lock your door."

One of my best tricks was to start locking doors and shutting them without me in the room. Then I would leave the house and go check out new comics at Dragon's Lair. Donald would start banging and kicking and screaming and there was no answer. I wasn't ever brave enough to do that when I was in a room. But for a while he must've thought I was getting really brave. It was fun to come home and walk past him like nothing. I would get my ass beat, but it was fun. Then once I came home and he had kicked in the bathroom door and no one was in there. Mom let Donald ground me for that trick, and I had to give up money from my savings to help pay for the new door. And Donald definitely paid me back.

Also I snore really bad. So I want to have a door between me and everybody else here. Nobody has said anything about it, but I wake myself up with it when I'm around others. In the first house there was a guy who minded—Dan. Dan isn't around anymore. I guess he went back home. People come and go. I think the big majority of us just met other ones of us hanging out on the street or at a canned food giveaway. Susan found me in the alley. When a new one comes in, he or she usually still has a good phone. Then we might pick up another new recruit from a text message or the newcomer might call one or two close friends and say if things are cool here. I always try to borrow a phone and call my brother and leave a message, which is also a way to let my mom know I'm all right and to let my stepdad know I'm still alive and still building my strength in order to kill him. But pretty soon the battery dies or the unpaid bill ends it.

We don't charge our phones. We don't take showers. We don't comb our hair. We don't wash our clothes. We don't brush our teeth.

We wipe our asses when we shit and that's about where hygiene ends for us. There is a look we're going for, and a smell, and a taste. We want to become rotten. We want to look wild. You get a kind of respect from it. People don't fuck with you. People don't even look at you. Even if you're a little guy. People can tell that you're not normal, that you don't play by the normal rules. So they can't assume that you won't growl at them if they make eye contact, that you won't rip their arm off if they tap you on the shoulder.

I wish we were vampires instead of werewolves. I think I would like a room the size and shape of a coffin. I read that hotels in Japan are like that, only a little bigger. I wish I could go to Japan. I would like to have just exactly what I needed and no more and no less. This is my only set of clothes. When we do finally do our laundry, when it finally gets to be too much and one of us has dog shit on our clothes or something we just can't stand, I walk around the house in a blanket. I feel like a sheikh. I don't know what I'm gonna eat tomorrow. Sometimes I steal a book from a house and that is my whole library for a while. I read it and reread it. I like being able to touch all the walls of a room at the same time. I like being able to reach the ceiling. If I were the god of our society, our houses would be much smaller or we would be a lot bigger.

I had a science teacher in late high school who said, "If the universe and everything in it doubled in size every night, we would never know it." He was trying to explain relativity or something. But I suddenly felt two hundred feet tall. I felt huge. My pencil was twenty feet long. Everyone in the room was a giant. I decided to adopt doubling as a belief.

I like to lie in a little room, alone, and try to sense myself growing bigger. Tomorrow I'll be over ten feet tall and weigh 280 pounds, and when I try to open the door to the pantry I'll crush the doorknob in my fist. I'll be able to open the canned tomatoes by squeezing them and I'll be able to step over fences and walk back home in a straight line and pick up my little brother and put him on my shoulders, and we'll walk across America like Johnny Appleseed telling people about how to become werewolves or vampires.

My biggest regret, besides leaving my little brother behind when I ran away, is not taking Susan to my room in the pantry. We just went upstairs to some empty room we'd trashed. I don't know why. I didn't even know what was happening, really. I was embarrassed. Our hands and our faces and our necks are gray with dirt, but the middles of our bodies are pale. We were fucking glowing and then I turned pink with shyness. I pulled her to me and started right in so she wouldn't see me blushing. I ended up rushing through the best moment to happen to me in a thousand years. But why be embarrassed if someone wants to have sex with you? If we come together again I'm gonna take her to the pantry. I have exactly what I need. A bed, a book, a candle, a box of matches. The candle makes just the amount of light you need to read and no more. It's like everything else I like. Just the right size.

I like matches because they come in matchboxes. Whenever I run out of matches I look around for more. If I can't find a new box of matches I ask around. I don't want a lighter. A matchbox is like a little room. When the matches run out I draw a picture of a bed in the bottom of the box and I draw a picture of me and Susan in the bed and I draw us a TV and a dresser and a dog on a rug and then I close the box and leave it behind. That's magic to make her become obsessed with me. I think she would like the way I lay out a room. If Susan came back to my pantry with me it would be twice as small because of the space she takes up. That's a doubling, too.

I love Susan. I love imagining the two of us lying naked in our bed with the candlelight making everything flicker and each of us with our clothes bundled up under our heads like a pillow and with books at our side, but we're not reading, we're just talking about what sort of room we want next, in what sort of house, in what sort of neighborhood, in what sort of city, in what sort of state, in what sort of country, in what sort of world, in what sort of planet, in what sort of solar system, in what sort of galaxy, in what sort of universe.

15

**Malcolm is the first one back.
Bobert, Tom, and Anquille are tied
for second, then some others.**

—Welcome home.
　　—Who is that?
　　—I'm over by the garage.
　　—I can't see you.
　　—It's Malcolm. I was the first one back.
　　—It's Bobert.
　　—And Tom and Anquille.
　　—We didn't see anything.
　　—It's dark.
　　—What are you doing?
　　—I'm spray-painting our mark on the driveway of this house.
　　—That's our mark?
　　—What is it?
　　—It's a wolf.
　　—Are you sure.
　　—Stand over here. Look at it from this angle.
　　—I see it.
　　—Where?
　　—That's the nose and that's the ears—

—What's that?

—That's the teeth.

—All right.

—What time is it, Malcolm?

—I think it's a little after eleven. It could be earlier.

—You want us to keep looking?

—No.

—I'm cold.

—I like a night like this.

—It's so dark.

—Not much wind.

—Just the sound of the highway.

—The highway sounds like wind.

—We didn't see anything.

—You said.

—What about you, Malcolm? Did you find anything?

—Just this guy.

—What the fuck is that thing?

—That's my dog.

—I didn't see him there.

—It's dark and he's black. Almost black. He's chocolate-colored.

—Does he bite?

—I guess if you kicked him or something you could get him to bite, but I've only been nice to him and he seems to want to be nice to me. He seems to want to be nice to all of us.

—Where'd you find him?

—I think he found me.

—Where?

—Well, just like you guys, I was out looking for the Peugeot and I went a little north, I sorta scooted by the edge of the elementary school.

—We were around that way, too.

—Rich people always want to live by nice schools. You see that in the movies. When rich people talk about buying a house they ask what school district it's in, and where the nearest school is, and what the test scores are.

—Well, that school is a nice school.

—But there's no Peugeots around, right?

—We didn't see any.

—I thought I would go down around toward the Speedy Stop and maybe stake out the parking lot for an hour, see if the Peugeot came by there. Gas stations are tar pits for dino-cars. The fossil fuels bring them in and the high prices bring them down. Haha. I'm being stupid.

—We didn't have a real plan. We just sat in the swings and watched cars drive by. But we didn't see any Peugeots.

—But on the way to the Speedy Stop I saw this mutt. He was wearing my belt so I thought I would follow him.

—I don't get it.

—This is the dog I was walking when I got hit by that car.

—Why were you walking a dog?

—I do it to fit in.

—He's a good dog.

—He likes you, Bobert. He trusts you.

—I like him, too.

—Why don't you hold on to his leash for a while. So he doesn't run away again in all the confusion that's gonna happen as everybody comes back.

—What confusion?

—Hey guys.

—Hey.

—See? Everybody's coming back already.

—Did you find anything?

—Look at this.

—Malcolm has a dog.

—Everybody go in and get packed up.

—Did you find the Peugeot?

—This dog found us a mansion.

—I don't get it.

—Dogs are domesticated. That means safe. Nobody dangerous walks a dog. Walking a dog is a real Norman Rockwell activity. I do it when I want to case a new neighborhood.

—Where do you get the dog?

—Some yard. This one was a couple blocks over that way.

—I hate dog-walking. Walking the dog was one of my chores I had to do when I lived at home. I was supposed to walk the dog before and after school.

—Did you?

—No one was ever home after school so I just said I did. I never really did. But when my mother would ask me, "Did you really?" I would just smile and say, "Ask Riley."

—I use my belt as a leash and then I just wave at the neighbors as I try to guess how robust their canned good supply is so we can come back when they're gone and take 'em.

—I was afraid Riley was gonna start talking one day and tell Mom that I had been lying for years. But dogs can't talk.

—Anyway, this is the dog I was walking when I got hit by that Peugeot. I was trying to move us from this neighborhood up north, past the elementary school. I think it's called Sherwood.

—That's what the elementary school's called—Sherwood Elementary.

—I know.

—So this dog told you about some new house?

—When I got hit by the Peugeot I dropped the leash, which is my belt, and the dog ran away. Then tonight, I see a dog running down the street dragging something behind him and I know automatically that he's my dog. I take off chasing after him and calling and waving my arms. Running my ass off. Just like I told you guys not to. Because if you run, what happens?

—The cops chase you.

—And sure enough, two or three blocks chasing this dog and a cop pulls around the corner. He rolls down his window as he pulls up to me and he asks, "Dog get away from you?" "Yes, sir," I say. And he's all like, "Watch this." And boom he hits the turbo and, like, does a big loop around the block to get in front of the dog and cuts it off at the pass. And I can see him up ahead of me in a red-and-blue flashing silhouette. This cop gets out of his car with some sort of treat. Probably a doggie biscuit he keeps in the glove box for just such an occasion. The cop gets the dog by the leash, which is my belt, and then I run up to him and the dog is all licking me. The cop hands me the belt and the dog is straining and straining to go and I can barely keep ahold of him. And the cop is like, "You need a better leash. A real leash." And I'm all like, "Yeah, well, I'm poor." And then guess what? The cop hands me a fifty-dollar bill and tells me to have a nice night.

—No way.

—Check it out.

—It's a fucking fifty-dollar bill!

—We can buy beer with it.

—We don't need to buy beer with it.

—What do we need to buy?

—Nothing for a while. Everybody go get your stuff. We're moving out.

—Moving out where?

—Well, the dog pulls me down the block. A couple blocks. And I go with him because I don't want the cop to see me fighting with the dog. The cop is sitting in his car, like, watching me. And I want it to seem like the dog is mine. Like we work good together. And so I go with the dog a couple of blocks and then all of a sudden the dog stops at a house and starts shitting on the lawn. Well, this makes me crazy nervous. Because the cop will arrest me for littering or something if I don't pick it up and I don't have a bag. But when I look back, the cop is gone. And the dog isn't straining at the leash anymore. He's just sitting on the lawn of this house. And the house looks deserted. And the more I check it out, the more it looks perfect for us. It's huge.

—So we're going to some random house this dog picked for us by shitting on it.

—That's about the long and short of it.

—This is bullshit.

—I don't see how this is any more bullshit than pulling ideas out of a hat. Or out of your ass, like yahooing some beer.

—It was good beer, though. Admit it. Right?

—Everybody go inside. Pack up your shit. But only pack the stuff that has sentimental value. You can leave all the food and all the granola bars behind. The place we're going to has everything.

—What does it have?

—It has a pool. And it has a wine cellar. It has a fucking huge collection of music. Good music, not just a bunch of jazz and bullshit. It has more food than we can eat. And it has cable.

—No way.

—Way. So don't come out here with a bunch of overstuffed backpacks. Nothing looks more suspicious to cops than a kid with a giant backpack in the middle of the night.

—You're obsessed.

—If you've got a giant backpack in the middle of the night, you're either going to night school or you're a runaway. And there's really no such thing as night school after ten p.m.

—How much cable does this place have?

—This is too good to be true.

—It is. And the only way to keep it that way is to stay ahead of the bad news. So let's get a move on.

—Wait.

—What?

—Explain it to me.

—What?

—How it all happened.

—What?

—What happens in your story between the point where the house looks great from the outside to the part where you tell us what kind of CDs we get to choose from.

—The house looked abandoned. There were no cars. I peeped in a few windows. Then I rang the doorbell and hid in the bushes. Then I started looking for a key. I tried all the obvious rocks and the welcome mat and all that. Then I looked in the mailbox and there was a little reminder note for the mailman that the Yorks are on vacation for a month in Israel. There was an emergency key in the way back of the mailbox. They left two days ago. We'll move in under the cover of darkness tonight, and tomorrow I'll go around to the neighbors and tell them I'm house-sitting.

—How much cable do they have?

—They have the whole package, three hundred channels.

—What are we waiting for?

—Midnight. I want to make sure everybody who wants to stick with us for one more house knows where it is.

—What time is it?

—It's about eleven thirty, by now, I bet.

—It's eleven twenty-three. Precisely.

—Are you drunk?

—For the next six hours or so, by my calculations.

—You were supposed to be looking for the Peugeot.

—I did.

—We did.

—We looked for the Peugeot at a party. Think about it. A party is a good place to look because a lot of cars from all over come to one part of the neighborhood.

—That's what Malcolm was saying about parking lots.

—Malcolm and I think exactly alike.

—Then we noticed it was getting on to midnight and we thought we would come back for the rendezvous.

—Where'd you get the watch, Susan?

—This nice guy at the party gave it to us.

—He *gave* it to you?

—He didn't want us to be late.

—Angel! Did you tell someone we were all meeting up here?

—No. What Susan means is he didn't want us to be late to meet back up with him. Susan told him we would meet up with him, later, at three a.m. And he made me promise we would be on time.

—And so you took his watch and gave it to Susan to make sure she gets there on time.

—What can I say, I'm a fucking romantic.

—You're not really gonna go back out. Are you, Susan?

—I dunno.

—It's a nice watch.

—I'm gonna give it back, Malcolm.

—She's gonna give it back. Susan's not a thief.

—So you're gonna go meet him tonight?

—It's not really any of your business what we do, Bobert.

—I guess not.

—Tell us the time again.

—It's eleven twenty-seven.

—All right. Everybody, you've got thirty-three minutes to get your shit together. And then we're leaving here at precisely midnight. If you want to know how much time you have left, ask Susan. She's the new time-keeper for all of us.

16

What the police officer really said to Malcolm.

—Good evening.

    —Evening, officer.

    —You mind stopping to have a word with me?

    —What?

    —What do you mean, what? I said stop.

    —I'm just walking.

    —I didn't ask what you were doing. Come 'ere.

    —What can I do for you, officer?

    —That's better. You pretend respect. At least. Now, tell me—what happened to your face?

    —I got run over by a car. Knocked down, really. You want a description of the vehicle?

    —Not particularly.

    —Then how are you gonna catch the bad guy?

    —I'll just look for anything with a face-shaped dent in it.

    —That oughta do it.

    —So why don't you tell me what you're doing out here?

    —See that dog up there?

    —I'm not even gonna turn my head.

    —It's just right at the end of this block.

    —It's dark. Describe it to me.

—My dog got loose and I'm trying to catch him.

—If I turn my head, I'll see a dog over there?

—Maybe not. He's black, so he's hard to see. Almost black. He's a chocolate pit bull.

—A pit bull?

—Not that kind of pit bull. He's a good pit bull. Like a Saint Bernard pit bull.

—Because he's big?

—He's bred to Serve and Protect—just like you. He's nice.

—To you. I bet. But even if he's the nicest dog in the world, it isn't gonna work—a pit bull running loose through the neighborhood. People panic when they see a pit bull.

—It's dark. Nobody'll see him. They won't even turn their heads.

—Where do you live?

—732 Glenwood Springs.

—You know what a patch zone is?

—No.

—It's interesting.

—I bet.

—A patch zone is what our department calls the area a police officer covers on his beat. If you're within a certain area, calls to that area are patched through to me.

—Any trouble on Glenwood tonight?

—I don't know. Glenwood is just one block outside my patch zone.

—So if I understand you correctly, officer, that means if someone put in a basic patch call for Glenwood, it's some other cop's problem, unless that other cop is already on a patch call and then it goes out as general 404 to whoever's closest?

—That means I don't know the area you're talking about as well as I'd like to. For instance, I have no idea who lives at 733 Glenwood Springs.

—I said "732."

—I guess you did.

—Nice try, though.

—Thanks. You want a dog biscuit? To help lure your dog back. I keep some in my glove box for just such an occasion.

—What's the catch?

—If I show you this picture of a few kids your age shoplifting beer from the Speedy Stop, you're not going to recognize any of 'em, are you?

—I left my glasses at home.

—But you can see your dog?

—I'm farsighted. It's the close-up stuff that looks fuzzy.

—Left your glasses at 732 Glenwood Springs?

—On the credenza in the front hall.

—You want me to give you a ride back real quick?

—I gotta catch my dog first. Before any of these people around here panic and start lighting up your switchboard.

—I wanna help you.

—Isn't gonna work. A lot of dogs, even the nicest dogs in the world, when they see a cop, they panic and they start to run.

—Even if he's the nicest cop in the world?

—Yep.

—If I search you am I gonna find any drugs or paraphernalia or anything fun?

—No, sir. Search away.

—I bet you left it at home on the credenza in the front hall.

—Left what at home?

—Still, I wanna help you.

—That's nice. But the best way to help me is to let me go. I don't want my dog to get away.

—How about I make a donation to a fund or something?

—What d'ya mean?

—Here's a fifty-dollar bill.

—Don't see a lot of those anymore.

—I want you to take it.

—What do I have to do? Is this about to get gross?

—You don't have to do anything.

—So I get it for nothing?

—It's for your dogcatching fund.

—All right.

—But there's a catch—

—All right.

—The way this donation works is, you get to hold it for a week.

—Then what happens?

—That fifty-dollar bill is a crystal meth detector.

—How's that?

—It's a heroin detector.

—I get it.

—It's an any-kinda-dope detector.

—So I hold on to it?

—And if you still have it in a week—the next time I see you, whenever—then you get to keep it.

—That's great. I'm clean. You just gave your money away.

—I feel pretty good about it. I feel like your little mind'll start telling you you can replace it with another fifty before the next time you see me. Your little mind'll start telling you, you can avoid me next week, you're not gonna see me. But I have a good feeling we're gonna be seeing a lot of each other. Now get the fuck out of here. Start walking and keep going until you disappear into the night and I can't see you anymore.

17

Malcolm and Tanya walk in front of the group and lead the way to the new house.

—Why'd you lie to everybody, baby?

  —So I could tell you the truth.

  —I don't like the difference you're making between me and them.

  —You think I'm using you.

  —I know you're using me. I just don't know what you're using me for, exactly.

  —I want the truth to be something we have just between the two of us.

  —I don't think the truth works that way.

  —I want them all to think that cop is my friend.

  —But he's not.

  —No one's gonna find out.

  —They'll find out eventually.

  —Only if you tell.

  —No. They'll find out no matter what. The truth wants to be found out.

  —The truth doesn't want anything. It's a description we give to words. Like, "that sounds sad." "That sounds angry." "That sounds truthful."

  —We have different points of view on this one.

  —What's your point of view?

  —I think sadness, anger, and especially truth—I think they represent the spirit of the event or the person the words describe. I'm sad you're separating me out from everybody else by lying to 'em. They're gonna hear that sadness every time I keep your secret.

—You want me to lie to you, too?

—I want you to separate me out by doing something nice for me. Pick me some fucking flowers. Steal me a necklace or something. Don't just take me aside and whisper to me. Don't just play bullshit games with traded shirts so everybody knows I let you fuck me.

—Everybody knows 'cause you're shouting.

—That's just the spirit of the truth trying to make itself heard.

18

Bobert and Tom bring up the rear as the group wends its way to the new house.

—What was the name of that street we just passed?

—I dunno. But that dog likes you. Every time you talk he looks up at you.

—I like him, too.

—What are you gonna name him?

—I'm not gonna name him anything. I think it's disrespectful.

—How is giving a dog a name disrespectful?

—I don't want to talk about the dog. I want us to pay attention to the route we're taking.

—We're going west.

—No. You have to pay more specific attention to the little details, the address numbers, the style of mailboxes they prefer, the flowers they're trying to grow in the gardens.

—The little corners of the curtains getting peeled back to watch a pack of crusty freaks walk by.

—Where?

—The little blue house over there with the gnome by the front door.

—Oh, did you see her drop the corner when I looked? That's good. The little details you notice are bread crumbs you can use to find your way back home.

—I don't want to get home.

—I mean to find me, to find the rest of us.

—Why should we be separated?

—It happens sometimes.

—Not for long.

—You weren't there when Malcolm was smashing up my game.

—That game belonged to everybody. Now none of us can play it. So that's something Malcolm did to all of us.

—But you weren't there. So it's something Malcolm did to me.

—I'll stick with you.

—Anquille is sticking with me, too.

—Then where is he now? I don't see him.

—He's trying to stay close to Malcolm. He's trying to hear what Malcolm hears and what he says. That's how Anquille is sticking close to me. It doesn't have to be physical.

—What do you want me to do?

—I want you to pay attention to the route we're taking.

—All right.

—I think we're going the wrong way.

—What do you mean?

—These houses are getting fancier and fancier.

—We're moving up in the world. That's how it works.

—I don't want to move into a fancy neighborhood.

—Why not? Nicer neighborhood means nicer house. Nicer vide games. Nicer couches for you to sleep on. Nicer pantries for me. Nicer towels.

—We stick out in this neighborhood.

—So.

—I hate that feeling. All the neighbors looking at us through their blinds. If we walk into a store in this neighborhood everybody's going to think we're shoplifters.

—We *are* shoplifters.

—We only shoplift when we have to sometimes.

—Sometimes counts.

—Of course it counts. Everything counts. But it also counts when people look at you like you don't deserve to be here.

—We don't deserve to be here.

—What about civil rights?

—What about 'em?

—Civil rights had to be passed because everybody didn't think everybody had the right to be in the voting booth.

—So you think there needs to be a "nice neighborhood" civil rights movement?

—I think there is. I think we're part of it. But I think Malcolm is leading us in the wrong direction.

—I don't think he should've broken our game. I think he's trying to make it up to us, to get us a new one, a better one.

—Look at this neighborhood.

—I like it.

—Is this the kind of neighborhood you come from?

—Fuck off.

—These people are gonna notice us more. Notice us until someone decides to do something about it. And "doing something about it," in this kind of neighborhood, means calling someone else to do something about it. Calling the cops. You already found one nosy neighbor spying on us walking. Spying on us when we're not doing nothing. Just walking home. For all that nosy neighbor knows we just got off work.

—We *all* just got off work at the same time?

—Have you been in a supermarket recently? It takes a hundred people to run a supermarket. Probably more. There's probably a bunch of people running the supermarket that you never see. It probably takes as many as there are of us just to watch the security cameras and wrestle the shoplifters to the linoleum.

—We should all apply for security jobs. We'd be good at security.

—Why couldn't twenty or so people who work at a fancy supermarket go in together on a house that's actually in the same neighborhood as the supermarket? If half of us worked the day shift and half of us worked the night shift it could work out pretty handy.

—I don't think they're gonna sign a mortgage over to a bunch of checkout girls and bag boys.

—That's my point! That's my point! We need to be around the bag boys and checkout girls and the security people. We don't need to be hanging out with the people who reject mortgage applications and turn down health insurance requests and deny our civil rights.

—What do you think Malcolm is up to?

—He's leading us into battle to cement his shaky leadership. But what he should be doing is taking us somewhere where we can get some more recruits.

—How are we going to recruit people?

—You were recruited. So was I.

—Recruited for what? What's the cause?

—It doesn't have words yet.

—We're just getting by.

—That's the center of it. The civil rights to not be looked down on just because of the way we live off the land.

—We don't live off the land.

—We do.

—We break into houses and we steal canned goods.

—Listen, if they cut down all the forests and poisoned all the streams and put up a bunch of ridiculous super-supermarkets—then I don't think it's right to arrest us for living off the land they gave us. People didn't shoplift in the Wild West.

—That's because you would get shot.

—It's because on the way from your house to the store you passed trees with fruits in them and fields with corn and woods with little rabbits and streams with trout.

—You make it sound like a supermarket, too.

—Food used to not come from stores. It used to be something that was around. So if they filled up the land with bullshit they can't say I'm bullshit for saying I live off the land when I help myself to what I find.

—I don't know what the fuck you're even saying. You don't know. So how am I supposed to recruit people?

—Do you want to be close to me or far, far away?

—I want to be close to you.

—Then pay attention to the route we're taking.

—I am.

—And look for recruits.

—You just said these aren't our sort of people.

—If we can't recruit the people then pay attention to the trees. We can recruit bushes to hide behind. We can recruit rocks to throw. Anything we can use when they try to come get us. Look over there.

—It's a back porch. What?

—The barbecue grill has a propane tank we can recruit.

19

Angel and Susan make a plan.

—How much farther do we have to walk?

—It's bracing. The night air will wake you up. I feel more and more alive the later it gets. Fuck!

—I feel like shit.

—Are you sleepy?

—I'm drunk.

—So you're not really gonna go meet that guy later tonight?

—Do you think we should?

—*We* didn't tell him we would, Susan—*you* did.

—You were there.

—Yeah, I was standing right there beside you, wondering what the fuck you were doing.

—He wouldn't let us go unless we promised.

—No one can make you do anything, Susan. No one tells you when you can leave a party. Or what you have to promise. Not if you're the sort of person who sticks to her word. That kind of person has willpower and nobody can ever manipulate her.

—Are you saying I don't keep my word?

—I'm saying Malcolm expects you to break it. He thinks if he tells us to stay inside that we have to. But you already told someone else you were going back out. You have to decide what sort of werewolf you're gonna be.

—What do you mean?

—Malcolm's not your boss.

—Neither are you.

—I don't care either way.

—You're trying to get me to cross Malcolm so that he'll look stupid. That's not cool.

—He doesn't need my help.

—Then why are you bothering me about it?

—You got me involved. When I asked Craig if you could borrow his watch so you could be there on time, I didn't know you were lying.

—You didn't borrow anything.

—It's only stolen if you don't keep your word. That means *you're* the thief. Not me.

—I'm not a thief.

—There's no bad karma from stealing food or anything you need to survive. The universe understands necessity. But if you steal things by lying or by stealing someone's affection—that can bring you a serious curse. You'll see.

—Will you go with me?

—You're gonna go meet him?

—Tell me what you think I should do.

—I'll tell you what I'm gonna do, Susan. I'm gonna wait until we get to this new house, then I'm gonna see how far it is and how safe it is, and wait until we get settled, and see what kind of bed I'm gonna be able to curl up in, and how late it is. Then, no matter what, I'm gonna make myself get up and go meet him, because I fucking said I would.

—I didn't take you for being a "man of your word" kind of girl.

—Doing what you say is the only kind of magic I know. It's the only real magic. If I say I'm gonna transform into a werewolf, then I have to do it. Otherwise it's just a fairy tale.

—Say you'll help me. Give me your word on that.

—I'll make sure that Craig gets his watch back.

—Cool. Thank you.

—You can just give it to me. If you're too drunk or tired then just give me the watch and I'll take it to Craig if you don't wanna go with me.

—I didn't say I don't wanna go with you.

—All right. We'll see.

20

This place is awesome.

—It's a two-story house.

—Three stories. There's a basement with a badass stereo system. The speakers are like four feet tall.

—And there must be five bedrooms upstairs.

—Did you see the clothes in the girl's room?

—The *pink* girl's room or the *baby blue* girl's room?

—I've never been in a house that has three stories before.

—There's *two* girl's rooms?

—And they both have cool clothes.

—Food in the kitchen. Food in the basement. And there's even a mini-fridge in the master bath.

—Who needs to eat while they shit?

—I'm gonna pawn everything brass in this house.

—The paintings are even cool.

—I think there's two girls. I think one of them must be off at college. And I think there's a young boy. Then I think there's a mom and dad. Or mom and stepdad. Or stepmom and dad. Or whatever. And then I think there's just an empty room for visiting dignitaries or whatever. It has a big fucking African mask on the wall.

—Did you see the stereo room, baby?

—Is it CDs? Or LPs?

—It's fucking *reel-to-reel*—and the shelves are lined with bootlegs.

—What kind of bootlegs?

—Everything. Old-fogy shit like folk music and Dylan. But there's also a lot of punk shit, old punk shit, Clash shows and Dicks.

—It's like a fucking library. Alphabetized. And there's a bunch of little portable reel-to-reel recorders. too.

—But there's no CD player?

—There's one in the living room but down in the basement it's only reel-to-reel.

—Fuck me.

—No, that's awesome, baby. It's special. Like French.

—And there's like a hoarder's stash of food and flashlights and blankets and shit down there.

—Thank you Y2K scare. Thank you bird-flu panic. Thank you stock-market crash. Whatever fucked-up thing turned these consumers into hoarders, I get down on my knees and thank you.

—Get up and let's go check it out.

—It's those silver blankets. And canned food and first-aid kits.

—They must be survivalists.

—I claim all the canned beef stew as dog food for the dog!

—What's the dog's name?

—You have to ask him. If he tells you, let me know.

—Did anybody see any backpacks?

—I dunno.

—In the girl's room.

—Who gives a fuck?

—We need to get all the bags, the backpacks and the small rolling luggage shit and the good purses, and we'll each make a bag for ourselves of the best clothes and the best food.

—We're not leaving this place.

—I'm not saying we have to pack up and leave immediately. I'm saying we should pack so that when we *do* go, we don't waste this house. We're each gonna want to take a little bit of this house with us.

—That's smart.

—I don't wanna go. We just got here.

—We don't have to go.

—I just want one place to be a good long home.

—We can try to make this that home. At least for the month they're gone.

—Turn off all the lights.

—How are we supposed to check out the new house?

—If you wanna stay here a long time then turn off all the lights so the neighbors don't see us.

Click. Click. Click. Click. Click.

—That's worse. The flashlights darting around a dark house and shooting beams out into the neighborhood night?! That's ten times more noticeable.

—Fine. Everybody turn off your flashlight.

—It's pitch-black now.

—Who's in here?

—Where are we?

—I think we're in the kitchen.

—Just open the fridge.

—Open the freezer. I want that frosty mist to be our only light.

—Aiiiieghhh!!!!!

—What the fuck?!

—Oh, my god, he's wearing the fucking African mask.

—You're gonna break it.

—That is scary as fuck.

—I thought you were some kind of monster.

—I am.

—Look at this freezer.

—That scared the shit out of me.

—It's wall-to-wall ice cream.

—Find the silver-spoon drawer.

—What do you wanna start with? The fudge ripple? Or the rocky road?

—You can't eat that.

—Why not?

—We have a bet, Mr. Malcolm, or so you forgot. Neither of us eats for three days and three nights. It's after midnight. Susan, please confirm with your watch. Our three days have started now.

—She's right.

—When you're right, you're right. Here. You eat it. Somebody eat it.

—Sorry.

—What's there to be sorry about? You and I both get hungry at the same rate. After three days we'll go out and get something incredible, for everybody.

—But there's so much food here already.

—Hey.

—It doesn't matter.

—Hey guys.

—Imagine how incredible it's gonna hafta be to impress you in the midst of this bounty. We'll have to steal live lobsters and one-hundred-year-old bottles of wine.

—And, Angel, I think there should also be a rule that neither one of us leaves this house.

—Guys!

—Hold on! I have to go out tonight. I told someone I'd meet them!

—But he might take you to a restaurant for your date. Or get you a corny dog at the fairgrounds and then you would have broken our rules but nobody would know.

—Fuck you.

—And who are you trying to impress with all your swearing, anyway?

—I don't give a fuck what you think about how I talk.

—I think Malcolm's right.

—Thank you, Anquille.

—This isn't cool. Look at me!

—What is it? What? Did you hear something, Susan?

—I just don't feel right.

—Are you gonna puke?

—No.

—What is it?

—I don't know.

—What do you feel like?

—I don't know. Look at my face and tell me what I look like.

—What? I don't see anything, Susan. What is it?

—I don't know. I think I'm changing.

21

What to do when someone starts to change.

—I can feel it. I swear I can feel it.

   —Susan, I want you to try to stay calm.

   —It's happening. It's happening right now.

   —I'm only gonna talk to you. Do you understand? You have to trust me.

   —All right, Malcolm.

   —You're my focus. But I'm going to ask everybody else to listen so they'll know what to do when someone starts to change.

   —All right. I'm cool.

   —Is that all right?

   —All right.

   —Susan, we need to find a safe place to put you.

   —All right.

   —I want Anquille and Angel to go find a safe place to put you.

   —All right.

   —Have you ever changed before?

   —No.

   —Have you ever had a seizure, or been knocked out, or had anything happen that you didn't understand that might have been a change?

   —I don't think so.

   —I want Bobert to stop the dog from barking.

—It's loud.

—Bobert's gonna take care of the dog. The dog can sense things we can't and you can hear the dog better than we can.

—I don't mind it.

—But the neighbors might.

—I think I'm starting to feel better.

—All right. You're gonna be locked up for three days.

—I don't want to be alone.

—We're gonna be right outside the door. Everybody is going to be focused on you. Tanya is gonna be responsible for feeding you.

—All right.

—And Tanya is gonna go get all that ready right now, and just get it lined up for you so that every six hours or so we'll get you some food and water.

—I'm hungry now.

—You're going to be very hungry. But Tanya will feed you.

—All right.

—That's right. I can hear your throat starting to close up.

—Is it? Oh, no.

—No, that's good. You won't be able to talk while it happens. While you're in the safe place that Anquille and Angel are getting ready, the whole three days we won't hear anything you say, we won't be able to understand anything you say. But we'll be there.

—A'right.

—I'm going to ask Bobert to be your reader.

—Uh-huh.

—He'll be with you the whole time.

—Uh-huh.

—I bet I'm not the best reader out of everybody.

—That's okay—isn't it Susan?—if Bobert just does his best? He's never been a reader before and you've never changed so I think it's actually gonna be nice for both of you.

—It's all ready, we put down blankets and pillows in the closet in the master bedroom.

—Angel and Anquille have it all ready for you. Are you ready, Susan?

—Uh-huh.

—You don't have to be scared. We're all gonna be with you the whole time. Just right outside the door.

—It's a huge closet. It might as well be its own bedroom.

—Now I'm gonna tie your hands and feet. All right. Just to protect Tanya when she feeds you. You don't want to hurt Tanya, do you?

—She can't talk anymore, baby. Can you?

—That's all right. Don't be scared.

—It's gonna be fine. It's gonna be okay.

—I'm proud of you.

—We're all proud of you.

22

Tanya has seen the archangel Gabriel.

There was a flier in a coffee shop. It said "Artists Wanted." I misread it to mean "If you want to be an artist you should call this number . . ." I usually read things really quickly and then always hafta go back and clear up my mistakes. It was a flier for a really cheap room. It was one of seven artist studios on one floor of an old flour mill. I still had some money at the time. Not a lot of money. Not enough money to live in an apartment for more than a month, but the studio I could afford for three or four months. I figured with that much time I could get things together so that I wouldn't go totally homeless.

I'm not an artist at all. I draw sometimes, but it comes out all messed up. Still, I called the number. I was the first one to tear off a little strip from the bottom. The guy said I must've just missed him because he had just posted the flier that morning. I said I could come by around noon. He said great. I went back to the flier and tore off all the other strips and ate them for good luck. Then I sat down with my coffee and tried to figure out my story. I decided to tell them I was a sculptor working with found objects. I figured that way I didn't need to have any supplies and I could just show up with my bag. Plus, I had been going through the trash, anyway, looking for stuff I could sell. I had seen plenty of stuff I thought was nice, but not actually worth anything at a pawnshop. So I knew there was a lot of material out there to work with. And what if I turned out to be an artist after all? Stranger things have happened.

The guy showed me around the studio and he was pretty straight about the situation. His name was Reggie and he said the ambient flour in the air was bad for asthma but it would keep you from starving while you worked. Haha. I never smelled it or felt it in the air or in my lungs. Reggie worked in oil, and he said the flour messed up his mixes or something. I don't really remember what he was talking about. He was pretty straight about the fact that everybody lived in his or her studio even though technically we weren't allowed to. We all had to share one big kitchen and one bathroom. He said the rent was cheap for an apartment but expensive for a studio, so I "have to decide." He said if the fire marshal or the landlord ever found out we were all living there then we would all get kicked out and we wouldn't get our rent back. But he also said that would never happen.

I tried to keep my door shut because I thought I would be in trouble if anybody found out I wasn't making anything. I went out in the day and went through trash around the university looking for cool stuff. I would bring home old textbooks and bicycle tires. I tried to also find useful stuff, blankets and good clothes. It got confusing. I remember dragging a banged-up old Japanese screen up three flights of stairs because I thought I could use it to separate my sleeping space from my studio space. But I didn't really have a studio space because I never made anything. I just stacked up the prettiest trash I could find on one side of the room and the most useful trash on the other side of the room.

I had an idea once. I don't know if it was while I was there in the studio or not. But I had an idea that I would make a calendar of my entire life and I would chart what drugs I was on during what years. I imagined this calendar as a giant mandala of pills radiating out from the first pink aspirin I took as a kid. I thought it would show patterns. I thought I would be able to chart certain life choices based on the antidepressants I was coming off of. I thought certain boyfriends would make sense because of the speed or the dope. I never made it, though. Hell, if I had all the pills I ever took all laid out and all the dope and everything, I wouldn't use it for art. Not most days.

I kept my door shut tight the entire time. I was so nervous about being found out. I came in by opening the door only a crack and sliding my body in, and mashing my tits and belly to fit. And I went out the same way. It made me a point of interest. The other artists there started saying, "When can I see your work?" I was afraid they were going in while I was out so I started going out less. I was afraid they were going to band together and break down my door and force their way in. It only takes one person to kick in a door, but groups band together to do it so that no one feels bad about it. I know that now. At the time I was just getting paranoid. Maybe "can I see your work" is just something artists say to each other no matter what. When I had to go out I would drape a big sheet over a trashed-out bike I had on the art side of the room. I figured the sheet made it look like a work in progress. I put hairs on the sheet to see if it was disturbed, but it was hard to remember where I had put the hairs and there was a breeze from the window, even when I closed it, so the fact that they were gone, I don't think it meant anything. When I was in the house I would act like I was gonna go take a shower and then as soon as I turned on the water I would act like I forgot my soap and have to go back to my studio to get it, but I never caught anybody in my room. I was on a lot of cheap speed at the time, maybe that would explain my actions on the calendar of stupidity.

All the other artists left their studio doors open most of the time and didn't mind if you leaned in the doorway and talked to them while they worked. They didn't mind if you sat in the corner against a wall and drank wine and asked them questions about what they were painting. It was pretty much an open-door policy with everyone except for me and this guy Paulie.

Because we shared a kitchen we all ate a lot of meals together. It was almost never planned—you would just hear someone yell out "spaghetti" or "pancakes" and if you were hungry you would come running, because there wasn't always enough for everybody who was hungry because it was almost never planned. The exception to the lack of planning was Paulie. Paulie, I remind you, is the only other artist besides me who was super private about his work. Except I wasn't an artist. And I'm still not. I figured Paulie wasn't, either. But one day there comes a knock on my door. I say, "Hold on," and I make a big show of noise and banging, like I'm putting away my work. And even though the sheet was never off, I mime like I'm throwing the sheet over the bike and then adjust it, just to take up the right amount of time. I don't really know why. I never even opened the door all the way. Nobody ever really wanted to come in. It was always like, "Hey, I'm going down to the Pic Quik for a six-pack. Wanna chip in?" Or "Did you happen to find a credit card on the kitchen counter?" A lot of them had credit cards.

Maybe it was my secret hope that one of them would push past me and say, "Hey, I have to marry you, so get on your knees on the bed and let's fuck and then be boygirlfriends forever and see a movie." That's the sort of abstract psychosexual cloud that drifts around my mind most of the time. It's the kind of thing that would look monstrous if it got out into the real world, but as long as it stays in the mist, it seems kind of romantic to me.

It was Paulie knocking on my door. The other secretive artist, as I said before. I didn't open the door more than a crack. He said he wanted to invite me to "a thing" he did. He was finished with a new piece. He said there would be a dinner and I could come. But I had to say for sure if I could make it. Plus Paulie said there were only going to be three people invited and I was one of them.

"You don't have to bring anything. The whole thing is on me. In my studio. And it's not a date. It's just how I make what I make. You'll see. *If* you can make it. Can you make it? It's at seven tomorrow night. Can you make it? It's not a date."

I told him he said that one too many times. Then we laughed and I said, "Sure," and shut the door.

I spent all day working. That day and the next. I started just by tying things together, literally. I had a ball of string I had found and I just started tying things to the spokes of the bike. It got kinda pretty, the string fanning out in a circle from the spokes of the bike wheel, like a skirt. And it was just tied to everything. Around the neck of a stuffed dolphin. To a number two pencil. To the tab of a Diet Coke can. I had this image that I would ride that bike to dinner and I would drag everything in the world along behind me. When I ran out of string I started taping things together with brown packing tape. I liked that a lot. A spiral notebook taped to the back of a stuffed dolphin tied to a bike. I got really excited by that. But I bet it all looked like shit. I don't know why I got all keyed up to start working. I wasn't an artist. I left it all behind. I wonder what they thought when they went in my room finally. I'm sure they had to clean it all out. Reggie at least. I still feel bad about that.

But the reason I know that I'm not an artist is that I went to dinner the next night with Paulie. At around seven fifteen I got up and went to his studio. I sort of thought Paulie might come get me at seven, but he never did. When I got to Paulie's studio there was a card table set up and four metal folding chairs around it. The studios weren't very big and Paulie's might have been smaller than mine. There was a bed in there, and a desk, and an easel in the center of the biggest wall, facing the door so you saw it when you walked in. On the easel was a painting of the archangel Gabriel. I don't want to say anything about it. We were all jammed up under that painting at the little card table. There were four of us. It was three men, Paulie and two others I had never met before. I opened the door to Paulie's studio and there beneath the archangel Gabriel were three men. Paulie was wearing a tie. Not super fancy, but a tie, still.

Paulie stood up and the other two guys stood up. They were gay. Paulie pulled out my chair and I sat down and everybody sat down. The other two guys were a couple so it did feel a little like a date. Paulie had made spaghetti and meatballs, but he had made it really good. And he had baked his own cornbread, which you might not think would have gone with the whole thing, but it was perfect. Maybe he didn't know how to make French bread? Everybody introduced each other and Paulie intro-duced the archangel Gabriel. He had just finished painting it. Then we went around the table and everybody said what they did. I said I was a vagabond and everybody laughed. John said he was a mathematician and I said I didn't know that was a job and everybody laughed. Ray-Ray said he was a dancer and everybody laughed. Paulie said he was an artist.

Gabriel was an archangel. One of seven in most traditions. In Juda-ism they are Michael, Raphael, Gabriel, Uriel, Sariel, Remiel, Jophiel, and Chamuel. I know that's eight, but that's part of the mystery that there is confusion about which one of those names mentioned in the Torah is not a true archangel. I could be getting this all wrong. Gabriel is special. He also goes by Jibril or Jibrail and he is the messenger of God. Some people even consider him the same as the Holy Spirit. To Catholics, Ga-briel's the patron saint of emergency dispatches. But in Judaism, Gabriel wasn't always the best messenger. He was once punished for not obeying a command exactly as it was given and he was hidden from God outside the heavenly curtain. In Christianity, Gabriel is the angel that tells Mary that the baby buried inside her is the son of God. In Latter-Day Saints, Gabriel is the same as Noah who built an ark and hid all the animals from the flood in that big giant floating wooden womb-boat. And then after the flood all the animals are born back into the world. Noah is his earthly name and Gabriel is his celestial name, sorta like when people from your hometown call you something different. Muslims believe that Gabriel revealed the Koran to the prophet Mohammed. Muslims believe that because Gabriel is the messenger of God and he has six hundred wings, you can never see his face behind them all. I'm just telling you what I remember, there was a lot a lot a lot more.

The spaghetti was really good and we drank a lot of wine, all of which Paulie paid for. And it wasn't like a lecture. Paulie asked us all to talk about what religion means to us. Our experience with spirituality. If we believed in angels. If we believed in signs from God. John said Ray-Ray was his guardian angel and told a story about Ray-Ray coming out of nowhere to physically defend him against a physicist who was being an asshole. I told a story I don't know if I ever told anybody about one time I was hiking in the woods, and I swear to this day I heard someone say my name, as clear as a bell, but there was no one else there for a thousand miles. I heard a voice say my real name, not Tanya but the name my mother gave me, the name maybe only a handful of people in my hometown would even remember. But there was no one else there for a hundred thousand miles. And I felt scared and special, like everything was going to be all right, and still scared—all at the same time.

Paulie said he was painting all the archangels. The way he did it was he painted them the best he could, and then he had some people over to "witness" the angel, and then he sealed the angel away in an ark, which was just a flat wooden box, and then on the ark's lid Paulie had written with a black marker a little sentence that says "I have seen the archangel Gabriel—" and we were all supposed to sign on as witnesses.

I helped Ray-Ray clear food from the table so Paulie could use the table to box up the painting. In the kitchen, as we threw the dishes in the sink, Ray-Ray said to me, "He's great. Isn't he?" I had no idea if he was talking about his boyfriend, John, or Paulie, because it was sort of like a date, the way Ray-Ray and John were paired up, leaving me and Paulie. But he might also have been talking about the archangel Gabriel. I just said, "Yeah, he's fantastic." And then Ray-Ray hugged me, like we had just had this big moment together, but I still had no idea what was happening. He could have been hugging me to express how happy he was to have found John and to be in love. Or he could have been hugging me one of those "you two are going to be so happy together" hugs about Paulie. Or he could have been hugging me because of the abiding presence of the divine in our shitty lives. Whatever he intended, he probably got more than he bargained for, because I hugged the ever-loving shit out of him. No one had touched me for a long time, and it felt good. I squeezed him like a maniac and started crying. And he said, "There, there, baby. There, there now." And he didn't rush me or get embarrassed, and I remember thinking, "Maybe Ray-Ray *is* a guardian angel. Wouldn't that be weird?" And now I try to be like him and remember his mannerisms and his kindness to others.

When we got back to the room they already had the cover on the angel and Paulie had a tack hammer and some brass nails. I really wanted to see it one more time, but I was embarrassed to ask. Paulie smiled at me and then got to work. The card table we'd eaten on was not the best workbench in the world. It wobbled as Paulie nailed the ark shut, and we all stood around in silence as the archangel was put away.

I asked Paulie, "Does anyone ever get to see it again?"

He said, "They have to have faith that you did."

"But it's so beautiful."

"Thank you."

And then we all signed off that we had witnessed the archangel Gabriel. And as soon as I signed, I went back to my little studio and packed up all my stuff. I was gone the next morning before the second month's rent was due. Paulie came by and knocked on my door again, in the middle of the night, after Ray-Ray and John left. But I didn't answer. Sometimes I still find myself thinking about my "sculpture," which is stupid, because it was just a bunch of stuff I found all tied together. And sometimes I find myself praying that I'll hear my name again. That I'll be found and that everything will be all right, as scary as that concept is for me. My real name. A name that almost no one knows.

23

How to be a reader.

—All right. Pay attention, Bobert.

—Don't hit me.

—If you don't want to get hit, pay attention.

—I am. I was.

—If you were then you would have ducked. Like this. Good. You're quick.

—Stop it.

—Stop whining. You should be listening to every word I say and soaking it in. Like a sponge. Good. I didn't even hit you that hard.

—I don't think you get to decide how hard the hit is. I think it's the one getting hit who gets to decide. Ow. Fuck. I knew you were going to do that.

—Then why did you say it? . . . Good. Now the most important thing to remember is to pay attention.

—I am. I was.

—Don't pay attention to me. Already you should have one ear focused on the closet. Do you know how to focus your attention? If I say the closet, can you imagine it?

—It's right there.

—That's just the door. The closet is what's behind that.

—All right.

—Don't pay attention to me. And don't just focus on the door. Susan

90

isn't gonna open up the door and tell you how she feels. You have to train your focus to go imaginary. But you can't just make up anything you want. You have to imagine Susan with some accuracy. That's sympathy. It helps if you like her. Do you like Susan?

—I just. I don't—

—I thought you might, Bobert. Now when Susan needs something—if something goes wrong—you've gotta get help from all of us. We all want to help Susan, but to do that we need you to focus your attention on her.

—I can do that with my focus.

—I'll stop talking in a second so you can really get zoned in, but start sending half your attentive forces into the closet already. All right? Good. Now the second rule is to never leave Susan alone.

—What if I have to go to the bathroom?

—We're gonna get you a can.

—I can't shit in a can.

—You *can*. Haha.

—No way.

—Get it?

—I'm not gonna shit in a can.

—What do you think it's gonna be like when *you* change?

—I won't care if someone takes five minutes to take a shit.

—You might. You don't know how you're going to feel when it's actually happening. That's one of the reasons I want you out here.

—So I can learn this, so when I start to change—

—I don't even know why I talk to you. You're so fucking smart you don't even need to hear words.

—What do I actually do? I just shit in a can and wait?

—You have to watch out that I don't get frustrated with you.

—But what do I do?

—You pay attention.

—I am.

—And you never leave Susan alone.

—Can the dog stay with me?

—No. The dog's too excited. This needs to be a calm thing for Susan. And you're a little too into the dog.

—We have a connection.

—That's great. You can have the dog again as soon as this is over. But right now you're Susan's connection. You're the only connection to everything she knows. She's going through some . . . I don't know what. It's really personal. You'll see. I guarantee that.

—I won't leave. No matter what. Just get me a can.

—And you have to keep talking, too. It's not enough just to be here. She has to know you're here. She has to *hear* you're *here*. Haha. Get it? I'm being a dork, but seriously.

—What do I say to her?

—Mostly it's reading. But if you run out of things to read and you don't want to reread something you've already read, then you just talk. You just don't stop talking.

—What do I read?

—We're gonna give you everything we can. I have some pages left over from the last time someone changed and everything else we're gonna write down, *right* now. Haha. We're each gonna write down what happened to us. The way we experienced it. Our regrets. The rules. Bad habits. Conversations we can remember. And as Susan hears it, she can use it, to make her change.

—Why don't I get to tell her anything? Why does it all have to be stuff you guys write?

—What did I just fucking say to you?

—Ow. Don't hit me.

—Why not?

—Ow. Don't fucking hit me!

—I just fucking said: You have to keep talking all the time. You can tell her anything you want. But take it seriously. Don't tell her dumb shit or lie to her or change the words in our shit on purpose. It might be funny to you, but it could end up being mean to her. Take it seriously. Like her life depends on it.

—I do.

—Then why didn't you fucking listen when I told you the first time you could talk to her.

—Ow. Stop it.

—All right. We're fucking around way too long already. You should be talking already.

—All right.

—I'll get everyone started writing stuff for you. You just start by telling Susan that's what I'm doing. Describe us all writing. All of us sitting in different rooms in this awesome house with all its games and music and books and cable. And we're all gonna be hunched over little pads of paper and scribbling away for her.

—Do I have to yell?

—Oh, no. Like the opposite. Her hearing is gonna get wild. She'll be able to hear the slightest whisper.

—Susan?

—She can't answer you. She can't talk.

—Susan, I'm going to be your reader.

—Now just to be super clear. If I come back here and you're not here, or you're not talking, or you're asleep, then I'm going to hit you once—as hard as I can, with my fucking baseball bat. Get it?

—Susan, Malcolm's leaving now and it's just you and me talking to each other. All right? Go on, Malcolm. I got this. He's walking out the door right . . . now. Now it's just you and me, Susan, and I'm just going to talk to you and tell you how I feel.

24

If you could change one thing about yourself, what would it be?

—I wish I didn't care so much what other people think of me.

   —Why do you care what other people think of you?

   —Fuck if I know.

   —I wish I could be more organized.

   —That's a funny thing for a homeless person to say.

   —Huh, I guess we are homeless. Technically.

   —We're more than *technically* homeless. If the cops come we have to run. If the people who own this house come home, we have to run. If a big fight breaks out among us, the whole thing is over.

   —That's why Malcolm wants us to pack a bag.

   —What do we have to fight about?

   —When we run, there are some of us who are gonna run right home.

   —And some of us who are gonna get run right into the ground.

   —I started packing my bag already.

   —I thought we were going to do it all together tomorrow?

   —I didn't want all the good stuff to be gone.

   —That's what we'll end up fighting about.

   —This place has too much good stuff to fight over.

   —That logic's not borne out by history.

   —Let me see your bag.

—Here, honey, do your best.

—Jesus, you *do* need to get more organized. It's all string and tape and shit.

—I know. But I can imagine my bag being perfect. A couple cans of beans. A can opener. A change of clothes rolled up tight. A book. A roll of toilet paper. My toothpaste and toothbrush in the center of the toilet paper tube. And the whole thing wrapped up in a trash bag.

—I can organize this for you.

—What good would that do?!

—I thought that's what you wanted?

—I don't lack the physical ability to organize my bag. I lack something else.

—That's right. For almost everything that's right. I mean, I can imagine being stronger. I can imagine being calm when I talk to the cops, but—

—I wish I was a natural leader. I wish I could just say, we're gonna take off for the woods and find a farmhouse and live off the land, and you guys would follow me.

—I wish I could fuck all night.

—I wish I could stop snoring.

—I wish could lose about forty pounds.

—I wish I didn't get so sulky. I wish I didn't sulk so much.

—I wish I could tell jokes. And remember jokes.

—I can't remember jokes, either.

—I wish I wasn't scared.

—I wish that when I saw something I wanted—I wish I would take it and I would do it with so much . . . intention . . . that no one would try to stop me, whether I was taking it from one of you, or in the Speedy Stop, or taking a gun right out of a policeman's hand. A stronger intention. That's what I wish for.

—Wait 'til you change. You're gonna love the change.

—You've changed already?

—Before you came.

—What's it like?

—Everything everybody is wishing for seems available. It's right there. What Tanya said, about physically being able to organize her bag, but something *else* is missing . . . That other thing isn't missing anymore.

You have the mental power to do with your body what you can think with your head.

—I wish I would change.

—Me, too.

—Me, too.

—You will. You will.

25

**Angel comes into the master bedroom
in the middle of the night and convinces
Bobert to help her.**

—What are you doing in here?

—Don't talk to me. Don't fucking look at me. You're supposed to be talking to Susan.

—Susan, what do you think Angel is doing in here?

—Is she asleep? Is that why you're whispering so soft?

—Angel wants to know if you're asleep. Are you asleep?

—Wouldn't you love it if that's all there was to this? Your friends grab you and throw you in a room, bring you food and water, talk to you day and night, take care of you, and all you have to do is sleep for three days. We could start a business where all we do is kidnap people and give them a three-day break from the crushing pressure of their shitty lives.

—Sleep as much as you want, Susan. I'll be here. I'll keep watch over you.

—You don't "keep watch." You can't see her. There's a door in between you and her.

—It's a turn of phrase.

—Say it into my tape recorder. I'm collecting turns of phrase.

—Stop it.

—Don't talk to me. Talk to Susan.

—Susan, Angel is standing here like a . . . I dunno . . . like a roving reporter. She's got a little black tape recorder, from like the seventies. It's the size of a loaf of bread sort of squished flat. Like a little black loaf of bread. And there's a little handheld mic attached to it by a long black cord and she's pointing it at me. And you can see the reels spinning so you know it's on.

—Tell her what I look like.

—Mascara. And glitterly makeup. And a too-tight T-shirt—it looks like a Powderpuff Girls shirt.

—They're called the *Power*puff Girls, not the *Powder*puff Girls. That's the whole point.

—It's looks like she got into the little girl's stuff—that's what she's wearing on top. But she's wearing the same tight jeans she always wears. And it looks like she found a pair of combat boots.

—From the wife's closet.

—They look used—they're really good sand-colored combat boots.

—I'm wearing the three ages of femininity. Girls on top. The wife on my feet. And me in the middle. I can't wait to show you the house, Susan. You haven't even been able to enjoy it yet.

—In just a couple more days, we'll open up the door and you'll come out and we'll make everyone else give us a tour of everything that's great about this house.

—You're gonna love it. There's a collection of tapes in the basement. It's all live bootleg concerts. Music seems to be somebody's thing in this house. Right now I'm recording over Bob Dylan and Joan Baez in the Rolling Thunder Revue from 1975.

—Stop it. That's a part of history.

—It's old history. We're making new history.

—Does anybody else know what you're doing? Does Malcolm know you're recording over shit?

—I dunno. I think almost everybody's asleep. They wrote all night. Did you read it all yet?

—I read everything y'all wrote tonight. It goes pretty fast. I've got some of the old pages Malcolm gave me from some of the earlier changes. But I was gonna save that for the middle of the night. I thought I would just talk for a while. How about that, Susan? I'll just talk to you for a while and then later, if I get tired, I'll have something new to entertain the two of us. And then we'll just do reruns until everybody wakes up to write some more.

—Tell Susan how I look.

—We already did that, Angel. Are you still drunk?

—You told her what I was wearing. But you didn't tell her whether or not you liked it.

—Angel's feeling goofy or something, Susan. She's goofing around.

—But I got nobody to goof around with.

—I can't goof around. I gotta watch Susan.

—Well, let's read the old pages. Let's get them onto tape so they can be preserved! I got out the tape recorder because I wanna record Susan's entire change. I wanna update our records from paper to something more modern. What time is it?

—I don't know.

—Ask Susan what time it is. She has the watch.

—What time is it, Susan?

—These pages are ancient. The paper's yellow. It's weird, isn't it, to imagine older werewolves? Who do you think is the oldest now?

—Anquille. Or you.

—It's not me. I'm eighteen.

—Me, too.

—I know you're not eighteen.

—How would you know?

—Susan told me. She told me the two of you hooked up.

—So?

—You think she's jealous? Listening to us out here? While she's all tied up in there?

—There's no reason to be jealous, Susan.

—We could give her a reason to be jealous.

—I'm supposed to keep watch.

—We could do whatever we want and then when she comes out we could just tell her we were joking and she would never know the truth.

—I'm not gonna try to make Susan jealous.

—Well, what about you? You jealous that she was gonna go out to meet some guy tonight?

—She's not going out.

—She might.

—She's tied up in the closet.

—You don't know that. You can't see her.

—I don't need to. I know. My attention is focused on her.

—But you're getting tired and once you fall asleep you can't control what your attention gets focused on. You fall asleep, you might start dreaming about me.

—I'm not gonna fall asleep. I'm Susan's reader.

—Fine. Then read something to her.

26

The Story of Doug.

—This is the story of Doug. Doug was the first one of us to change. Not the first change ever, but the first change in our group. This was back when we all camped out behind that bar on Navasota called Nasty's.

—That's in San Antonio.

—How do you know?

—I know where famous bars are. I make it my business to know. I'm gonna write a book someday about getting thrown out of all of 'em. Wouldn't you buy that shit? A history of the circumstances under which I get thrown out of all the most famous bars in the world. The White Horse in New York. Heinold's in Oakland. Harry's New York Bar is in Paris. And Nasty's is in San Antonio. It's not famous. But I think I've been kicked out of it.

—Did you know Doug?

—No, I think that was back before I was a part of the group. When I had a separate life.

—"The guys at Nasty's knew we were camped out back there. The cops knew. It's different now with the cops. I mean, this is before we were breaking into houses. The cops would come back and visit us, but not really chase us."

—I don't know which is worse, getting chased by the cops or getting "visited."

—"We kept a little campfire fire going back there. And everybody had a little area. If it rained we would put up a tarp, but if you built a permanent shelter—of any kind—if you propped up a corrugated aluminum sheet of metal as a wall and sloped a tarp down from it to make a triangle, the cops would come along during the day while we were away and tear it down."

—What do we do with Susan if the cops come?

—You're safe, Susan. The cops won't come.

—Did Malcolm say anything about that what if?

—Susan, if the cops come we have a plan about what to do with you.

—No, we don't.

—I'm just trying to tell her good stuff.

—But it's not true.

—It is true. If the cops come I'll make it true.

—You're in love.

—Shut up and listen. "Doug was having a rough night. We *all* drank a lot. Especially in the winter, 'cause, as you know, it does get cold down here in winter. And we were sitting around the fire and Doug just all of a sudden got really mean and started hitting people."

—Sounds like Malcolm.

—You think Malcolm wrote this?

—I mean, this guy Doug turning mean and hitting people. That sounds like Malcolm.

—Yeah, but who do you think wrote this?

—Could be Malcolm, I guess.

—'Cause it sounds way nicer than Malcolm. Kind of sad.

—You mean nostalgic.

—Maybe.

—Keep going.

—"Doug was going crazy. He was falling into the fire and hitting people."

—That's what Susan would be doing if we let her go.

—Susan wouldn't hit anybody.

—Wanna bet?

—Everybody's different.

—But the change is the same.

—Let me finish. You keep saying "keep going" and then you interrupt.

—Fine.

—"Doug was the sweetest guy in the world and even, usually, a sweet drunk. But once he started changing, he was swinging a log from the fire, flaming on one end, and he hit this woman named Val—"

—See? Doug was sweet like Susan.

—Shut up.

—Go on.

—"And then Malcolm just became Malcolm." So it's not written by him. It's by somebody about him.

—It could be propaganda. He writes it from some other point of view about how badass he is and then gives it to you as a historical artifact.

—Maybe.

—Go on.

—See?!

—I won't say another word.

—"He started telling us to get one of the ropes we used to put up the tarps and he lured Doug away from the fire. He tackled him and we tied him up and Malcolm started talking to him."

—What was that sound? Did you hear that? Oh, sorry. Go on.

—"And in the firelight you could see Doug's teeth grow longer, all of them, not just like fangs, but like his mouth was growing out like a snout. And he bit Malcolm more than once, so there was blood. And Doug's eyes were crazy. I mean, we didn't know what was happening back then, but you could tell Doug wasn't human. Not when he was changing. And his hair thickened up. Like every hair follicle on his body doubled in size."

—I bet it itches.

—"Doug was shaking and struggling. And Malcolm was straddled over him, sort of riding him, keeping him away from the fire. And he was asking him over and over again, stuff like 'What are you fighting against?' And 'What are you afraid of?' And 'What's the most important thing in the world to you?' And we were all so scared we started answering Malcolm's questions—for Doug—to Doug."

—All right. Is that it?

—It says: "He changed back after three days, but he was so burned, and that got infected. He wouldn't let us take him to the hospital. He just wanted to stay drunk for his last few days and have us tell him about the change and imagine what he could have done with all that power." That's it.

—All right. Let's rewind it and see what we sound like.

27

Tanya tells Malcolm what she found when she went to feed Susan.

—Malcolm, baby, wake up.

—I'm awake.

—Bobert's gone.

—Where?

—I don't know.

—What do you mean, he's gone?

—I'm telling you straight—I woke up and I couldn't get back to sleep. I went down to the kitchen, and they have fresh fruit. So I decided to make Susan a snack.

—That's a problem.

—It was fine. There was nothing wrong with the fruit.

—The problem is—if they left fresh fruit out that means they expect someone to come eat it.

—Not necessarily. Rich people let shit go to waste all the time.

—I bet we should be expecting a maid or a cleaning lady or something. We'll just have to plan for it.

—The point is—Bobert's gone.

—All right. I'll get up. Keep telling me while I get my jeans on.

—I cut up the fruit and put it on a plate and took it up to Susan. I could hear Bobert reading to Susan, like whispering. He didn't say anything to me when I told him I was going to feed Susan. I figured he was just in the zone. Just focused. So I told him I was gonna go in, but he didn't stop reading. Whatever. But then I asked him to hold the tray for second while I got the door unlocked. By then my eyes were adjusting and I was putting two and two together. And I saw, in his chair, it was just a tape recorder playing Bobert's voice and the door to the closet was open.

—Is Susan all right?

—I don't know. I came to get you.

—Fuck. This is all we need right now.

28

House meeting.

—Turn off the lights.

    —No. I'm not gonna turn off the lights. Get up.

    —What the fuck, Malcolm?

    —Get up. Is everybody here?

    —Don't hit me with that thing, Malcolm.

    —I'm not hitting you. I'm tapping you. I'm waking you up. You'll know when I'm hitting you.

    —What the fuck is so important?

    —I don't see Angel.

    —She's probably passed out in some other room.

    —We're having a house meeting.

    —What time is it?

    —Susan's missing.

    —What happened?

    —Bobert took off.

    —I left a tape recorder playing.

    —Where were you?

    —I went to go to the bathroom.

    —I told you to go in the bucket.

    —No one ever brought me a bucket.

—Then ask somebody for a bucket. Call out. Start screaming. I would have come running.

—There was nobody to ask.

—Are you sure?

—Yeah. You were all asleep.

—We have to find Susan.

—All right. Everybody search a different room. Just search the house first. I don't think she's gonna get far. We'll meet back here in five minutes if nobody finds her. And somebody let the dog out. He probably needs to shit. Not you, Bobert. You stay and talk to me.

—The dog likes me.

—I don't care. Your privileges are revoked. Everybody else start looking! Bobert, no. You stay and talk with me.

Search. Search. Search. Search. Search.

—No one ever brought me a bucket.

—You should have asked somebody.

—There was nobody to ask.

—You shoulda asked the person who brought you the tape recorder.

—That was Angel.

—You think I don't know? I can hear her on the tape. In the background. Breathing.

—You can hear that?

—I'm a good listener.

—What are you going to do to me?

—What do you mean?

—Are you going to beat me up?

—You want me to tell you what we're going to do to you?

—Yeah. Just tell me. Then I don't need to worry about it. I think once you say it, then it's over, in its own way.

—I like that theory.

—If you say you're going to hit me, then I know it and it's like it's already over. Even if you say everybody's gonna hit me, one by one, or something. I can take it. If you hold me down. Or even if I have to just stand here and take it. Whatever. Just tell me. Or are you going to brand me?

—What do you mean, brand you?

—Like bend up a coat hanger into shape and heat it up on the stove and brand me, like an animal. You could use the wolf shape you spray-painted on driveway of the other house? Just tell me. I don't really care.

—I'm gonna send you home.

—How?

—We're gonna make you leave.

—But I don't have to go home. I can go anywhere I want.

—You don't have to do anything you don't want to do. Including look after Susan.

—If you kick me out I'm gonna call the cops and report this house.

—If you send the cops to this house, we won't be here when they show up. You know that.

—Don't kick me out.

—It's like you said—once I say it, it's already done.

—I'm sorry.

—At least you're not getting branded. That sounds messed up. Where'd you hear about that, anyway?

—Give me another chance.

—I am.

—I'm gonna die wandering the streets. I'm no good at it.

—Don't wander the streets. Go home.

—I don't want to go home.

—If you don't go home we'll have no way to get in touch with you.

—You don't know my home address.

—Write it down before you leave. Then, in one month, I'll write to you and tell you where to meet us. I promise.

—What about Angel?

—Don't sell her out. In the first place, you don't need to. And in the second place, it only makes me like you less.

—Why does she get to stay?

—I didn't say she did.

—But she does. Doesn't she?

—She didn't break any rules.

—But she distracted me. She gave me the tape recorder. It was her idea. She said it was my voice that mattered and as long Susan could hear my voice it wouldn't matter if I took a break to go to the bathroom.

—It was your job to stay. In some ways it was Angel's job to try to talk you into leaving. But it was your job to stay. Nobody told Angel to do anything. She didn't, like, violate the will of the group.

—But why do I hafta go home?

—Where else are you gonna go?

—Why can't I just live in the backyard, in the bushes or something?

—No. If you don't go home, you are never gonna see us again. I'm telling you it's already done.

—Who's gonna take care of the dog?

—That's disrespectful. The dog can take care of himself.

—What if I change while I'm home?

—You got any brothers or sisters?

—I have a younger brother.

—Then let me give you a piece of advice: Don't eat him.

—We found a trail—

—The dog found it—

—Susan's shoes are on the other side of the fence, and then her socks are in the street!

—Get the fuck out of here, Bobert. Now! Before I change my mind.

—Change your mind.

—Are you sure? I could change my mind into something worse. I could change my mind into we all kill you.

—I'm gonna die just getting home. I'm terrible on the streets.

—You know what? Here's fifty bucks. Get a cab. Or else try to live on tuna for a month and keep track of us. You won't be able to. And if I see you anywhere around here I'm going to personally kill you. Take it. I don't need it. I don't need money. I do better when I have to scramble to figure shit out.

—Thanks.

—Don't fucking thank me. That's disgusting. Just leave.

—Can I say goodbye to everybody?

—Just leave your address. Write it down.

—Where?

—Find a fucking piece of paper. Write it on the fucking wall, for all I care. Write it down. Now.

—Ow. Jesus! Fuck. Someone. Help. You broke my arm. Don't hit me again.

—I'm only gonna hit you that one time. Like I told you. Just so you know I'm true to my word. So you'll know I will write to you and tell you where we are. And so you know I will kill you if I see you snooping around here. All right? Now finish it. Good. Now leave.

—You better write to me.

—I said: Leave.

—He promised to write to me, everybody. Malcolm promised to send me your address in a month.

—All right. Now, everybody else. Let's go get Susan before she hurts somebody.

29

Someone new catches Susan up on what happened while she was changing.

—The dog found you in the Speedy Stop.

—How?

—Everybody said it was the dog, but we were just following a trail of your clothes.

—My feet are all cut up.

—You ran across pavement without any socks or shoes.

—Who are you?

—I met Tanya at a coffee shop. I told her I liked her drawings, and we started talking. She was so nice. The way she called me "baby" and was just nice to me.

—When the dog found me in the Speedy Stop, was I awake?

—You didn't look like it.

—Was this recently that you met Tanya in a coffee shop or, like, years ago in college?

—A few days ago.

—Weird.

—She brought me home. To the last house. Before we moved. I met everybody. I met you, too.

—I guess I don't remember anything from the past week all that well.

—You took off your shoes in the backyard and your socks were in the street. And then we found your shirt down the road.

—Oh, no.

—Yeah. You took off everything in a straight line pointing to the Speedy Stop. Your pants were in the intersection at Cresswell. And by then your feet were bleeding pretty good.

—It's funny. I'm embarrassed, but I remember it felt so good.

—I bet. That's the reason they made up embarrassment. To keep us from doing the stuff that feels good.

—What did I want at the Speedy Stop?

—By the time we caught up to the dog, we found you in the middle of a big pile of beer and potato chips and candy and shit. It looked like you had been running, trying to smash through the glass doors, but the magic eye saw you and opened the doors and you just crashed right into the big potato chip display and all the shit around it fell down onto you. You weren't trying to eat any of it. You were just in the middle of it. It was kind of funny. It was kind of a good thing you smashed into it, too, because the next thing to crash into was the glass wall of fridges and they don't open automatically.

—Why was I running?

—I dunno. Why do people run?

—To get away from shit.

—Why do kids run?

—Because it's fun.

—Maybe you were just having a new kind of fun for you. Or an old kind of fun you forgot about.

—I'm all cut up.

—Malcolm's guess is that Angel cut the belt off you with a big knife from the kitchen. We found the knife block tipped over in the kitchen, and all the knives were scattered on the kitchen counter, and when we put them back the biggest one was missing. But Angel wasn't trying to free you. She just wanted to get the watch off your wrist. But once your hands were free, you clawed the ankle rope off yourself. Plus, who knows what happened to you between here and the store. You might have killed an alley cat or attacked an old lady.

—I know I said I don't remember anything, but I do remember some things.

—Did Angel take the watch from you?

—I remember Malcolm coming up to me in the store. I would have sworn I was still in the closet. But it was so bright. He was glowing from the fluorescents behind him, and I remember him brushing the hair back from my face and asking me if I wanted to get out of there, and I tried to say yes because I thought I was still in the closet. And he just kept brushing my hair back over and over for forever.

—Then you let him have it.

—I don't remember that.

—You went for his face, clawing and scratching. You bit his arm, bad. It looked like you wanted to kill him. But he got you by the hair and held your head away from his face so that you couldn't bite him and then you started scratching the shit out of his arm.

—I don't remember that.

—Malcolm was totally calm. He didn't call for help or ask us to do anything.

—That's unusual.

—Is it? I don't know him very well yet.

—Yeah, I guess you could say he's our leader, but the main way he shows it is by bossing people around. Asking for help. Making other people do this and that.

—Tanya said you didn't have a leader.

—You said she was drawing? I didn't know she drew.

—It's all portraits of you guys.

—Do they look cool?

—Yours looks like you.

—I wanna see it.

—Ask her.

—I remember thinking this was my chance. That now I could go somewhere I always wanted to go to. I don't remember Angel cutting the belt or getting free. But I remember a feeling, like, now a door in my life is open, and I can go get something I always wanted. Like, if I wanted for Tanya to show me something all I had to do was go get it, or if I wanted money from a bank, or sex, or anything, I could just have it.

—You looked calm when the dog found you. But as soon as Malcolm touched you . . .

—Now I just feel like I want to get that way again. I mean, I'm tired, too. But mostly I just want to get that way again. Not just to change, but to change and be free.

—You would have killed Malcolm if he hadn't held on to you.

—Is that how I got so cut up?

—No. Malcolm didn't fight you. He just held on to you as you tried to kill him. You got cut up on your own.

—I wouldn't kill anybody. Ever.

—You weren't yourself.

—I feel like if I wanted to I could have gone to a stranger's house and just walked in and gone up to the bedroom and gone to sleep and nobody would have bothered me. Like everything available in the world belonged to me.

—You're lucky you didn't get hurt.

—I did.

—I mean, you're lucky you didn't get hurt to death.

—What did I look like?

—You should ask Tanya to show you her drawing.

—Is it me now or me changed?

—You looked totally different.

—Did I have more hair?

—No. But you looked totally different.

—Did I look bigger?

—No. I guess you were about the same size.

—Did I look scary?

—I was scared. But not because of the way you looked. It was because you suddenly possessed this really broad range of expressions all at once. Like, most of the time, most people, we're happy when we're happy, and sad when we're sad, and we have to move along really slowly to get from one to the other over the course of a day. But you could go instantly from calm to totally attacking to happy to see me and fall into my arms to carry you out.

—You carried me out?

—Yeah. The lady behind the counter recognized some of us from when we stole the beer, and she wouldn't shut up, so Malcolm finally hit her until she shut up.

—I remember you were with us when we stole the beer.

—Yeah. I've been here for a while. I like it here. I think I'm gonna stay.

—Even after what happened to me?

—After what happened to you everybody woke up and had a house meeting and went out looking for you. Nobody's looking for me at all. That's why I want to stay.

—I remember Malcolm pushing my hair back from my face and asking me to put my arm around your shoulder, and you helped me walk home.

—Yeah. That's right.

—And then Tanya fed me something.

—Slices of apple dipped in some fancy organic peanut butter they have.

—I remember wanting to eat for her. To make her proud or something.

—She likes feeding us. Nothing makes her happier than providing for us.

—And Tanya told you to take over being my reader for the last two days.

—And now you're back to normal.

—Where's Angel?

—She's gone. Malcolm thinks she's starting a new house on her own. He says she's watching us. He says she's biding her time, waiting for an opportunity. He says she's going to come swooping in with a new group of kids and—

—Where's Malcolm?

—He's around. He's still not eating. He says he's going to be true to his word. And do something for us with all that hunger. Today's his third day without food.

—Where's Bobert?

—He went home.

—Really?

—Malcolm said he had to, for a month, so he'll remember what he's missing here.

—What day is it?

—Tuesday.

Part Two

NEIGHBORS

30

Bobert's little brother follows him around the house.

—What was it like to live on your own?

   —I wasn't on my own. I was with friends.

   —You know what I mean—to be out in the world, doing whatever you want to?

   —I'm not gonna tell you anything different than I told Mom or the police.

   —That was all bullshit. I could hear you from the other room and you were lying so bad.

   —I'm not gonna tell you anything different, 'cause if I do, they can use it against us.

   —Bullshit.

   —You think so? I bet you fifty dollars that in the next twenty-four hours Mom is gonna come ask you what I've told you. If she does, that's proof they're trying to use you against me.

   —You're on. I'm not gonna tell on you.

   —That's not the bet, Tim. Besides, you don't have fifty dollars.

   —Neither do you.

   —That's another bet you'd lose. See?

   —Where the fuck did you get fifty dollars?

   —When did you start cussing so much?

—The day you ran away and fucking left me here.

—Well, you can cut it out. I'm back.

—That doesn't mean you can boss me around.

—You know it's not like there are no rules outside this house. We had a lot of rules. We were trying to develop a kind of discipline so that we could do important stuff.

—That's the dumbest thing I ever fucking heard.

—Why don't you make a list of who *can* boss you around. That way when I want something done I'll go straight to *that* person and talk to them.

—I'm the only one who's in charge of me.

—Then you're the one I want to talk to about not cussing so much when you talk to me. You can cuss when you talk to somebody who'll be impressed, but don't waste your time on me. I wanna hear you sound like my little brother. The guy who stays up late at night whispering so no one hears us, who'll talk with me about anything. We don't have to try to impress each other, or sound tough, or try to pretend we don't have any emotions.

—Dad takes off. You take off. I can cuss as much as I want.

—Here. I don't like the way you're petting the cat. Give him to me.

—Why?

—You have to be soft with animals. You have to be gentle. An animal only understands physical touch. An animal doesn't understand talking.

—How come you know so much about animals, Bobert?

—Nobody calls me Bobert anymore. They all call me Rob.

—Who?

—The friends I was staying with.

—Why'd you leave?

—I'm just lying low a while. They're gonna send for me.

—At school they call me "the Orphan."

—You got Mom.

—I think that's their point. I have Mom but she doesn't count as a mom.

—You got me.

—I didn't.

—You do now.

—For how long?

—See how he likes being pet? Steady and regular but soft. See?

—How long until they send for you?

—I'm not going to tell you anything different than I told Mom.

—What's it like to be back home?

—It's different. It seems like everything goes faster here. And there's a lot of food in the house. I never realized how much food we have. I always used to think there was nothing to eat. But we have a lot of stuff. If you were starving and you came across this house you could live for a month. But it smells weird here.

—Shit.

—Don't cuss.

—It's just—I don't want our house to smell.

—It doesn't stink.

—Yeah, but that's one of the shitty things about being poor. You go over to other people's houses and they smell great. And then you go over to somebody's house, like John Longoria's, and it smells weird, and the first thing you think isn't "John's gross." Instead all you can think is "I hope my house doesn't smell this weird when people come over."

—Who comes over?

—Yeah, well, that's the other shitty thing about being poor.

—Stop cussing. I'm serious. If you don't know you're doing it we could make a rule that every time you cuss I hit you. That way you'll start to develop a consciousness about it.

—What's the big deal? What's the big fucking deal?

—I don't like it. Isn't that enough? I just don't like it. I want my little brother to be nice.

—I don't care.

—Well, that's the main difference about being back home. Where I stay, the people I stay with, they all care about one another. They're all nice. In their own way. And everybody's equal.

—Then why did you leave?

—You know what? I'm going to set up a game for this. I'm going to write down a list of everything I'm eventually gonna tell you: where I was, what I was doing, who I was with, why I'm here now, and when I'm going back. And then every time you ask me a question you already asked me, I'm going to cross a fact off the list and then you'll never find it out.

—Whatever. I don't really give a shit.

—And every time you cuss. That's one, too. Now stop following me around. Take the cat back and leave me alone for five minutes. Here. Ow.

—What'd you do to your arm?

—I'm not gonna tell you anything different than I told Mom or the police.

31

Malcolm drags everybody down to the basement to show off his discovery before they all go to bed, except for Tanya and Malcolm, who stay behind to discuss it, but not like you think.

—What the fuck is that?

   —It's a gun safe.

—How do you know?

   —It fucking says BROWNING AUTOMATIC in curly, fake, old-timey writing.

   —What's a Browning?

   —It's a kind of gun. Right, Malcolm?

   —I knew there was something in this house we hadn't found yet. That's what I did while I wasn't eating. I went over the whole house inch by inch, to occupy my time. Your brain gets a little weird when you don't eat. So I thought I would use that feeling to explore small things. To look at all their books. To see how many knives they had. I had no idea I would find guns. But I did. I knew I would find something exactly like this.

   —But you don't know if there are actually guns inside the safe?

   —Why else have a safe this tall unless you want to hide rifles? And why else put it down in the basement, in a utility closet with the hot water heater in the back of the house, out of the way of the kids?

—We won't know what's in it until we open it.

—Not tonight. I'm too excited. I'm too tired. I have to eat and then sleep. But tomorrow we'll search all the drawers and cabinets. We'll gather together all the important looking papers and we'll go through them looking for a combination to the safe.

—I thought you had already explored all the small stuff.

—I wasn't looking for a number. I didn't notice it because I wasn't looking for it. I probably saw it. I know I did. I probably picked it up and held it in my hand and looked at it. But I don't remember where.

—I bet the safe is full of Krugerrands.

—What's a Kruggerand?

—It's like gold bullion. It's money for survivalists!

—Too bad it's locked.

—It's a fucking safe, you idiot, of course it's locked.

—We'll get in there.

—How?

—Why don't we call the Eye-5 News Hotline and ask to borrow their helicopter? Then we hook the safe up to the whirlybird and haul it up to the stratosphere. That way the Quick Response News Crew will be in perfect position when we cut the safe loose and it shatters on the pavement. They can look down on us and capture on film the way we scoop up all the guns like kids picking up candy from a piñata.

—What are we going to do with the guns—if that's even what's in there?

—Point 'em at people.

—Who?

—Bad people.

—The Peugeot man?

—Among others.

—Angel?

—I don't know that pointing a gun at Angel would do any good. I think you'd have to pull the trigger at her.

—I don't wanna shoot anybody. Necessarily.

—Where do you think Angel went?

—Not far.

—What makes you think she's still around?

—I just know.

—Have you seen her with your own two eyes?

—No, but the little hairs on the back of my neck can sense her. I think she's watching us.

—From where?

—I think she's got some place in the neighborhood she can stay.

—Where?

—If she doesn't have it yet, I bet she's looking for it. I bet she's living in some kid's tree house or she's shacked up with some dude from some bar. She's gonna take over somebody's life so she can be nearby and watch us.

—What does she want?

—I bet she wants to start her own family, or to take over this one.

—All right, everybody. Let's let Malcolm get some rest. He's done enough for tonight. I'm gonna feed him and put him to bed. Everybody go find a bed or a best friend who's already got one. Let's pack it in for the night. Come on, baby. You'll thank me tomorrow. When we're searching all over the house tomorrow, you'll come across some nice stationery and a fountain pen and you can write me a thank-you note.

—Good night, Tanya.

—Good night.

—I call the older sister's room.

—You have to call it by name.

—I call Rebecca's room.

—How do you know her name?

—I read her journals.

—That's awesome. Were they good?

—There's good parts.

—Good night.

—Good night everybody.

—

—

—I'm scared, baby.

—I got it all under control. I'll take care of you.

—That's sweet. But it's not true.

—What are you afraid of Tanya?

—Angel wants to destroy me.

—Why would she want that?

—Well, there's plenty of songs about love at first sight, lifelong romance, and soul mates meant for each other. But the opposite is also true: A lot of times two people meet and it's just perfect hate.

—It's probably the same chemicals that makes 'em both happen.

—You ever read *Othello*?

—In college, I guess.

—I bet they have a copy here.

—They have two. Rebecca has a copy and there's a collected Shakespeare in the dad's office. I noticed all sorts of little shit like that when I was starving to death.

—I'll get you some food. But what do you remember about the play?

—It's about a black guy and a white girl.

—Right. It seems like that's the stuff that doesn't fit right. Black vs. White. Man against Woman. But get one of those copies and take a look. The real trouble is between two people who are exactly the same. Two white guys. The bad guy, Iago, is only going after Othello to get back at this other white guy, Cassio. Take a look—it's weird. I think Angel and I are like that. We're exactly the same.

—You telling me you wanna go out and start your own family? Or take over this one?

—Take a look at the story again. Seriously.

—You think Angel wants to kill you so she can get ahold of me?

—Angel doesn't give a fuck about you, Malcolm. She wants everything I have. Not just you, but my mind and the way I go about living in the world.

—Why?

—I hath a daily beauty in my life that makes her ugly.

—What does that mean?

—It's from the play. Read it.

—Just tell me what it means. Jesus. I don't want to go reading books to understand what you're trying to say.

—It means when Angel and I look at each other we hate ourselves.

—So you think she's going to try to tear us apart.

—I do. I think she's gonna try to destroy our pack.

—Why doesn't she just call the cops?

—She might. But not now. If she calls the cops we all just get split up and run away. But if she does it right—if she can manage a way for the cops to come and get me and leave all of you together, especially if she can save you from the cops while I get taken away . . . I think that's what she's gonna do.

—Well, I'm not gonna get together with Angel.

—I don't care if you do.

—Why the fuck would you say that?

—It's not about you. It's about me and Angel. You should read the fucking book.

—All right. I will.

—But not now, baby.

—You're right.

—You better believe it. What make you think I don't already control this house? They support you because I do. So you better watch out.

—You're right. I should be getting myself ready for Angel, so I can protect you from her.

—How?

—I need to make us safe. And then I need to get into that gun safe and get those guns.

—Good. But eat something first, baby. Tomorrow we'll figure out the combination.

—I'm not hungry.

—I don't care.

—Once you get past a certain point it feels like you could just not eat forever.

—Well, I'm gonna bring you back to your appetite.

—How are you gonna do that?

—Chicken and dumplings. Rolls. Iced tea.

—That sorta sounds good.

—Wait 'til you see me eating it all right in front of you. You'll get your hunger back.

—All right. You start cooking. I have to go out and take care of something.

—What are you gonna do, Malcolm?

—I gotta make us safe. I have to run back by the last house and make sure we didn't leave any evidence we didn't mean to.

—You better hurry. I'll start eating without you.

32

Angel wakes up with Craig.

—Get up. Wake the fuck up. Wake up.

—Whoa.

—Yeah, "whoa" is right. You need to shake the cobwebs out, sleepy-head.

—Who are you?

—I'm your new girlfriend.

—Did we meet last night?

—What do you *fucking think*?! Am I in your bed?! Am I wearing anything?! Are these bruises on my wrists and my ribs—are they real?

—Ow. Don't hit me.

—Are you *serious*?

—Yeah, I'm fucking serious. Don't hit me.

—Don't you remember anything about last night, cowboy?

—No. You were fucking force-feeding me drinks.

—Look at my arms and my ribs. You see these bruises?

—I didn't do that.

—You did. This is what you're into.

—No way.

—You got drunk enough to forget your manners—then you started to wanna mess me around.

—I don't wanna mess you around.

—You did. You got drunk and then you wanted to play "don't hit me."

—I have to go to work.

—Wait.

—Ow. Don't hit me!

—Yeah. That's how the game's played. Only last night the roles were reversed. You were pitching and I was catching.

—Look, I'm sorry—

—So you *are* starting to remember?

—No. I don't know what you're talking about.

—Then I'll show you.

—Show me what?

—Find your fucking handcuffs and I'll jog your memory.

—I have to go to work.

—Fine. We can talk about it when you get home.

—You're not gonna be here when I get home.

—I am.

—Fuck you.

—I'm your new girlfriend. I'm gonna stick with you until you remember me.

—Why do you wanna be my girlfriend if I was so mean to you?

—'Cause I'd never let a total stranger treat me the way you did.

33

Malcolm takes the dog out.

I got back, ate the best meal of my life, and then collapsed in the bed. I was planning on the best sleep of my life, too. But the dog woke me up. It wanted to go outside. It kept standing up on its back legs so it could get its front paws on the edge of the bed and lean forward until it could lick my face. At first I thought it was in love. I thought the dog wanted to get in bed with Tanya and me. But when I tried to lift the dog up into the bed it growled at me and backed away. Tanya told me to take it outside.

As soon as I got up and opened the bedroom door, the dog bolted out of the room. Maybe it should have been obvious to me that this was why the dog was licking me. It's funny, animals and humans can do the exact same action and mean the opposite thing by it. If Susan had been lying on our bedroom floor, reaching up onto the bed, licking my face, etc.—that wouldn't mean Susan wanted to go outside; that definitely would have meant Susan wanted to get under the covers with us.

The dog ran away when I opened the bedroom door because it wanted me to follow. I know the dog wanted me to follow it because the dog came back and barked at me when I paused in the doorway to get my head on straight. The dog knows it's going to need me to open more doors to get outside. This is how a dog says "follow me," by running. But I didn't run away from home so I could be followed. I ran away to be gone.

The less said about my family the better. I try to do push-ups and sit-ups every day because that's one of the simple things I can do to change the way I look, to make me look less like the rest of my family. I keep my hair cut in a mohawk. I try to smile a lot. And I never look directly into a TV screen. If it ever happens that I'm unlucky enough to be standing next to my family ever again, you're not gonna see any resemblance. They're clean, clean-shaven, no tattoos, clean clothes and trimmed nails. I'm wild.

The dog's funny. It runs over people in the living room. When they yell and swing their arms to get the dog to leave them alone, the dog wags its tail and jumps back over 'em. The dog is playing and the people aren't. But they're both engaged in the same activity at the same moment in time.

My thoughts are getting shorter and shorter as I get farther and farther from the bed. I'm tired. Not eating for three days will really wear you out. I'm impressed if this is something Angel actually did with any regularity. She's out there feeling the same way I am, more or less, if she kept her word. Starving makes you wild and then that first meal tames you into a seriously sluggish bad mood.

The back door on this house has at least four locks. A lock in the door-knob, a couple of deadbolts, and a chain latch. All this on a door with a big glass pane in the middle of it so you can see who's there. Whoever installed these locks ought to be sued for malpractice.

The dog bolted into the bushes after a cat or something. Animals know what they want when they want it. Wish I did. Always.

I want Tanya to get up and come to the window. I want her to stand there, naked, and look down on me in the backyard. I want us to take a little time to look each other over at a distance. I want her to fall in love with what she sees. Then I want Angel to come flying out of the bushes, attacking me with a hammer. But I want to catch Angel's wrist with my left hand and punch her with a right cross and send her into the pool. We're all naked in this fantasy. Angel drowns. The dog comes out of the bushes and howls at the moon. All the rest of the gang is in the kitchen, watching me through the windows at the kitchen sink. Everybody is applauding me. And Tanya is up above, looking down on me from the bedroom window, smiling.

None of that's gonna happen. Tanya's asleep. The rest of the gang is asleep. The dog isn't going to come out of the bushes unless I go back into the kitchen and find a piece of meat or something to lure it back. The dog would come to Bobert. The dog liked Bobert. But the dog only *needs* me.

I don't know if Tanya's right about all our troubles being between her and Angel. I don't know if she's right in her description of what *Othello* is really about. But I do know Angel's as smart as Iago. At least in the sense that Angel's not going to jump out of the bushes and swing a hammer at me. Angel's gonna lay a trap for me and I'm going to be the one that jumps into it.

I want to kill somebody. I want to see what it's like. I assume it's no big deal. At least I tell myself it's no big deal. But I get really excited when I think about it. Here's how I imagine it now: A man is washing his dishes at the kitchen sink, and all of a sudden he gets a sensation that he's being watched. He gets a chill down the back of his neck. He looks behind him. There's no one. He looks out into his backyard, and there's me, completely naked. No weapons. But I have a smile on my face. Most people smile because they're happy. I smile because I'm an animal that's getting what it wants. The man can't do anything but watch as I walk to the back door. I don't even try the handle. I punch my left hand through the glass and unlock all four locks without taking my eyes off the man. I use my left hand because I don't care about it. I'm keeping my right hand useful for the task and that's all that matters. The man I'm fantasizing about killing is terrified. He probably yells at me. He probably runs to get the phone. He runs to another room with a better door and locks it between us. But his actions are in conflict. If he wants to calm me down, he shouldn't yell at me. If he wants to hide, he shouldn't call the cops and tell them where he is. If he wants to get away from me, he shouldn't back himself into a corner.

I walk through the house slowly. I open the door to the bedroom. I lift up the covers and Tanya is there, naked, asleep, but growling at me to get in next to her, to pull the covers over both of us and get warm. The dog followed me back in and now it lays on the floor at the side of the bed, perfectly content. The dog knows I can be trusted now to give it what it wants. This is my house now. No matter what Tanya says. I'm not gonna give it up for Angel, or the man who owns it, or his family, or the cops. This is my house. I put my right hand on Tanya's breast and pull her to me and swear myself to sleep on it.

34

Bobert and his stepdad have a little talk about the way things are now.

—Leave me alone.

  —Come 'ere.

  —You don't want me to.

  —I do.

  —You don't.

  —Why don't I?

  —I changed, motherfucker.

  —Come back here. Come back here right this instant. Don't talk to me like that. Don't walk away from me while I'm talking to you. Bobert. Bobert!

35

And on the third day, all the werewolves gathered in the kitchen to make a plan.

—Morning.

    —Morning, sugar. You look great. Who got you smiling like that?

    —I love this house.

    —Me, too.

    —I feel like we can be totally different people here.

    —Me, too.

    —It's been three nights and nobody's trashed the place. Last night nobody got drunk. Nobody broke anything.

    —I broke the Jacuzzi tub in the back bedroom, but it was an accident that could have happened to the normal family.

    —If we were a normal family, we'd call a plumber.

    —But we're not, baby.

    —We just keep using what works. Keep eating yogurt 'til the fridge breaks down, keep watching TV 'til it stops working. Then we'll get a tape all knotted up in the reel to reel player . . . until eventually almost everything is broken and we'll all be jammed up in the bathroom, waiting for the last lightbulb in the house to burn out so we can say we got every last drop out of this place before we move on.

    —How'd you break the Jacuzzi? Were you taking a bath?

—I thought I'd clean up. I didn't wanna get the sheets dirty in the little girl's bed.

—It's not just me. This house is changing all of us.

—How do you feel, Susan?

—I could use a cup of coffee. But otherwise, I'm cool.

—I'm glad you told us to go to bed last night, Tanya.

—Did you do it?

—No, but now the coffee tastes *so* good.

—I haven't had coffee in months.

—Why didn't we make any yesterday morning?

—We were all sleeping.

—I can't believe I ever lived without coffee.

—The smell is what woke me up.

—It woke everybody up and lured them into the kitchen.

—So what's on the agenda today, Malcolm?

—Well, why don't we get a couple of people on breakfast duty, cooking up a big meal—

—We're all gonna eat together?

—Like a family?

—What's got into you, Malcolm?

—I can eat again. I took care of some business last night. I had a big meal. Then I got a good night's sleep. I got my head on straight. Now I know what I want. And it starts with eating a big meal with everybody.

—I can cook, baby.

—I'll help.

—While you two do that, the rest of us are going to turn the house over.

—What do you mean?

—We're done just eating and sleeping and drinking and fucking. We're gonna make a plan and live by it.

—What's the plan?

—First thing we need to do is to go through the house.

—You already did that.

—We all have.

—We need to do it again, methodically, and make a mental inventory of everything we've got here. Here's how we're going to do it—

—Pull out a drawer. Turn the drawer over. Kick through the shit with your foot.

—No. The point is *not* to make a mess.

—We can be neat. We have been, pretty much.

—First thing is: Everybody think through what you personally would need if we all took off to live in the woods.

—Why do we have to go live in the woods?

—We don't.

—But the point I keep trying to make is not to let this house go to waste when we *do* have to leave. Which we will. Eventually.

—So like: food, water, clothes.

—Right. And I want you all to be especially on the lookout for any money, or medicine, or pills.

—Some of us already found some.

—Well, then tonight, after everybody's had a chance to go through the house *methodically*, we're all going to share what we've found and divvy it up.

—I don't wanna share.

—What if somebody finds something better than what you found, honey? You'll want them to share with you, won't you?

—I guess.

—Also, collect any clues you find about who might come visit us here. What kind of people might be stopping by? Maids, relatives, house sitters, whatever.

—And anything that gives us a basic family bio—news clippings about little junior's last track meet or whatever.

—Why do we care about that?

—We need to be able to have a basic conversation about family business with whoever they have checking up on the house.

—What makes you think someone's gonna stop by?

—Tanya pointed it out to me—we've been eating fresh fruit. So I think someone's coming by to check up on things.

—We should get our story straight in case someone stops by.

—That's what I'm saying, you fucking moron.

—I guess the house hasn't changed you *that much*, Malcolm.

—We can do it tonight. We'll have a big story circle and work out who we are and what we're doing here and we'll plan out the whole fairy tale while we're baking cookies and then Malcolm can take the cookies to the neighbors tomorrow.

—That seems like a dumb idea.

—We'll talk about it tonight.

—I wanna start digging through their shit!

—Don't trash the place. Don't pull things out of drawers and just throw 'em on the ground. Keep the shit from each drawer and each shelf all together so you can put it back neatly.

—We should do it like a practical joke. Empty out one drawer and then move that stuff to the next drawer up and on and on as we search the house, so when the family comes back everything is just one drawer or one shelf off.

—Malcolm probably won't let us.

—Can we do that? Or is that against the rules, Malcolm?

—I think that's funny. We should do it. It's got a little bit of cruelty in it to keep us focused. That's discipline. Let's do it. As you search the house, put everything back perfectly, but in the wrong place. Everything goes back one drawer up or one shelf over.

—This is gonna be awesome.

—And everybody keep your eye out for the combination to their safe. They must've written it down somewhere. Maybe in a filing cabinet with tax returns or something. It might not say, "This is the combination to the safe." But it's going to be three numbers. You know, like a combination lock. 35-12-14. Whatever.

—What do we get if we find it?

—What do you want?

—A blow job.

—From who?

—I'll give you a blow job right now, baby.

—I want to be allowed to drive their car around town.

—We'll see about that.

—Everybody's gonna want something different.

—All right. We'll each write down what we want and put all our wishes in the hat and whoever finds the combination gets to pull a wish from the hat and we'll all do everything we can to make it come true.

—The hat is back!

—What do you think about that idea, Malcolm?

—I think it sounds fine.

—I thought you hated the hat, Malcolm?

—I don't hate the hat.

—He just wants to be the head of it!

—Haha!

—How do we decide who gets to start searching which room? I mean, the combination's not going to be in one of the kids' rooms, so if you want to win the prize—

—You don't know where the combination's gonna be.

—When I say *go*, everybody run to the room you wanna search. If somebody else is already in that room go somewhere else.

—Or fight 'em for it.

—No. I don't want a big fucking, bloody mess all over this house. You get disqualified if you trash the house or do something stupid.

—What qualifies as "something stupid"?

—Use your best judgment.

—No, baby, I'm the judge. Use *my* best judgment. Don't do anything you think is going to piss me off. And don't rush. Be quiet and thorough.

—And whoever finds the combination let out a howl.

—We're gonna stay and cook breakfast.

—You don't wanna try to win the prize?

—I already have my prize. The whole group of you acting like a pack. It's beautiful.

—Is everybody ready?

Nod. Nod. Nod. Nod. Nod.

—Then . . . on your mark. Get set. Go!

36

Tanya and Malcolm discuss the plan.

—Breakfast was good.

—Why do you say it like that? I don't know why you say it like that. You know I can cook, baby.

—I know you can cook one-on-one, but cooking for an army is a whole other thing altogether.

—I wanna talk about our army for a sec.

—What?

—I just don't know if guns is such a good idea.

—We haven't found the combination yet.

—I don't know if I want to.

—What are you scared of?

—I'm not scared. It's just not what I want.

—All right then, let's hear it.

—If I had to add one thing to this group it would probably be a camper van, or another two or three dogs.

—We'd look cool rolling into a country truck stop in a rickety old camper van farting exhaust, lurching to a stop with a backfire. Then the door opens up and four or five pit bulls tumble out.

—Why don't we do that? Why don't we run away? Now. Before what's going to happen next happens.

—This *is* what happens next.

—This conversation?

—This house. This taste of good fortune. We're going to have everything we need to run away.

—Then let's do it. Tonight, after we get everybody together and go through all the stuff. Let's take the best and go?

—The best people or the best stuff?

—Both.

—How are we gonna figure out who the best people are? Not the best people to hang out with and drink beers with, but the best people when things get tough?

—So you're gonna make things tough as a way of sorting everybody out?

—That's what happens next.

—You think they'll find the combination?

—What's the number one fear a person has when they lock something up?

—I dunno.

—The biggest fear is that they'll never get into it again. I mean, why else do ninety percent of the houses we squat in have keys under the mat? No one wants to be shut out of anything, much less their own belongings.

—But have you thought through what a gun is gonna do to us, baby?

—That's what I need you for. To worry it over for me.

—Fuck off.

—No, I'm serious. Tell me what you're thinking.

—Are my worries gonna change your actions?

—I can't tell until you share 'em with me. But, sure, if you've got a bad enough worry, I'll stop things in their tracks.

—Well, one of my worries is you won't be able to stop things.

—I'll shoot my gun in the air. That always gets everybody's attention in the movies.

—If there's only one gun in that safe, things are gonna be easy. You can be the only one who gets to hold it and things are perfect. But what if there's two guns?

—You can be my deputy.

—You're full of shit. You'll probably give it to Anquille. Or somebody who can shore up your leadership with some of the fringe people.

—Maybe some days. Maybe day by day I'll decide who gets the second gun. I mean, I don't imagine we'll even have the guns out most days.

—Just special days.

—Sure. Full moons and the like.

—You really wanna go busting into the Peugeot house, don't you?

—Yeah. That'll be a special day for sure.

—Okay, here's another worry: You break into that Peugeot house with a gun and someone's gonna get killed.

—I just wanna scare him really bad. I swear. Plus it'll bring the group together. Why do you think people come and go all the time?

—Why don't you tell me?

—We need a common enemy.

—Just trying to get by is the common enemy.

—Doesn't work. Or else all humanity would be united around that shit. You have to put a face on "trying to get by"—so we can see who's standing in our way and share a common point of focus.

—And Peugeot Guy's the focus?

—The planning for it. The training.

—We don't plan or train for anything.

—We're going to. For this.

—But think about it, Malcolm: What if Anquille decides he doesn't like you being the one who gets to decide who gets the guns? What if Anquille decides to get up in the middle of the night and get the guns himself and then—*bang*—he's the new leader?

—Maybe I won't give him the combo.

—Everybody is gonna have the combo.

—Maybe.

—What if Anquille finds the combo and decides not to share with you?

—That's why I offered a prize.

—The prize wasn't your idea. It was my idea.

—But it was my idea to make you my deputy.

—What if Angel comes back?

—I know Angel's coming back. She's gonna try to dethrone me before I solidify things.

—I'm not gonna feel safe 'til we're all a long way away from here, bouncing down the highway in our camper van.

—I promise.

—I don't need you to promise shit about that. I'm gonna make it happen myself. I just hope you're still around to see it.

37

Angel gets caught going through Craig's pockets.

—What are you doing?

  —I'm looking for my keys.

  —Come back to bed.

  —I can't. I have to get to work. You want breakfast?

  —No. I'm on a diet.

  —Really!?

  —Why do you say it like that?

  —You don't seem like the kind of girl who diets.

  —You don't seem like the kind of guy who would know which girls diet and which girls don't.

  —Sorry.

  —Don't apologize. Come back to bed and let's fight about it.

  —Do you see my coat anywhere?

  —How can you lose anything in this house? Everything's white and clean. The countertops are empty. Your bookshelves are alphabetized. I bet you shit at the same time every day, don't you?

  —I like to put everything back in its place. I usually hang my pants on this hook in the closet and leave my keys and my wallet in the pocket, so when my keys aren't in my pants pocket they could be anywhere.

  —Let me help you look.

—Thank you. As soon as we find my keys I'll take you anywhere you want to go.

—Why do you want to get rid of me so bad? I'm trying to be a good girlfriend.

—I don't want to get rid of you. I just have a lot of shit to do today.

—Maybe I can help?

—My life isn't something you can help with. I have to go to work. I have to get back to my regular life.

—All right. Calm down. We'll find your keys. Then you can get some of your stuff done and relax and we'll talk about *us* later.

—How are you gonna help me? You don't know where anything is in my house.

—What was the last thing you remember unlocking?

—I don't know. I was so fucked up when we came home last night.

—Are they still hanging in the front door? Or in your car?

—I walked to the party last night. I knew I was gonna get fucked up, so I walked.

—That's why I can't have a car. I mean, besides the fact that I'm completely broke. I don't have the kind of responsibility it takes. If you gave me gas money I'd probably just develop a taste for diesel.

—Haha.

—See? I'm funny. And I'm helping you look for your keys. That's all nice. Isn't it?

—I'm not trying to get rid of you. I like you. I had a good time last night. But now it's *today* and all the stuff I'm supposed to do today is weighing on me.

—What's this?

—I told you about that.

—You did not.

—I did.

—You have a video camera and a TV and a microphone and the whole thing set up and pointed at the bed.

—Why would I not tell you about it? It's out in the open. It's not hidden or anything.

—Did we make a sex tape?

—I swear to god I told you.

—I'm not accusing you. I just don't remember. I was just as fucked up as you were.

—Listen, this is turning out to be the worst morning ever—

—Look. That's us. Oh, my god! I can barely unzip my jeans, they're so tight. Jesus. I look cute, though, don't I?

—I don't know how to say this—but I don't want things to get weird between us.

—They are, though, aren't they?

—Yeah.

—Why do you think that is?

—'Cause now we're sober.

—And you feel different about me.

—No. It's just—it's like two different worlds. What we did last night was last night, and now I'm sure we both have stuff we need to get done. If you want we can get together tonight and talk. Or I could call you later in the day.

—You don't think there's any way this could turn into a normal relationship?

—I don't know. Is a normal relationship what a girl like you really wants?

—It's funny. I don't feel any different when I'm sober. I want the same things at night that I do in the day. And I think I can get those things from you. Wait. Where are you going?

—I'm not going anywhere until I find my keys.

—No, I mean on the video—look at that—I have my shirt off and my pants are unzipped and you're leaving the room.

—I think I had to piss.

—Oh, shit. Now I'm embarrassed. As soon as you left the room last night I started going through your pockets.

—You took my keys.

—See? I didn't want you to get away last night and I don't want to let you go today. I'm the same drunk or sober.

—Give 'em back.

—Let's see if they're still in my pockets . . .

—Stop fucking around.

—I'm not. These jeans are pretty tight. This might take a while. Why don't you entertain yourself by watching what we did last night. Look at that. Maybe that's what happened to your keys.

—Stop it.

—I'm taking something out of my jacket and putting it under your bed. I'm hiding something under your bed. What do you think it is?

—Are you gonna give me my keys back?

—That depends. What kind of car do you drive? If it's something fancy I might want to borrow it to go see a friend.

—I'll take you to your friend's house.

—I want to surprise him. I want to show up in three days, when I'm really good and hungry, and let him know I have a new boyfriend and that we're starting our own family together. Ow. Look at that.

—Turn the TV off.

—You're the one who recorded it. What? You only wanna watch it on your own?

—I have responsibilities I have to get to today—

—You didn't leave me standing there with my shirt off, ready to roll, because you had to pee—you left to get your handcuffs.

—You kept saying you needed to be thrown in a closet. That you wanted to be tied up and fed. I had no idea what you meant.

—You keep sounding like you want to apologize to me. But I liked it. What you did—is what I like. Why does it make you feel so bad? I'm not a victim. I look plenty willing to put the cuffs on, don't I?

—I'm going to give you five minutes and then if I don't have my keys back I'm going to call the police.

—Ow. You fucking hit hard. What does my face look like today? I haven't looked in a mirror yet. What will the cops have to say about that?

—You told me to.

—I bet I fucking *dared* you to. And you did it. Look at that. Every time you hit me I put my hands closer to the edge of the bed where I hid whatever I hid.

—I have to go to work.

—I wonder if what I hid under the bed is still there.

—Go look. Is it my keys?

—Holy shit—It's a fucking knife. It looks sharp.

—You were into what we were doing last night.

—I still am. Only it's not over.

—What do you want?

—Why don't you sit down. And hey . . . why don't you put the cuffs on, too? Why not?

—What are you going to do?

—I'm gonna take your cell phone out of my pants pocket and hold it up to your ear while you call in sick to work today. And then we're going to record over what we did last night with what we're going to do right now.

38

Susan, Anquille, Tom, and a few others come up with a new definition for "Wednesday."

—Did you find anything yet?

—I haven't found the combination to the safe, but I think I've found just about everything else in the world.

—They got so much cool stuff I didn't know I wanted. Toys, clothes, books, DVDs.

—I can't even make up my mind what I wanna steal from 'em.

—Have you looked in the medicine cabinet in the master bedroom?

—No.

—I pulled all the pills from it, but the lotions alone would take you an hour to alphabetize.

—The little girl's closet is something else.

—There must be a whole factory in China that stays in business 'cause of her.

—Did you see their pantry?

—Bobert would have loved his new room in this house.

—What about it?

—There are two rows of shelves. The front row is on rollers like one of those sliding puzzles. You can move them out of the way to get what's on the back row. But the back row is so deep, Bobert could have made his bed back there and been double protected by the door and the rolling shelves.

—Or he could have had a guest room.

—I gotta go see this superpantry.

—Bring us back some Pop-Tarts, Anquille!

—Meet us in the master bedroom!

—I love this house. It's so, so, so cool.

—You think everything is cool.

—I already moved all the drawers in the master bedroom.

—I just wanna hang out in there. It's just a fun place to hang out.

—I swear the bed is bigger than a king size.

—What's bigger than a king size?

—Obese size.

—Emperor size.

—Nero size.

—Oh, gross. Look what I found.

—Is that a used condom?

—Well, they *do* have a sixteen-year-old daughter. She's having trouble with Jeff, but she doesn't want to dump him until she knows for sure if Dylan is into her. Dylan is a total unicorn. OMG.

—That journal should be one of the things we take with us. That could keep us entertained for days.

—So do you think this condom is full of Jeff or Dylan?

—Put it down.

—Where?

—Oh, gross. It's leaking.

—How old is that?

—Not that old. It still has juice in it.

—Throw it under the bed.

—That's disgusting.

—Where'd you find it?

—Right on the dresser. Right there.

—You're right. It's a shame Bobert's not here to join in all the fun.

—Bobert didn't go back home. He wouldn't. I know.

—Where else is he gonna go?

—Salvation Army.

—He'd hit the road. Go West.

—He did go home. Bobert wrote his home address down for Malcolm.

—Bobert told me his stepdad was a complete and raging asshole. He wouldn't go home. I'm telling you.

—But he has a younger brother.

—You think Bobert went home to get his brother?

—I think he went home because Malcolm destroyed his PlayStation.

—We should steal his address from Malcolm and write him and let him know where we are.

—That's why Malcolm made him write it down. He's going to write Bobert in a month. But until a month is up Bobert is banished for helping Angel.

—Helping Angel what?

—Helping Angel set you free and messing up your change.

—That's bullshit.

—Malcolm isn't the fucking CEO of us.

—We're all digging through the house, looking for the combination. Why are we doing it? 'Cause Malcolm said so. So don't be so sure who your CEO is.

—You're right. This is bullshit. I'm gonna go back to the last house, before things got fucked up, and live on my own. Fuck Malcolm.

—Don't you want to find the combination and get a free wish?

—Fuck that. This is my wish. To do what I want, when I want to. Anybody wanna go with me?

—I'll go.

—You guys are fucking stupid.

—

—They're fucking stupid.

—Why?

—If they would keep looking for the combination then they could wish us all back to the old house.

—They could wish Bobert back, too. That'd be cool.

—Too late.

—What?

—Look what I found in the pantry—

—It better be Pop-Tarts, Anquille.

—What is it?

—It's a set of instructions for the maid who comes every Wednesday.

—Bullshit.

—It was up on the top shelf of the pantry.

—I was in the pantry.

—Next to the applesauce.

—I hate applesauce.

—That's why you didn't find it.

—It's got the numbers to reach them in Israel. And it's got the neighbors' numbers. And the alarm code.

—There's an alarm?

—It's off.

—No shit, Sherlock.

—But the instruction manual notes: There's a "personal panic-button key fob" in the second drawer down of the credenza in the vestibule. And some Mace.

—What's a vestibule?

—But the book is wrong. The key fob and the Mace are in the third drawer down now.

—Haha.

—I hope they do come home and I hope they do panic.

—What's a credenza?

—That's the part in the music when everyone stops playing so the main person can just solo.

—Haha.

—Don't be such a prep-school dick. She's asking because she doesn't know. You're trying to make her feel bad for exposing that. In fact, you're trying to double that bad feeling by giving her the definition of another word she doesn't know. But *nobody* knows every word. There are so many more words than one person can carry around. Asking what something means is how words travel. No, seriously. A dictionary is like an orphanage. When she asks what it means, she's adopting that word. That's a good thing. All right? I don't want to ever hear you make any of us feel stupid for asking what a word means again, or else I'm gonna jaw-jack you.

—I get it. You want me to ask what jaw-jack means and then you're going to hit me.

—I'm gonna hit you either way. You might as well learn something.

—What's a jaw-jack?

—Ow.

—A credenza is like a long, low chest of drawers.

—Stop fucking around.

—What else is in that instruction manual?

—Then there's the names of the people at the security company and the passwords, and then look. The combination to the safe!

—No fucking way?!

—You win, Anquille. You win.

—Wait. Wait. Wait.

—What?

—What day is it?

—It's a Wednesday.

—Does it say what time the maid comes?

39

The werewolves take a vow of silence.

—Everybody down to the basement. Now! Everybody. We're gonna get the safe open ASAP and then we'll figure out what to do about the maid.

—What do you mean "figure out what to do about the maid"? If we get the safe open we can shoot her.

—Come on, baby. Quick. Down to the basement.

—Malcolm, what about the dog?

—Leave it. For now. Maybe she'll bark when the maid shows up and give us a warning. Hurry up. Is that everybody?

—Where's Tom?

—I think he took a walk.

—You're fucking kidding me.

—No, I think he and the newest kid wanted to go back to the old neighborhood.

—That's just fucking perfect!

Smash. Smash. Smash. Smash. Smash.

—Calm down, Malcolm.

—You're right. All right. Let me get to the safe. Where's Anquille?

—I'm right here.

—Shut the door. If anybody opens that door from the outside, grab whoever it is, drag the body down the stairs to the center of the room, and then I want to see all of you hitting and kicking it until it stops screaming.

—What if it's Tom and Carl?

—Fuck Tom and Carl. They shouldn't have gone wandering off without permission.

—Now we have to get permission to take a walk?

—Of course you do! Of course you do!

—Calm. Be calm.

—All right, Anquille, why don't you read me the number from the book and we'll see if you have the winning combination!

—Why does Malcolm get to do the combination?

—What the fuck do you care?

—Why are you always sticking up for him, Tanya?

—Malcolm and Tanya are married now.

—When two werewolves drink nothing but each other's sweat for three days they become bonded for life—

—Shut the fuck up so I can concentrate. And back the fuck up so I can see. I can't see shit.

—Calm down, baby. Back up and give Malcolm a little light to work by. Back up.

—I still don't see why he gets to do the combination!

—*I* found the combination. It's *mine*. It belongs to *me*. And *I* say Malcolm can do the opening.

—Now you've got Anquille sticking up for you.

—He wants to get married, too.

—Three-way marriage!

—The combination is 84-87-12.

—Is that what you're gonna wish for, Anquille?

—I dunno.

—You should wish that every single one of us gets placed into a passionate, nurturing three-way marriage.

—Are we divisible by three?

—They can be interlocking. Anquille will be married to Tanya and Malcolm. Malcolm will be married to Tanya and Susan. Susan will be married to Tom and me.

—I'm not marrying you.

—Don't worry about it 'cause that's not what I'm wishing for.

—I wish that you would wish that everyone would shut the fuck up.

—I might.

—You know there are people who pay money to go somewhere quiet for a weekend, like a silent retreat, where no one's allowed to talk?

—That would suck.

—We'll see. I haven't made my wish yet.

—Well, Anquille, I'm afraid you may not get to make a wish.

—What do you mean, Malcolm?

—This combination's no good. I tried it and the safe didn't open. It doesn't work.

—How can it not work?

—Maybe it's like a code or something. Maybe you have to add one to each number. So the real combination is 85-88-13. Maybe that's why they were so cavalier about writing it down and leaving it in a notebook lying around the house where any common burglar could find it.

—You're probably right, baby.

—Shut up, Tanya. It's embarrassing to watch you two work.

—Have you read the whole book? Has anybody read through this whole notebook? Maybe there's some page in it where it tells us to add one to every number?

—Or maybe there's another set of instructions hidden somewhere else in the house that tells us how to read this set of instructions.

—This sucks! I hate this! I hate it!

—Don't get angry. Just try it again.

—It's 84-87-12.

—All right. Back up. Jesus.

—What does "cavalier" mean?

—Everybody just be quiet—please—while he tries again.

—Is that your wish?

—Anquille doesn't get his wish if the combination's no good.

—It's just a practice, to see what it would be like if we were all silent and we let Malcolm concentrate.

—

—

—

—It still doesn't work?!

—No.

—This total fucking bullshit!

—Calm down, Anquille. Let me try one more time.

—

—84.

—

—87.

—

—12.

—Nothing.

—No guns for us, I guess.

—So I don't get my wish?!

—You just would've wasted it on making everybody be quiet.

—You don't know what I'm gonna wish for.

—You're not gonna wish for anything. The combo doesn't work.

—Do the different codes. Add one to every number.

—We don't have time. We have other shit to worry about. The note-book says the maid is coming today.

—If we figure out the code and get the guns we don't have to worry about her.

—That's not gonna happen. If we can't get the guns we need a new plan of action and we need it quick. Listen. Everybody. Here's what we're gonna do. One, we go upstairs and we make things shipshape. Everybody pick a room and clean it up. Sleeping bags and clothes all get put into closets or under the beds. Two, then we meet in the living room and get our story straight. We'll figure out something to tell the maid that will get her to leave us alone.

—Maybe we should all get out of the house for the day?

—Or we could all hide.

—Wouldn't that be fucking creepy?! A maid just doing whatever she does—wandering from room to room, half-assed dusting—

—watering the plants—

—sweeping—

—while *unbeknownst to her*, in every closet, someone's hiding—

—and we've all taken a vow of silence—

—we've all sworn to one another that if she opens the door and finds one of us, we'll grab her and drag the body downstairs screaming—

—and everyone will come running to the living room to attack her—

—and each of us has a different weapon, a steak knife, or a golf club—

—or a hammer—

—and we're just waiting, watching her between the slats of the closet as she straightens up around the house.

—That's awesome. That's what I wish.

—The combination didn't work. You don't get what you wish.

—Then I'm gonna stay in here and keep trying that combination until I do.

—I tried three times, Anquille!

—Then I'm going to try adding one to each number, like you said, and then two, and so on and so on until I get it.

—All right. We'll come let you know when we figure out what the plan is for dealing with the maid.

—All right. I'll be here.

—And you let us know as soon as you get the safe unlocked. Don't open the door all the way without all of us. Promise?

—All right.

—All right.

40

Tom and Carl work out the new world order.

—Do you wanna be alone?

    —No.

    —'Cause I don't have to go with you . . .

    —I don't care.

    —Well, if you don't care, then I'm gonna go with you.

    —Fine. But I don't wanna talk shit over with you—about how things are going in the house . . . and my emotions and shit.

    —I don't wanna talk about how things are going with you, either.

    —It sucks, though, doesn't it?

    —Yeah.

    —Always being followed everywhere and watched.

    —You're not talking about me, are you?

    —No. I'm talking about Malcolm.

    —And Tanya.

    —Yeah.

    —But if you're talking about me, I can just go back.

    —No, let's just go, come on.

Walk. Walk. Walk. Walk. Walk.

    —We're not leaving for good, are we?

    —Where would we go?

    —We'll just stay at the Baxters'. And one by one as people get pissed off at Malcolm, they'll come over and join us. And maybe Bobert'll come back.

—The Baxters' was, like, two houses ago.

—I wasn't here then.

—Now we call every place the Baxters'. I think Bobert started it.

—Yeah, well, I liked the last place, whoever's place it was. That's where we're going right?

—Yeah. We're going back to the Baxters'.

—We're gonna start our own group?

—I don't know. I just wanna get away from Malcolm. I hate feeling like even the people on my own side are against me.

—We were all trying to get away from bullshit like this in our regular lives. None of us is competent enough to be a waiter and make enough tips to just live like a person. So we end up bumming around. We find one another. And now we're back at the beginning.

—I don't wanna be worried about someone catching me doing something normal and yelling at me—I mean—something I just do without even thinking about it. Like staring out the window, looking at birds. I don't want to worry that Malcolm or Anquille or someone is going to yell at me for compromising our safety or whatever, 'cause some neighbor is gonna look at our house and see a strange man in the window.

—Anquille's on our side. He would be in our group—if we started our own group.

—You think so?

—Yeah.

—But what if it all happens again? I mean, if I have to worry about something normal, like looking at a bird, then I have to think about everything I do, everything I *might* do. That's the opposite of being in tune with nature. That's the opposite of following your instincts. And that's the opposite of being a werewolf.

—Who yelled at you about staring out the window?

—Anquille.

—It was probably his window. He likes to claim things in a house. Weird things. Light switches.

—I wasn't even right at the window. I was lying on a couch in the upstairs study watching a grackle in the pecan tree.

—Maybe it was Anquille's grackle?

—He yelled at me for putting my shoes on the couch.

—That has to be it. It was his couch.

—That's stupid. Trying to protect upholstery that doesn't even belong to you? I told him I wanted to keep my shoes on, in case we have to run for it all of a sudden. Like if that cop came and busted us.

—And what was his answer to that?

—Malcolm stepped in and told me to do what Anquille said.

—That's weird.

—He said Anquille had been here longer.

—We never really had a rank for longevity.

—Are you kidding me? You call things by words we don't know. We're on our way to the Baxters' from the Baxters'. That kind of shit. You have all these rules about what's *werewolf*. Malcolm just makes it official. Anquille tells me to take my shoes off his couch and Malcolm enforces it. He said me wearing my shoes was "sending the wrong signal."

—What signal?

—If I can't take my shoes off, then Malcolm's not a good leader. He's not made us safe. And no one will trust him. Not the rest of you guys, or the cops, or the neighbors.

—And what did Anquille say?

—He said, "Get your shoes off my couch."

Houses. Trees. Grass. Birds. Clouds.

—We're getting close to the Baxters', aren't we?

—Don't *over*use it!

—What do you mean? You mean, sometimes it's all right and sometimes it's not?!

—I don't know. Just shut the fuck up.

—You want me to go back?

—I told you. I don't care.

—You don't have to be a dick to me just 'cause Anquille was a dick to me and you're his friend. That's not loyalty. That's just being a dick.

—I just hate everybody. I hate Malcolm so much I have to be a dick to you. I have too much emotion to only be a dick to the people who deserve it. I'm probably gonna transform in like five seconds and then turn on you and kill you.

—See that bougainvillea right there in front of the green house? If you make a move on me I'm going to run over there and pick up one of the bricks that make the border around the bougainvillea and bash your fucking brains in.

—See that garden hose? If you came at me with a brick I would pick up the garden hose and keep it to a length just a little longer than your arms and I would beat you with the metal tip until you dropped the brick and then I would use the hose to strangle you.

—See that recycling bin? I would pull a six-pack of beer bottles out of the recycling bin and throw five of them at your face until I backed you off from the hose and then I'd break the sixth one on the curb and cut your neck and your wrists wide open.

—While we're pointing out all this shit, did you notice we're just around the corner from our last Baxters'?

—So you can say it, but I can't?

—I've been here longer. Haha. Just kidding. I'm trying to make a joke of it. You know. As a way to say sorry.

—Do you think we could kill Malcolm in one of those ways we just said and take over?

—No.

—Why not?

—He's thought of all the ways we might kill him—and a hundred more, besides that. When Malcolm walks into a room he counts up all the sharp pencils and then keeps track of where they are. That's what he's like.

—We should make our own group.

—There's no chance to talk to anybody about it. Malcolm is always watching us.

—We need to distract him with something.

—What is Malcolm distracted by?

—Tanya.

—Angel.

—And Peugeots. That's about it.

—If we did make our own group who would you take into it?

—I would keep you.

—Me, too, with you.

—And I would want Bobert back.

—Can we invite Anquille, too?

—Do you trust him?

—

—I'm mean, I'm not saying you shouldn't.

—

—If you trust him he's fine by me. You've known him longer. I mean, if you like Anquille, he's in. You, me, Anquille, and Bobert. And maybe we should have some girls, too.

—Shut up. Look.

—What?

—Isn't that the Baxters' house?

—Holy shit.

—Malcolm did come back and set it on fire.

41

Arson investigators talk to Bobert's mom.

—How long has your son been back home?

  —You know the answer to that.

  —I have to ask.

  —Why? Do you have a list of questions you have to work through?

  —I do.

  —Did you write the questions yourself?

  —I wrote them with my partner.

  —I see. And she's asking the same list of questions to my son right now and later you're going to sit around a table like this and drink coffee and compare lists.

  —I can't drink coffee anymore.

  —Neither can my husband.

  —This is Robert's stepfather?

  —You know the answer to that.

  —No. I don't. I had no idea Robert's stepfather couldn't drink coffee.

  —He's got a tattoo, too. That sounds funny, doesn't it? "Tattoo-too."

  —What's it a tattoo of?

  —We're off the list now, I assume.

  —We are. I'm just interested.

  —Are you a big fan of tattoos?

  —My oldest daughter is a tattoo artist.

—In town?

—In Tempe.

—Well, then, she wouldn't have been the one to give it to Roger.

—Probably not.

—It's a fish with wings.

—Huh.

—Roger says it means "to each his own."

—Cool.

—You think so?

—If he likes it.

—He got it when he was a kid.

—We do dumb shit when we're kids.

—I didn't.

—When my daughter told me she was going to become a tattoo art-ist . . . I was grateful. She spent a lot of time, like Bobert, as a runaway. So "tattoo artist" was like—well, it's an actual job. Maybe not what I would have picked for her. But she has a house and I know where she is, con-ceptually, at all hours of the day. When she was homeless I asked her once to go to some other town, so she wouldn't be my problem. I know that's a shitty thing for a dad to say. But now that she's a tattoo artist I keep asking her to move back here. I told her I would line up every fire-man and cop in town and we'd all get tattoos and she'd have business forever.

—I bet she liked that.

—She's thinking about it. You know she used to hate cops, and now we might become her livelihood. She was addicted to meth.

—We do dumb stuff when we're kids.

—I thought you said you didn't.

—I married TJ and had Bobert. I mean, Robert.

—He's gonna be all right. The thing is, it's not just kids he was hang-ing out with. We think some of the gang he was squatting with, we think they're older, and we think they might be dangerous. They set a house on fire and the only clue they left was Robert's home address, your address. Someone spray-painted it on the side of the house, on the bricks of the chimney, so it wouldn't burn. I think they did it on purpose to cover their trail. I think they were willing to hang Robert out to dry to protect themselves. I mean, how long until they do something even stupider to some other kid?

—Two days.

—What?

—I'm cooperating. I'm answering your questions. From the list. Bobert's been home two days. What's next?

42

Tanya is becoming grateful.

What are my options? I don't have any skills, so I can't get a job. I wouldn't last a month if I struck out on my own, I already know that. No one in my family will even take my calls anymore. I think I called one too many times. If I walk into one of those agencies for homeless girls, I could probably get a shower and clean clothes, but then what? I can get a shower and clean clothes here. What's the next step after that? The distance between where I am now and anything remotely normal seems almost infinite. And I'm scared. That's the real truth. If I walk out that door, I won't make it a half block before I get hit by a brick from behind and wake up with Malcolm on my back, holding me down by the neck asking me just what I think I'm doing. I can imagine that happening in the middle of the night and I can imagine that happening in broad daylight with witnesses coming out of their houses everywhere to watch. Oh, baby.

Here's a weird idea: How long would it take us to live our lives if we could keep jumping back to any previous point and start over from there? It would take forever, right? If I had been nicer to Mike Hronek in middle school, would I have a family now? If I had just told my parents the truth about my grades in junior college, is there any way they could have helped? For some reason it seems so much easier to make the right choices in the past than it does in the present. Right now I can't imagine how I'm gonna get out of this. It seems like the only way to escape a bunch of freaks is to become normal. I don't know how to get there, but I feel like I'm starting to want normal things. I look at an alarm clock and it seems like a poem about desire; there are people that want to get up at a certain hour so that they can go get something. A cup of pens next to the phone almost broke my heart the other day: Who's calling? What do they have to say that's so important you have to write it down? And I can't even look at all the picture frames. I turned them all over in the master bedroom. This family's been everywhere. They're out there, right now, snapping new ones. I can feel it, like somebody's pinching my stupid, sentimental heart.

I want a family. But I don't want babies. I am a baby. I can't feed or clothe myself, much less take care of anyone else. Everything I need to survive I have to steal from whatever kind of mother or father is around at the moment: food stamps, Salvation Army, the houses we squat in. I think every house we break into is another womb and my bad behavior is a kind of umbilical cord connecting me to my sustenance. If I start acting right and obeying the law, I'll be cut off from everything I know how to do, from the only way I know how to get by. That's how you get born into adulthood, you just jump out into it, kicking and screaming and crying, only you're not naked, you're wearing a shitty, sweaty polyester-fiber Arby's uniform. I'd rather wear dirty jeans and a old T-shirt so thin you can see through it, and three or four flannels on top of that and a hoodie on top of that I can pull up over my head and block out all the terrible stares I get because of how bad I smell. I'll have to wear some kind of a uniform someday. If it's not an Arby's uniform it'll be one of those dull bright-orange jumpsuits from prison.

If I got to jump back to junior college, still living off my original mom and dad, instead of collecting shitty punk albums it takes longer to figure out what they're screaming about than it did for them to write the lyrics, I would make fashion my main goal. I would make a line of clothing made entirely out of the fabric they use to make those prison jumpsuits. I really mean "dull bright-orange." It's kind of a miracle they figured out how to take a color like that and make it so drab. But can you imagine a line of clothes made out of that stuff? Business slacks and button down shirts and little knee-length skirts that all proclaimed: "I'm a wage slave." Not only would it be cool to see, but then when prisoners broke out of jail they could just blend right in. It's probably not an original idea. Somebody probably already did it and the government shut him or her down because they didn't want to have to redesign their prison-wear.

All joking aside. There is seriously somebody whose job it is to design prison wear. That's a shitty job. I don't know what he or she tells him or herself to get through the day, but it's probably a pretty weak line of bullshit. "I'm only doing this to help those less fortunate than me have more comfortable lives. This will lead to something better. At least I'm on this side of the job."

It's the same line of bullshit I tell myself. I keep thinking I'll find a way to turn this pack of idiots into a family. I keep telling myself that I'm helping out the misfits like Anquille and Susan. That I'm protecting them from Malcolm. But I need Malcolm. Without Malcolm I would have just drifted from the artist's studios into the Salvation Army into some kind of program into some kind of addiction into some kind of serious crime into jail. I guess that's what this is, just part of my downward slide, but I don't see it that way—not always. I keep thinking that this can be saved somehow. We don't have to keep banging out beers and squatting in other people's houses. I know that in, like, the sixties hippies would turn abandoned factories and shit into apartments and put in plumbing and electricity. The way they did it, through this process of stealing a building and learning how to make it work and keeping the government at bay and fighting off other squatters who came late to the project, these hippies grew up without ever having to put on an Arby's costume. They were our parents in some cases. We could turn into those kinds of hippies if we had Malcolm's leadership abilities but didn't have all the dumb leadership ideas that come out of his mouth.

If I could jump back to my last stay at home and just keep my mouth shut when my mom started laying into me about how stupid I am— She's right. I am that stupid. I've had all these opportunities and I burned them down. If I could just keep my mouth shut through my mom's deluge of emotions—I bet there's like a tearful hugging session at the end. Or even a stony silence for a few days followed by a long thaw. If I could get back just that far, then I could re-enroll in junior college and then college and then medical school. Every step along the way I'll ask my mom, *Is it too late?* And every time she'll say, *No, baby, it's not too late for you.* And in medical school I'll take just enough classes to learn how you can anesthetize someone and cut out his vocal cords so he can never talk again. Then I'll jump back to this point in time and do it to Malcolm. And then I'll tell everyone that I'm the only one who knows what Malcolm wants and that I now speak for him.

I'm surprised that in the whole history of this weird world this has never become a thing—cutting out people's vocal cords. I think people's voices are the most annoying things about people. Listen. Really listen to whoever is reading this to you. Even if it's me. The grunts and wet little corners of the sound. The verbal tics. Language is disgusting. It's the root of all our problems. I think eventually we'll get rid of it. Maybe we just haven't gotten there yet. There's seven billion people on the planet now. The noise is just gonna get worse and worse. Maybe when there's twelve billion we'll have to start silencing babies at birth. Then I'll be famous for thinking it up. A bunch of silent people standing in line at Arby's. Pointing at the picture of the roast beef sandwich they want. A silent person in a dull bright-orange Arby's uniform nodding quietly. Only rich people will be allowed to keep their voices. And if somehow you're able to be nice to your Mike Hronek and to let your mother do the best she can with you and to stay away from your Malcolm—if somehow you're able to do all that and get through junior college and college and med school without getting distracted by all your weird ideas (none of which make you an artist! You'll learn that, too) and somehow you manage to get rich as a doctor—then there'll be a surgery to restore your vocal cords. Then, at the age of twenty-seven or however old you are, you'll be able to speak for the first time. What do you think you'd say? I know what I would say if I could have all that. I wouldn't curse the system or speak up about injustice. Fuck all that. I'd say, "Thank you."

43

What to tell the maid.

—Tell her the Yorks said we could stay here.

—She'll call 'em to check.

—Tell her the Yorks' oldest daughter said we could stay here.

—She might not call 'em, I guess—if she likes the older daughter.

—Tell her the Yorks' older daughter will pay her if she'll keep us a secret from Mom and Dad.

—Pay her with what?

—We have a fifty-dollar bill.

—Since when?

—Malcolm has it.

—No, he doesn't. He gave it to Bobert.

—It's a magical fifty-dollar bill. If you have faith in it, at the hour of your greatest, fifty-dollar need, it will appear.

—It doesn't matter. The maid's not motivated by money. Not little amounts. She could steal everything in this place if she valued quick cash over job security.

—We just need a note from the older York daughter written directly to the maid asking her to have mercy on us.

—Who do we say we are in the note?

—We can be her camp counselors.

—How do we know if the girl even goes to camp?

—We have her journals.

—Go get her journals so we can get some facts and her handwriting. Maybe we can be long-lost relatives—

—Or the relatives of a boyfriend.

—How many of us should we say there are in the note?

—There's just three of us.

—And everybody else will hide in the closets.

—Why three?

—Because one is a loner and that's dangerous. Two is a couple and that's sexual. But three is a community. It's always in the individual's best interest to help the community—in case you need help yourself.

—What are we going to do about the dog?

—We have to let it go, baby.

—No way.

—Go get it. We'll teach it to hide with one of you in a closet. A dog can learn. We'll teach it a signal that will make it run to its hiding place and one of you will be responsible for giving the dog a treat and hiding with it in the closet.

—I'll go get the dog.

—Who's gonna write this note from the Yorks' older daughter?

—I can write in that loop-de-loop script and draw hearts on it.

—And who's gonna deliver this note to the maid?

—I nominate Malcolm.

—We should have the York's older daughter, in the note we're gonna make, say how long we can stay. That way we don't have to argue with the maid about it.

—What's the most believable amount of time we can get away with?

—We should tell her we'll be gone the next time she comes over, in a week.

—We need more than a week.

—What for?

—I thought you were gonna write to Bobert to come meet us. If we keep moving how's he gonna find us?

—I told Bobert it would be at least a month. I'm not going to write him until we're settled somewhere we can stay for a while.

—I don't think you're ever gonna write to Bobert.

—If you have faith in me, at the hour of our greatest need, Bobert and his brother will show up wherever we're staying at the time.

—Which is it? Are we gonna get settled somewhere? Or are we gonna keep pushing our luck until we get to the hour of our greatest need?

—Often it's one that leads to the other.

—What if the letter from the Yorks' older daughter doesn't work?

—Then you should tell the maid we're werewolves and she should run before thirty wild animals come pouring out from the closets and under the beds.

—You should tell the maid we're werewolves and she's welcome to join up. It's gotta be better than cleaning other people's houses.

—I'll tell her both things: We're werewolves and she should join us before we attack. Then she'll be in the hour of her greatest need and how she handles it will settle things for us.

44

The last recorded conversation between Angel and her new boyfriend.

—Let me go.

   —Go where?

   —Please. Please. Please.

   —I heard you the first time.

   —This is my home.

   —You asked me to meet you here. You let me in.

   —I don't feel right.

   —You don't look so good, either. Your skin is turning kind of gray. And you smell. Or else we both smell. Smell me. Do I smell?

   —I need help.

   —What kind of help do you need? I don't know medicine, but I can do other stuff.

   —What's gonna happen?

   —You're gonna sit there and look at the camera and keep your fucking head up.

   —I'm tired.

   —We have almost seventy hours of footage already. Is that crazy or what?

   —I need to eat something.

   —I'm sorry. I thought we'd be done by now.

—I'm supposed to meet someone after work today. Today's Wednesday, right?

—That's right.

—She'll be expecting me.

—But we've been calling in sick.

—This isn't someone from work. This is someone from somewhere else.

—We'll call her, too.

—I don't have her number.

—Now I'm jealous. Do you have, like, a standing massage appointment or a dance lesson you haven't told me about?

—If I'm not there she'll worry about me.

—I can imagine. I'm worried about you and you're right here in front of me.

—She'll call the police.

—We don't want that.

—So you just have to let me go.

—All right.

—I haven't eaten anything since Sunday.

—Me, neither. I haven't eaten anything since Friday. That's five days. I've never been this far before.

—I can't go as long as you.

—You won't have to.

—Can I eat something now?

—All right.

—Will you at least loosen the handcuffs?

—All right.

—You keep saying all right, but then you don't do anything.

—Keep your fucking head up.

—What do you want?

—I want to get a good clear shot of your face.

—For what?

—For the moment when you start to understand what's happening. I want to see you change.

45

The maid reaches for the personal panic-button key fob only to find it's not there.

—Don't be frightened.

　—Jesus! Jesus!

　—I'm a friend of Rebecca's.

　—You scared me. Oh, my god!

　—I'm a friend of Rebecca's. It's all right. It's all right.

　—What are you doing standing in the middle of my living room?

　—Rebecca said it was all right.

　—She what?!

　—Rebecca said I could stay here.

　—Does Linda know?

　—Rebecca said you wouldn't care.

　—Do Linda and Jake know about you?

　—Rebecca gave me a note to give to you.

　—How long have you been here?

　—Not long.

　—Were you here last week?

　—I got in yesterday. From Mexico. I'm doing some research. For my dissertation.

　—You can't stay here.

　—Rebecca said it would be all right.

—But I don't work for Rebecca.

—She gave me a note to give to you.

—No, she didn't.

—She did. It's right here.

—Okay, but I have a note from Linda that says if anything happens I am to call her, immediately.

—This is isn't anything happening.

—Are you sure?

—Yeah.

—'Cause at first I thought it was me getting killed by some burglar. But now I see it's only me getting fired.

—Maybe this is you getting a couple of weeks off work?

—A couple of weeks?!

—Read the note.

—What has Becca gotten herself into this time?

—She wants to seem cool.

—You're telling me.

—I'm Jeff's older brother. You've met Jeff, right? The young man Rebecca's dating.

—Jeff?

—Yeah.

—I thought she was done with Jeff.

—You know how kids are.

—I'm beginning to figure it out.

—Do you have kids?

—Three.

—Well, Becca told Jeff that a couple of us—

—A couple of you!

—There's three of us.

—I'm calling Linda.

—We're grad students.

—I don't care if you're the Marines, you don't get to do whatever Rebecca says. Rebecca is not in charge of this house. Linda is. And when Linda's not here, I am.

—Will you please just read the note?

—No. I'm not reading shit!

—What are you freaking out about?

—There's people in the house! You want me to read about it?! The minute I look down at this note you're trying to hand me, you're gonna hit me over the head with a shovel. So, no. No. No. No!

—Anquille. Tanya. It's all right. I've told her we're here. It's all right.

—It's not all right. It's not.

—It is. My name's Malcolm.

—Oh, Jesus.

—Hello.

—This is Tanya and this is Anquille.

—I'm calling the cops.

—All right. Good. Let's call the police.

—We should leave, baby.

—Why? We have a note from the homeowner.

—Rebecca doesn't own the house. She's a sixteen-year-old girl.

—She gave us permission to stay here.

—You're just going to end up getting Rebecca in trouble. And Jeff.

—We are?! *You're* the one who wants to call the police.

—I have a job to do!

—You're just angry. You're mad that you won't have this great big house all to yourself anymore.

—Excuse me? That's it. I've had enough.

—Me, too. We tried to have a nice conversation. But now things are gonna change.

—You don't even know, son.

—I know more than you think. So stop and listen to me. What are you looking for in that drawer? The panic button or the Mace?

—How do you know what's in this drawer?

—Because I moved it.

—When I come back, I'm coming back with the cops and you better not be here.

—Shut the door. I know you've been using the house like it was your own and now you don't want to share it.

—What do you mean?

—We found a used condom in Linda and Jake's bedroom.

—You were here last week, too. Weren't you?

—And we're staying. I moved the personal panic-button key fob and the Mace one drawer up so you wouldn't have to bend over in the middle of a crisis. Go on, check the next drawer up.

—All right. I see.

—Now you can call the cops if you want to. Call Linda. But we're not going anywhere. Whoever you call, we're gonna tell them our side of the story, too. We have a note from the homeowner and you've been having sex in the master bedroom.

—All right.

—All right? We can stay?

—Let me read Rebecca's note.

46

Dear Carlene

Whatever you do, don't be mad. I love you. Hearts and unicorns. I kinda made a promise that you have to keep. I always feel like I can trust you. This one is a big one. I told these guys you were cool. I said they could stay here for as long as they need to. Sorry sorry sorry sorry sorry sorry sorry sorry sorry.

These guys saved my life. I don't want to talk about it. Remember when I was having that tough time? That *really really really* tough time. You don't know how bad it got. I kept it to myself. Then it got worse. I was on the internet looking for ways TO KILL MYSELF!!! I didn't want it to hurt. And I didn't want it to cause a lot of trouble for Mom and Dad. And I didn't want it to make a mess for YOU. It turns out there's about 10 million ways you could do it. I'm not going to—but now I know that car exhaust is the best in the business :). BUT DON'T WORRY. I'm all right now. I mean, I'm writing this, right? That proves I'm alive!

But Jeff knew how much trouble I was in. And Jeff told his brother, even though he had SWORN never to tell! But Jeff's brother was cool about it and didn't freak out and just asked me questions about my life and how bad things were and how long it would be until things got better until eventually I was telling myself that it wasn't all that bad.

So when Jeff said his brother needed something I totally, totally volunteered, even though I know I am wrong—but I'm also right! Malcolm and his friends are totally trustworthy. And they're Christians, too. They're theology doctors. They're doing a report on how it is here in our communities—something about the number of churches versus the number of homeless kids. That's why they need a place to stay! What Would Jesus Do?!!

Do not tell Mom and Dad. They will kill me. And I think I have already proved to you that I DON'T WANT TO DIE. So here is the plan I propose: 1) Do not tell Mom and Dad. 2) Let them stay in the house. 3) DESTROY THIS NOTE 4) If anything goes wrong you just deny that you knew anything about it! 5) If you have to discuss this with anyone, discuss it with me. My cell is 274-487-3773. This is a secret cellphone that Mom and Dad don't even know about. 6) Do not tell Mom and Dad about the cellphone, either! 7) I will owe you one, big time. 8) They promise to clean up and do whatever you say! 9) I love you forever.

If you do tell Mom and Dad I will be back in a kill-myself place. And now I KNOW HOW TO DO IT (and not just by car fumes but other ways, too).

Please please please please please please.

—LOVE, HEARTS, and UNICORNS,

Rebecca

47

Everybody gets together and takes off their clothes.

—She put down the letter, then she opened the top drawer of the credenza again, like to double-check and make her decision. Then she closed the drawer again and announced we could stay.

—But there's rules, baby. Tell 'em all the rules.

—Let's hear 'em.

—We have to stay on the ground floor. No one is supposed to go up to the second floor and no one is supposed to go down to the basement.

—That's bullshit.

—How is she gonna know?

—She doesn't even know how many of us there are.

—She doesn't know anything.

—Another one of the rules is she's going to come check on us whenever she wants and if she sees anything *funny* then we're out of here.

—She's bluffing.

—She's not really gonna come check on us.

—I think she will. I think she'll come back and she'll bring her husband or the cops. I think she was scared and she wasn't thinking straight.

—I could smell how scared she was from the hall closet. That's my hiding place, back up in the coats. And I swear I could smell her perspiration all the way across the room. The harder she tried to hold all her emotions in, the more it oozed out her sticky little armpits.

—You can *still* smell it. In this area and under the door and down the walkway.

—She better be scared. I was ready to pounce.

—She isn't scared of you. She doesn't know about you. She's scared of what she's been doing. That condom you found in the front bedroom didn't just appear there. She's been having fun in this house the same as us. She has more claim to it, but she also has more to lose by it.

—As soon as she calms down she's gonna realize we're not who we say we are. It's obvious.

—How is it obvious?

—If we can smell her—which I'm not convinced that you could—then she could sure as shit smell you.

—And look at us—we don't *look* like friends of the Yorks' older daughter.

—How do you know?

—Look around at the photographs on the wall, baby, on the *credenza*.

—Do any of you guys have any pictures of yourselves? We could slip one into a frame and then point it out as proof.

—That might work if the dad was coming back to check on us, but this is the maid we're talking about. All she does all day long is dust the pictures. She'll know if we switched one out.

—Then we have to make ourselves look more like the people already in the pictures.

—All right. We'll all take showers and wash our hair and wash our clothes. People trust clean people.

—How many showers are there in the house?

—I counted three.

—Let's get going. We need three volunteers to peel off their clothes and start scrubbing up.

—We can go more than one at a time if we want. We don't have to do it the way normal people do.

—That a good idea. Everybody strip down. I'll go first.

—I'm not gonna shower with you.

—It's not just for the shower. You can shower alone or six at a time for all I care, but we should wash as many of our clothes as we can in one load. We only have a limited amount of time.

—This is awesome.

—Don't be a prude.

—I hope the maid comes back *now*.

—Look at the lines on us, between the dirty skin and the clean skin.

—We smell worse naked. How is that?

—We're stirring up all the fumes that were trapped in the cotton.

—I always thought this was what was going on. After I went to bed I thought you all took off all your clothes and had some weird party. I never wanted to go to sleep because I didn't wanna miss it.

—Now you're here. Welcome to the weird party.

—All right. Calm down everybody. We're naked. So what? We're animals. Take a look around at one another and get used to what we look like.

Look. Giggle. Cough. Look. Relax.

—Where are we with the plan?

—You three, go take showers. You, start washing this pile of clothes.

—And then what? We're just gonna enjoy this house for as long as we can and them move on?

—I don't want to go.

—You wanna kill the maid?

—I don't wanna kill anybody.

—Me, neither.

—Nobody said that if the maid opened the door to the hall closet and found me, I had to kill her.

—Anyway, killing her wouldn't do anything. I mean, it would make her not alive. But it wouldn't allow us to stay in this house any longer, or make us any safer.

—The biggest thing we got going for us is a willingness to get in trouble. When she said she was going to call the cops and I said *fine*, she was temporarily stunned. 'Cause then she has to talk to the cops, too, and Linda and Doug have to come home—

—Linda and Jake—

—Linda and Jake have to get dragged into this and the older daughter gets in trouble—

—Or so she thinks.

—And it's all a big mess.

—So what she's hoping is that we just go away.

—And eventually we will.

—But until then we're going to make it seem like we're playing by her rules.

—I'm going to go back down and keep working on cracking the combination to the safe.

—No, Anquille.

—I can figure it out.

—I know. But first we need to figure out what our routine is.

—What do you mean?

—Well, first off, there's the maid's rules. Like with all the other rules in the universe, we need to figure out *how* we're going to follow them.

—You're pretty.

—Shut the fuck up and stop looking at me.

—Focus.

—The maid doesn't want us upstairs, but I already have all my stuff up there.

—Which is great. But maybe we just make a counter-rule that no one turns the lights on upstairs. That way if the maid does a drive-by she doesn't know we're up there.

—Why do you get to make all the rules?

—They're *counter-rules*.

—Well, by my *count*, Malcolm makes all our *rules*.

—Jesus Christ! What the fuck am I saying! I'm saying let's all have a meeting and make all the rules together, so everybody will have a say in the final outcome and support it and shit—

—Everyone except for Tom and Carl—

—All we ever do now is meetings.

—When Tom and Carl come back, and they will come back, you can give 'em the list of rules you made all by yourself. I'm not gonna say another fucking word.

48

Bobert and Tim check the mail.

—Are you bored, Rob?

    —I dunno.

    —Well, you were sitting in that chair staring out the window when I left to go to the park, and you're still sitting there, still staring. Did you do *anything* while I was gone? 'Cause if not, you're probably bored.

    —I'm just waiting.

    —What are you waiting for, Rob?

    —Nothing.

    —Why do you keep looking out the window at the front yard?

    —I'm not.

    —Are you expecting somebody?

    —I don't know anybody.

    —You know me.

    —I know you. And I know you're gonna keep asking me questions until my ears fall off.

    —Are you looking to see if the mail's come yet?

    —It's usually here by now.

    —You've become totally obsessed with the mailman.

    —Have not.

    —Have so.

    —Has it come yet?

—Why do you wanna know?

—Stop bugging me, Tim.

—How am I bugging you?

—All these questions!

—I'm worried about my big brother. Is that so wrong?

—What are you worried about?

—You're eating weird.

—Oh, Jesus. Now you're watching what I eat?

—I made cookies with Mom and Donald last night and you didn't eat any of 'em. I know you don't like to have anything to do with anything Donald touches, but they were chocolate chip.

—I'm practicing being hungry.

—Because you're gonna take off again.

—I'm right here. Sitting on the couch. Petting the stupid cat. Right where you can see me whenever you're in the house.

—Don't pet the cat so hard, Rob. You know she doesn't like it.

—So now you're the big cat-petting expert, huh?

—Ever since you showed me.

—Poor fucking cat. We're petting the shit out of her and she doesn't know why.

—I thought you didn't like cussing that much, Rob.

—I appreciate your pointing it out to me. I didn't even know I was doing it.

—I'm just trying to show you that I listen to what you say.

—You listen to what I say. You watch what I do. You keep track of what I eat. You're like my own personal security system. Mom doesn't have to worry about me running away again as long as you're on duty.

—I don't tell Mom anything you do. She'd tell the cops and then they'd take you away and I'd be back to square one.

—Why would the cops take me away? I haven't done anything.

—I know they're asking you about some burned-out house.

—You know everything about me, don't you, Tim?

—Every day, as soon as you hear the mailman come, you walk out to the mailbox, get the mail, and go through it. You're looking for something in the pile of mail as you walk from the mailbox back to the house. But it hasn't come yet.

—How do you know it hasn't come?

—Because you're still sitting here, waiting.

—I'm expecting a bill.

—For what?

—I'm expecting to pay for my crimes.

—Haha.

—Seriously, Tim, leave me alone.

—Tell me what you're waiting for.

—Fuck off.

—Don't cuss.

—Don't keep me to my word. That's the worst. I can't have you listening to everything I say and taking it totally seriously word for word.

—Maybe you should start paying a little more attention to me.

—What do you mean?

—You're looking right around me, out the window.

—I'm waiting on something, Tim. I told you.

—I know, I went up the street so I could start waiting a little bit earlier than you.

—What are you talking about?

—I didn't go to the park. I went up the street. I introduced myself to the mailman. His name is Steven. He likes chocolate chip cookies. He gave me the mail and I'm not giving it to you.

—Give it to me, Tim.

—Not until you tell me what you want to be in it.

Fight. Fight. Fight. Fight. Fight.

—Where is it, Tim?

—Get off me. Get off me.

—Where is it?

—I didn't bring it home. I knew you would kick my ass and search me.

—Was there any mail for me?

—I can't tell you, Rob. Not until you answer my questions. I promised myself no matter how bad you hurt me or anything. And I'm gonna hold myself to my own word. That's what you said mattered.

Silence. Silence. Silence. Car. Silence.

—I'm waiting for a postcard.

—From your friends?

—Telling me where they are.

—The ones that burned down that house.

—Probably, I don't know.

—And you're going to go meet them?

—Probably.

—Take me with you.

—Did it come today?

—It's all bills and shit for Mom and Donald.

—Did you hide the mail in the knothole in the tree?

—I rolled it up and slid it into the birdhouse.

—How are going to get it out?

—I'm going to break the birdhouse open.

—They're gonna be pissed off. It's gonna be covered in shit.

—Don't cuss.

—Okay, sorry. They're gonna be *angry*. It's gonna be covered in . . . shit.

—Take me with you, Bobert. I'm not going to let you go otherwise.

—You'll tell.

—I won't.

—Just as bad, you'll watch my every move and give me away by accident.

—Please.

—Okay, okay. Okay.

49

Tom and Carl return with news of what they found. Malcolm interrogates them.

—Why is everybody naked?

   —We're wearing blankets.

—Some of you.

—You're telling me you never wanted to see what we all look like without our dirt on?

   —You all smell funny.

—All the soap in this house is scented. I guess they prefer lavender to humans.

   —It smells like there was an accident at the potpourri factory.

—We're trying to make ourselves seem like we live here so the maid won't be able to sniff us out the next time she comes back.

   —The maid was here?

—We gave her a fake note from the older Baxter daughter saying we had permission to be here.

   —But Malcolm thinks she's gonna come back so we all have to smell normal so we can hide better.

—Our clothes are in the dryer.

   —The ones that didn't disintegrate when they touched water.

—Where were you two?

   —We found the Peugeot house.

—Are you sure?

—Why would we say it if we didn't mean it?

—That's a good question, Tom. Why would you say it?

—I guess to show everybody that we're just as werewolf as you are, Malcolm.

—You have any proof?

—Look. Carl is gonna open his fist so you can see. But it might blow away, so look quick.

—What's that?

—Is he bleeding?

—No. It's flecks of red paint we scraped off the Peugeot using Tom's old house keys. I've been holding it in the palm of my hand the whole walk home. We wanted to show you guys some kind of proof.

—You scraped this paint off with your old house keys, Tom?

—Yeah. Right into Carl's hand.

—That doesn't prove anything.

—Well, we couldn't bring the hood ornament. It wasn't on the car 'cause Malcolm's already got it.

—What's in your other fist, Carl?

—Anger.

—Haha.

—Okay, where's the house at?

—It's over by the elementary school.

—You mean it's over by the last Baxters' house.

—Yeah.

—So you were feeling nostalgic when you disappeared.

—I didn't disappear. Carl and I just wanted to take a walk.

—I'm not mad. You found the Peugeot house. It's a miracle, Tom. Do you think you could show it to me on a map?

—Yeah. I think so.

—I didn't expect this. I'm surprised at you. I wanna give you a surprise, too. But I can't think of anything just yet.

—Don't do anything to us, Malcolm.

—I'm not going to do anything to you, Carl.

—So then what's next? Are we gonna go play a prank on this asshole, or are we gonna settle into a quiet suburban lifestyle?

—Let me ask you one question, Tom.

—What?

—Why are you still carrying around your old house keys?

—I dunno. Why do you care?

—Are you gonna run home when things get tough?

—No.

—Then why do you carry them?

—I'm just used to it, I guess. It's a habit. About twenty times a day I pat down my pockets to feel if I have my keys. It makes me feel better.

—I don't accept that.

—Why do you care what I carry, Malcolm?

—Because you're also carrying me and you're carrying everybody who's a part of our family. We have to trust that there's no going back. That you're not gonna get so nostalgic that you run all the way home. If we go over to the Peugeot house and offer to teach him a lesson we have to know that you support that lesson. This is gonna be our first exploration of an occupied house. That's new territory for us. I wanna go to this new territory with you. But I'm worried. I don't want to go into this new territory with you while you're walking around carrying souvenirs from your old habitat.

—I don't even know what you're talking about, but I'm ready to go.

—There must be a reason why you carry those keys. That's all I'm saying.

—He used them to scrape paint off the car, Malcolm.

—I understand that, Carl, but that's not why he carries them. He didn't know you two were gonna stumble upon the Peugeot, did he? If he did, he would've had to have known where the Peugeot house was all this time. And that would be treason, right? So I still have to wonder, why do you carry those keys, Tom?

—I can use them as a weapon. I can put 'em in my fist like this, with the keys sticking out between the knuckles to make them a weapon no cop in the world is gonna be suspicious about if we get stopped and frisked.

—Maybe. But I guess what I want to hear from you is: If things get tough and we need a place to lay low after we make our first exploration of an occupied house—what I'm wondering is if, *maybe*, we can use your keys then?

—We can just lay low here, can't we?

—Unless the maid comes back. And I'm convinced she will. She doesn't trust us. She gave us rules, so she's gonna wanna see if we violate them. And if she doesn't come back right away, someone else will—the cops, the paperboy. We'll fill you in on the plan for what to do if someone does show up and somebody will help you find a hiding place that isn't already taken.

—You're all gonna run and hide if someone comes over?

—That's what I'm asking *you* about, Tom. *If* we do need to hide, in an entirely different house, in an entirely different neighborhood, do you think we could borrow your keys and find temporary refuge at an occupied house?

—You want to lay low at my parents' place?

—I dunno. Maybe. I wanna know if it's an option.

—Sure. But what are we going to do with my family?

—We're you're family, right?

—Sure. But what are we going to do with my parents?

—I mean, it could happen in so many ways. Either you could use those keys to unlock the door to your old home and go inside and tell your parents we're gonna lay low there for a while and give them some rules, like a bedroom or a bedroom closet or something they're not allowed to leave. Or else you could just give us the keys and you could stay out on the front lawn until we're done and then we would come get you.

—Done doing what?

—I don't really know. And I won't really know until we finish up our first exploration tonight. So think about it. All right? All right? Why don't you answer me, Tom?

—Leave him alone, Malcolm.

—No. Wait. Carl, you seem to be spending a lot of time with Tom. Does he look weird to you?

—No.

—His skin's turning red and he's sort of shaking and he won't say anything to me.

—He's angry.

—No, Carl. I think Tom's changing.

—I'm not changing.

—What a surprise.

—I'm not changing!

—No, Tom. Listen. This is going to be great. You're going to feel weird, but it's a great time.

—I'm not changing.

—Have you ever changed before?

—No.

—Then how do you know what it feels like?

—Leave him alone, Malcolm.

—Some of you guys help me. Tom's changing.

—Stop it.

—He's resisting it so be careful. Hold him down while I tie up his hands. Stop fighting, Tom.

—Fuck off!

—I'm gonna have to put a gag in his mouth so he doesn't swallow his tongue.

—Can I be his reader?

—That's perfect. Yes.

—Where should we put him?

—This is bullshit.

—Shut up, Carl. Put him in the big closet in the master bedroom upstairs.

—I'll get him some food, baby.

—What do you want me to do?

—Susan, why don't you take Carl and explain the plan we came up with for if the maid comes home. Everybody else get your shit together. It's eight p.m. now. We'll go find the Peugeot house at midnight. I'm gonna go see how Anquille is doing with that safe. Tanya, Tom's food can wait. Why don't you come with me? Give everybody a chance to talk without us spying on 'em.

50

Susan explains to Carl the plan for if the maid comes home. Anquille joins them about midway through.

—Okay. No one's allowed to turn on any lights upstairs or down in the basement. The upstairs lights you can see from a block away and the basement lights shine through the garden windows.

—So?

—We're only supposed to be on the first floor. You can still go anywhere you want, you just can't turn a light on. And everybody is supposed to plan a hiding space. If the maid does come by we have an alarm system and everybody will scramble for his or her hiding space.

—What's the alarm system?

—We'll turn the stereo on really loud. That'll cover the sound of all of us diving into the hall closet.

—I was gonna hide in the hall closet.

—Is it gonna be cramped in there?

—Have you seen the hall closet? It's huge.

—Everything in this house is bigger than it needs to be.

—It's cool. We can both hide in there.

—Susan and Carl are a couple!

—Fuck off.

—We all take shifts being the lookout and watching for the maid to show up. The lookout sits in the leather chair by the front door. From that chair you can see all the ways into the house. All the *normal* ways into the house. Down the front walkway, and to the side door, which you can see through the kitchen window.

—You should disable the garage door opener so we'll have more time if somebody comes that way.

—That's a cool idea, Carl. We'll get somebody to do that.

—It's my idea. I can do it. I used to do it to my parents all the time. If I wanted to smoke dope or watch porn or something, the minute my parents left the house I would climb up on a kitchen chair and flip the switch so the garage door wouldn't work. When my parents came home they would just end up sitting in the driveway, honking. Later I would volunteer to take a look at the garage door opener. I would *say* I couldn't find anything wrong with it, but secretly I would flip the switch back so it would work again. My parents just thought it was balky. They bought a different brand, but I can do the same thing on any brand. My parents ended up believing it had something to do with "radio interference" blocking the signal from the remote opener.

—That's cool. I'll tell Malcolm it was your idea so you'll get credit and maybe he won't be so hard on you.

—I don't care. As soon as I can get Tom, I'm outta here.

—After he's changed he might not want to go with you.

—Tom's not really changing. I think Malcolm just wanted to shut him up.

—We'll know in three days.

—What do you mean?

—When Tom comes out he'll be able to tell us if he really changed or not.

—I'm not going to wait three days.

—That's not cool. Don't go in and try to get him. Remember what happened to me?

—He's not changing.

—It doesn't matter, Carl. You think you're right, but you have no idea. I didn't think I was changing, but something happens once you're alone in the dark. Tom has permission to change now. That's what it is: permission to change. If you go mess with Tom now, somebody's gonna get hurt. And that's true either way. Whether Tom decides to change or not. Somebody's gonna get hurt if you try and mess with him.

—Maybe.

—Maybe's cool. Just stick with "maybe" for three days, all right?

—All right. I'll wait. What do we do in the meantime, if the maid comes?

—It's so simple. You just press play on the CD player. It's already on and the signal song is cued up. The volume's turned up all the way so wherever you are in the house you'll hear it.

—Boo.

—Jesus Christ, Anquille. You scared the shit out of me.

—Sorry. Just goofing around. Malcolm told me to take break.

—Take it more calmly. That's not cool.

—You said you'll hear something. Hear what? What are y'all talking about?

—You get into the safe yet?

—My finger muscles are sore from spinning. The pads of my fingers are sore, too.

—No luck yet?

—Not yet. I'm up to plus or minus seventeen. I've been doing add one/subtract one, add two/subtract two. I'm being real careful, 'cause I don't want to feel like I missed a number.

—So, Anquille, you know the maid came by, right?

—Yeah. She saw me. I introduced myself to her.

—Well, if you're the lookout when she comes back or if anyone else comes by, you sit in that chair, you look out the front window, through the house to the side door in the kitchen, and out the garage door windows. If you see anybody pull up from any direction you press play on the stereo to start the signal song and you run and hide.

—Now let's go find you each a hiding place that nobody's taken.

—Wait.

—What?

—What's the signal song?

—Oh, I was looking through their music. They have good music. It should be something by the Pogues.

—No fucking way.

—The Pogues are awesome.

—Yeah, but if we made them the signal song then we can't listen to them any other time—even in some other room at low volume, we can't listen to a bootleg on the reel to reel, 'cause someone will get confused. So we made it something totally shitty that we would never listen to.

—What is it?

—It's Sting singing "Mack the Knife."

—I like that song.

—You would, Anquille.

—It doesn't really fucking matter. If you hear the song, you run to your hiding place. And you stay there as quiet as you can be while Malcolm and Tanya and Anquille try to convince the maid to give us one more week.

—Anquille doesn't have to hide?

—The three of them are college students. That's what the fake note from the daughter said.

—This is never going to work.

—If it doesn't—if one of us screams out: "It's happening," or if the visitor opens one of the closets and finds your hiding place, you come out, ready to attack, screaming "it's happening," and everybody'll come out and join you. Don't try to kill anybody or anything, we're just gonna tie up the visitor long enough for us to get out of here.

—So then we're gonna go to Tom's house next, huh?

—We're not gonna let Malcolm hurt Tom's family.

—Seriously Susan, if it came down to it, would you join us against Malcolm?

—Who's *us*?

—You are—if you're promising not to hurt Tom's family.

—Just 'cause I have a half ounce of mercy for Tom—that doesn't mean I'm an *us*.

—So you're with Malcolm?

—I'm not with anybody.

—Malcolm's dangerous. Look. I'm gonna open my other fist.

—What's that?

—It's soot and ash from the Baxters' place. Malcolm did go back and set it on fire, probably when he was crazy from being hungry for three days. I rubbed this hand in the ashes of it and then kept it in a fist the whole way back so I'd have some sort of proof.

—Y'all need to reconsider what you consider proof.

—Malcolm's out of control. That's the point. He's not gonna tie up the maid if she comes back. He's not gonna *prank* the Peugeot guy. He's gonna get a gun from that safe and kill him and then it's going to be all of *you* who go to jail.

—How are *we* gonna go to jail for what Malcolm does?

—Bobert's address was spray-painted on the chimney, on the bricks, as a clue to get him in trouble.

—Maybe Bobert put it there so we could find him? Hell, maybe Bobert burned the house down because he was mad at Malcolm for enforcing some discipline.

—That's bullshit.

—You guys need to get on board with what we're doing here. Find a hiding place and then take a shower. You stink.

—Malcolm's gonna shoot the Peugeot guy and write one of our names in blood.

—He can't shoot the Peugeot guy. He doesn't have a gun.

—He doesn't have a gun *yet*.

51

Malcolm and Tanya open the safe.

—What did you tell Anquille, baby?

—I told him to give up. I told him he'd never figure out the code. I explained that it wasn't just a matter of figuring out what number to add to the combination, but that it might be adding one to the first number of the combination and two to the next number and three to the last number. Or it might be adding someone's birthday to the combination, the day, the month, and the last two digits of the year . . . It's impossible.

—So how do we get into the safe?

—It's simple. Watch this.

Spin. Spin. Spin. Click. Open.

—Holy shit! Will you look at that?

—Wow. Money and guns. I guess it figures. These Baxters seem to be some sort of survivalists.

—How'd you do it? How'd you figure out the combination?

—The combination was written in the book. It always worked. I only acted like it didn't when I tried it in front of Anquille. I said the right numbers but I just spun the dial randomly so everyone would think it didn't work. The only thing I wasn't sure of was whether Anquille would double-check me. It turns out he trusts me.

—That's gonna be my downfall, too.

—How can you say that? I just made you rich and well-protected.

—How much do you think is in here?

—Oh, I don't think it's very much. It's probably just a few thousand or less. Two thousand, is my guess. I mean it's a lot to us, but I bet the Yorks don't even count it as part of their assets.

—That's a lot. We could pay the rent on a place for a few months.

—That's a weird idea.

—It's not. It's normal. You're the one who's weird.

—You don't know what I want to do with it.

—You wanna use it to keep yourself in power.

—I wanna find someone, an artisan, someone who works in leather and metal, maybe one of those Renaissance Festival freaks who build chain mail and jerkins. I wanna hire that person to make us a really beautiful set of matching leather straps and a harness and a muzzle. I wanna formalize our transformational practices and get it all official. That'll do more to keep this group together and grow it.

—You wanna consecrate our rituals.

—Yeah, that's a beautiful way of saying it.

—It's a kind of a beautiful thing to wanna do, Malcolm.

—See? I can be surprising.

—You can be surprising with money, but the guns you're gonna use in the traditional way, right?

—No one's gonna get hurt. I'm only going to use them for protection.

—That's the traditional way people get hurt by guns.

—Give me a kiss, Tanya.

—You really wanna leave everybody alone up there?

—They're not alone. We got a maid, a cop, Angel, and probably two or three nosy neighbors keeping an eye on the house for us.

—I don't trust Tom. Do you think he really found the real Peugeot house? I mean, how? It's weird.

—Bobert probably told him about it.

—Bobert knew where the Peugot house was?

—And Anquille, too.

—Is that it?

—And me. I heard them talking about it and I thought—later, when it's the right time, I'll reveal it to the group.

—And now's the right time?

—No, it's way too early. But I think that's what Tom wants. He wants to show everybody how scary this is gonna get. He wants to break us up.

—But you're gonna go to the Peugeot house, aren't you?

—You are, too, Tanya. We're all gonna go. We're gonna find a street map somewhere in this house and we're gonna draw up a plan. We gonna break up into groups and we're all gonna take a different route so we don't seem too noticeable. We don't want this cop who's already suspicious of me to bust all of us. So when your group gets to the Peugeot house you're gonna hide somewhere nearby, in the bushes or in the shadows and you're gonna wait until all the groups are there, in position, watching the front door. And then you're gonna see me running down the block toward the Peugeot house. I'll be transformed, hair covering my entire body. My eyes wild. Running at top speed. And it's gonna look like I'm on fire. Shooting guns off at the moon. Screaming bloody murder. And I'm gonna run right past you all and kick the door down and go into that house. And whoever wants to can come with me as I explore. But even if you stay outside, you'll know which room I'm in, because I'll be lighting it up from the inside. You'll see the curtains glow and you'll know I'm in the living room, I'm going up the stairs, I'm in the bedroom, and I'm on fire. But first I want you to kiss me. I want you to kiss me and kiss me. I want you to kiss me and I don't wanna think about anything else. I want you to kiss me and fuck me again and again right now without thinking anything. Right now. Kiss me. Please.

52

Angel and Craig get married.

—If you decide to stay with me we'll have a big family. We'll move out to the country. We'll live off the land. We'll grow corn all around the house in every direction to make a green wall. We'll keep goats that we'll train to eat only weeds in among the corn. Old farmers will laugh and tell us it's not possible, 'til they see the way we train 'em. When a goat kid bends its neck for a weed, we'll pet it. But if it opens its mouth for an early stalk of corn, we'll slap it on the face. We'll take the time to make the kids learn. We'll perfect nature. We'll keep bees without a mask. When the mailman comes he'll cry when he sees us standing there in a cloud of bees, perfectly understood by our insects. Unstung. A honeycomb in each hand. Offering him the opportunity to join us. Offering him a handful of gold if he can only get over his fear and reach out. Honeycomb and a cup of black coffee in the morning.

—

—We'll get a lot of mail because people will write to us for advice. That's what I want to do for a living. I want to give advice. Big picture or little details. I want to be the person people come to. "How should I live?" In perfect nature. "What should I eat?" Raw meat and vegetables. Honey. Coffee. Cigarettes are good for you because tobacco is native to this place. Put money in the next envelope you send me if you like my advice. "Does he love me?" Does he make you come? It only takes time and attention. If you love something, make it come. I love coffee. I pour the cream in real slow to watch it swirl. I let the honey drip down into it from a mile above. If I have whiskey, I put a finger in to warm the coffee up. I expect the same from a man. And you can expect the same from me toward you, if you decide to stay. "What time should I wake up?" As often as you can. Your mind should want to be awake. If you have a dream you should wake up right away and write it down and send it to us to read.

—

—That'll be our only TV, reading America's dreams to each other. You can read everything from east of the Mississippi and I'll take the west. If you decide to stay with me those'll be our subjects. We'll teach our children to read from these dream letters. We'll teach 'em spelling and psychology and geography. Imagine raising children on nothing but letting 'em play outdoors and reading to 'em from a great big compendium of dreams. If those were the only two sources of input they were allowed: running around and listening to Mom and Dad read dreams? Perfect nature.

—

—And we'll have lots of children. We'll have seven children. We'll have three girls and three boys and one that's just wild. We'll set it loose the day it's born. We'll put out food at night on the back porch. We'll lie awake in bed at night and listen to it while we eat, holding each other. Proud. Frightened. The seventh child will be a test of our faith in perfect nature. At any moment it could break into the house and kill us all, eat the children, fuck me to death while it fights you back from saving me. But that won't happen. We'll trust in perfect nature and the seventh child will be kind to us and the goats. We'll tell the rest of the brothers and sisters, "You have another sibling. Out there somewhere. Running wild but close enough to keep an eye on you." And we'll say, "Your father and I believe," if you decide to stay with me, "that this other sibling," in perfect nature, "if you ever get in real danger," come with me, "will break down the door to save you."

—

—That's why I spent all this time training you. Breaking you. Preparing you to make this decision. So that when you decide to stay with me it can be perfect nature and we can come together forever.

—

—Amen.

53

Tanya shows Susan where she is on the map.

—Where are you going?

—Nowhere, honey. Not for a couple more hours, anyway. What time is it?

—'Bout ten. What are you looking at all those maps for?

—Malcolm said to find a city map and I remembered seeing somebody else move around a bunch of maps in this big flat desk in the Baxters' office when we were shifting everything up a drawer. But these aren't city maps.

—What's it maps of?

—I don't know.

—Does it look like any place you'd wanna go?

—I think this is Mr. Baxter's job.

—That's cool. What is he? Some kind of land-lawyer?

—What does that mean?

—How should I know? There's more kinds of jobs in the world than I'll ever understand.

—That's what college is for, sweetie. So you can make up the job you wanna get.

—I wanna do something for animals.

—Like what?

—Animals haven't done shit to anybody and they get all their land taken away and treated like they don't own anything. Animals own just as much shit as we do. They own trees and caves. And they have contracts with bushes for berries and nuts for the winter. They just need someone to translate their contracts into human language and to draw up the deeds to their homesteads.

—Haha. So, what? You wanna be an animal-lawyer?

—It's like "lawyer" has become a suffix you can put on anything.

—I'm gonna be a "sandwich-lawyer."

—I bet there's such a thing. He probably works for some mayonnaise company.

—What about a "dildo-lawyer"?

—Totally. Whoever makes 'em—the manufacturers, they have lawyers. Why wouldn't they?

—How about a "magic-lawyer"?

—In Las Vegas.

—One of these maps is from around there. Look, Vegas is over there.

—What's the area all covered in red?

—It's probably where an evil spell has been cast over the land and Mr. Baxter is suing the magician who cast the spell.

—It might be where people have died, or been poisoned.

—Same thing. Right?

—Tanya, I don't wanna go out and beat up the Peugeot guy.

—You don't have to do anything you don't want to do, baby.

—I know. That's cool. But sometimes it's just easier—

—What's easier, baby?

—It's easier to do what other people want than to want on your own.

—What do you wanna do, Susan?

—I dunno.

—You need a lawyer to represent your desires. What would that be? A "love-lawyer"?

—They all work in divorce court.

—No, I mean the opposite. This is somebody who goes around and represents your desires. Say you love a boy, and you know you would love him better than his mom and dad, and you want to take him away to be a wife to him—well, the lawyer of love will go to his mom and dad and make your case, and lay out evidence for how great you are.

—You're talking about Bobert. That's cool. But maybe it's not his mom and dad the lawyer should go to, but to all of you. Then Bobert wouldn't have been sent away. Or he would be brought back immediately.

—Either way. The lawyer of love has done a good job. I'm convinced at least.

—I'm not gonna go with y'all to the Peugeot house.

—That's all right. I think that's *why* Malcolm's doing it. To get rid of some of us.

—But you're going?

—Yeah.

—You wanna see this guy get beat up?

—I wanna see him get scared.

—Why?

—I'm not a good person, baby.

—I don't think that's true.

—I keep thinking about this Peugeot guy hitting Malcolm with his car. And Malcolm was walking a dog. You love animals. Think about that. This guy just shoved Malcolm to the side. I think everybody does that to us. People have been doing it to me my whole life. *I've* been doing it to me. I've been taught to do it to *myself.*

—That's what I'm saying. I've been doing to myself, too.

—But now you've changed.

—Yeah.

—So you're gonna go become a love-lawyer for animals? You wanna go around saying, "This dog could have a better home across the street where the kids would love it more and that Mr. Baxter would take it for more walks and that Mrs. Baxter would buy it better food."

—That's the difference between me and you guys. Malcolm's not a lawyer, he's a cop. He's not gonna try to persuade the Peugeot guy about what the law means. Malcolm's gonna enforce the law as he understands it.

—That's fun to think about—adding the word cop to everything, like "sandwich cop." Or "dildo cop."

—That's cool. If "sandwich cop" sees you put mayo and peanut butter on a sandwich he shoots you in the mouth.

—No, Susan. It should be that if sandwich cop sees you throw away half a sandwich, with all the starving people in the world—that's when he shoots you.

—Yeah. That's it. That's the difference between me and Malcolm.

—And me. I'm on Malcolm's side. I think we need to stop lawyering about shit and start policing what we believe.

—You think Mr. Baxter is protecting all these maps from apartment buildings and sandwich shops and shit.

—I bet you ten million dollars it's the opposite, Susan. I bet you it's the exact opposite. You don't get this house for being good.

—Yeah. All the buildings have lawyers. But in that whole red area, all the rabbits and bobcats and shit, they don't have anyone.

—That's what Mr. Baxter does. That's what all these coordinates and maps are about. Mr. Baxter protects the companies that ruin land with gas leaks and illegal dumping and shit.

—I told you. I told you! They ate the whole world and now there is nothing left. This is why there's nothing left. Jesus.

—Listen.

—What?

—Is that the signal song?

—No.

—What is it?

—It sounds like somebody's doing aerobics.

54

At least half the werewolves down in the basement standing in front of the flat screen TV moving in sync with a workout DVD.

—*Five, six, step together . . .*

—What are you doing, baby?

—What does it look like?

—*One, two. Relax and twist. One, two. Relax and twist.*

—And what are you wearing?

—These are workout clothes.

—It looks like you're transforming into suburbanites. You're all wearing their clothes and doing whatever the TV tells you to do.

—*Exhale on the jump and strrrrrretch. Exhale on the jump and turn.*

—Ignore the DVD. It is what it is. A girl in spandex is yelling at us to *feel the burn.* But the exercises, that's what's important. It's training.

—That's cool. But what are you training for?

—*Climb the ladder. Climb the ladder. Climb the ladder. Climb and jump.*

—It's physical training.

—And it teaches us to stay in rhythm.

—That'll be great the next time we have a dance-off with the cops, baby.

—Haha.

—Fuck off.

—Being together can help our synchronicity on hunting parties, and shit like that.

—Join in or shut up.

—You wanna?

—Why not?

—Tanya's in!

—Yay!

—Come on!

—Susan's taking off her sweater. She's in, too!

—All right. Now we have a pack!

—*With right foot. Push. With the right foot. Push. Now left foot pivot, right foot push. Left foot pivot, right foot push.*

—I can't believe we're doing this.

—It's fucking exhausting.

—*Punch and punch and jab and punch. Kick and turn and jab and punch.*

—And the Baxters do this shit every day.

—Mrs. Baxter does.

—The whole fucking Baxter clan. All of them. On every block. We think we're so tough, breaking into houses, living off dog food and shit we steal. But these suburban motherfuckers are working out and lifting weights and jogging and shit.

—No wonder they're taking over the world.

—It shows you what we're up against.

—We're not *up against* anything.

—Well, you're sure as shit not one of them.

—*Kick and take a step and plant. Kick again and step and plant.*

—We might be taking advantage of the Baxters, but this isn't some huge war against them.

—Then what do you call it?

—I don't know. I just want to be left alone. I want to go out on my own, but the Baxters have destroyed the West. And outer space isn't a real possibility yet.

—You want a separatist movement.

—Yeah.

—*Knee again then duck and punch. Knee again then duck and punch.*

—Well, you could start by separating yourself from the Baxters' houses and food. You want to be left alone. But you're wearing the Baxters' clothes and you're sleeping in their beds.

—Where else am I going to go? They ate the whole world.

—Shut up.

—Fuck you. You shut up.

—No. Shut up and listen.

—Someone's here.

—Who is it?

—Sting.

—Everyone to your hiding place!

55

Oh, the shark has pretty teeth, dear.

—*Oh, the shark has pretty teeth, dear, and he shows them, pearly white* . . .

—Hello? Hello?!

—*Just a jackknife has MacHeath, dear, and he keeps it out of sight* . . .

—Hey, Carlene. Back so soon. I thought we had an understanding.

—Turn that music off.

—No. We had an understanding. I know we did. And playing our music doesn't violate that understanding.

—*When the shark bites with his teeth, dear, scarlet billows start to spread* . . .

—I saw lights on in the basement, through the garden window. You weren't supposed to go down there.

—*Fancy gloves though wears MacHeath, dear, so there's not a trace, mmm, of red* . . .

—We thought we heard a noise down there. We just went down there to check it out.

—I could see the lights from the TV. You were watching a movie or something.

—So the rest of our time here, you're gonna spy on us every second of the day?

—The rest of your time here is over.

—*On the sidewalk, Sunday mornin', baby, lies a body, oozin' life* . . .

—I'm sorry but we can't possibly leave now.

—You can and you will.

—*Someone sneakin' around the corner, is the someone Mack the Knife?*

—One of us is sick. He can't go anywhere. He's got this fever and we have to wait at least until it passes.

—Who's sick? You're saying "he." But I can see all three of you. Is it someone else? How many of you are there?

—*From a tugboat, by the river, a cement bag's droppin' down.*

—You caught us. There's another somebody up in the master bedroom. We hid him in the closet because we didn't want you to find him.

—This is outrageous.

—*Yeah, the cement's just for the weight, dear. Bet you Mack, he's back in town* . . .

—You can go look in the closet and see for yourself.

—Malcolm, don't.

—Don't what? What's in the closet that you don't want me to see?

—Nothing.

—I'm not scared of you.

—Don't go look in the closet. It's a trap.

—I'm going to find out what you've done and then I'm going to call the cops.

—Don't.

—Give it up, Anquille. The more you say "don't," the more determined she's gonna be.

—*Looky here, Louie Miller, disappeared, dear, after drawing out his cash* . . .

—I'm dialing 9-1-1. On my phone right now.

—It's happening!

—*And MacHeath spends like a sailor, did our boy do somethin' rash?*

—Carlene. Just hang up the phone and leave.

—I am going to take care of Linda's house. That is what I'm paid to do. Out of my way.

—It's happening!

—*Sukey Tawdry, Jenny Diver, Lotte Lenya, Sweet Lucy Brown* . . .

—I wouldn't open that door if I were you.

—What's in there?

—Let her find out.

—*Oh, the line forms on the right, dears, now that Mack, he's back in town . . .*

Attack. Attack. Attack. Attack. Attack.

—*This is the 9-1-1 operator. What is your location?*

—Pick up her phone. Hang it up.

—*What is the nature of your—*

—What the fuck did we do?

—Does 9-1-1 know where we are?

—They'll probably be able to figure out who she was. Then they'll call her land line. Get the husband or the kids on the phone. Then they'll end up here eventually.

—What are we going to do?

—Everybody get your bags and meet me in the basement.

—What about Tom?

—Untie him. He was faking it. He wasn't changing.

—No. I am. I feel weird.

—Hey, listen up everybody. Tanya and I have a map of the neighborhood. We'll show you where the house is. Then we'll split up and head out in different directions to the Peugeot house. We'll meet up at the playground over there.

—What are we going to do to the Peugeot guy?

—You'll see.

—We're just going to scare him.

—Then where are we going to go?

—Tom? What do you think? Where should we go next?

56

Susan wants it to keep happening.

We heard the call, "It's happening," and everyone fell out of his or her hiding place simultaneously. I didn't want to be the one who wasn't there. I wanted to be screaming too. And I was. I was happy. I was laughing. Nervous-happy. Excitement-laughing. It was so cool. All goose bumps like my individual hairs were trying to thicken and become werewolf again. The change was really sudden this time, like physically screaming with my whole body, like all my individual cells screaming. It was a choice. But it was like a way of making a single choice that could account for everything for the rest of the night. Like snorting a long, long line of coke and waking up fucked with a bloody lip and you don't know where your purse is.

We heard the call, "It's happening," and instantly we were streaming out of the closets and up from under the beds. Everyone was running through the house in the same direction, like platelets in the blood, jamming ourselves through the hallways, slamming into the walls at a turn as a way of stopping and changing direction. All of us running together, sometimes pushing the person in front of you to go faster, sometimes pulling someone back to get ahead. We were all screaming, "It's happening, it's happening, it's happening."

Good thing the master bedroom is big. We couldn't all fit through the door at once, but I put myself into the pack surrounding the door and eventually got squeezed through. It was loud in the room. Punctuated loud. Not solid screaming. You could hear the maid and you could hear people hitting her and kicking her if they could get a clear shot. Some of us were still saying, "It's happening," but it was like a murmur now.

There seemed to be a system. It happened naturally. We heard the call, It's happening, and we all forced our way to where the action was. The maid was on the floor in the corner, jammed up between the bed and the wall. People were standing on the bed and on the dresser to try to get a look at her. Everybody was pushing to get closer to her. When someone would get to the front of the pack that person would be pushed off the edge of the bed or the dresser, on top of the maid. Whoever was there before would crawl out backward or climb up over the new attackers. Each attacker only had three or four seconds to land a blow or spit in her face or rip at her clothes. Everybody watching would go *oooh* or go *ahhh*, depending on how cool or cruel what you did to her was.

I was the first one to bite the maid. Then everybody had to do it. It was like steak, sure. Everybody was saying it was like steak. Afterward. Nobody was really discussing it while it was happening. Everyone was screaming. The maid included. "It's happening." "Aieieieiei." "Ohhhh." "It's happening." "Aieieieie." "Ahhhhh." But afterwards everybody kept saying it was like steak. But the difference between biting a steak and biting the maid was that the maid was alive. When I had my teeth in her I could feel her try to pull away. It made the bite worse. I realized it was an evolutionary thing. The better my teeth are at inflicting pain, the more damage my bite is going to do to living prey, because pulling away does as much damage as biting.

I don't really remember much more. You make some kinds of choices and then everything else is decided for a certain amount of time. You wake up with a little blood on your face and an upset stomach and a feeling like you want the choicelessness to last a little longer. Even as it was fading I was hoping that we could just keep going, running out into the neighborhood like wild animals, running down the streets screaming, "It's happening." As long as it was happening it hadn't happened. That's what I wanted. I wanted it not to have happened. I wanted it to keep happening.

57

Malcolm tries to manage things as the werewolves split up and make a run for it.

—We didn't kill the maid, so stop crying.

—I'm going home.

—*She* attacked *us*.

—She didn't do anything.

—She was spying on us. She was watching the house. She was out to get us. Literally. She was sitting out there in her car watching, waiting for us to do something that would allow her to call the cops in a way that wouldn't get her fired.

—*We* should call the cops. We should call 9-1-1. So they can come get her.

—We will. But first I have a surprise for you.

—No more surprises.

—Are you sure? This is a good one.

—What is it?

—One at a time I want you to run down to the basement and pick out something you like. I got the safe open.

—No way!

—Sorry, Anquille. You should have kept at it.

—Whoever got the combo to the safe was supposed to get a wish. That's you, Malcolm.

—I know. I've been thinking about it.

—What's in the safe?

—Guns, money, and paperwork. Pretty much everything that's wrong with the world. I assume none of you want any paperwork. But everybody can go get one thing, either a gun or a handful of money. There's cash or there's gold coins. There's more money than guns. But I think, on average, everybody'll be happy.

—What are you going to wish for, Malcolm?

—This is a map of the neighborhood. This is where we are now. This is the old Baxters' house and the Speedy Stop. And here's the Peugeot house. I *wish* that everyone here would go down to the basement and find something he or she wants. Then I wish you would get the bag you packed and leave this house, take a random direction through the neighborhood, and meet me at midnight at the playground of the elementary school across the street from the Peugeot house.

—That's at least two wishes.

—I know I'm not gonna get everything I want. But even if you're not gonna go with us to the Peugeot house, if you didn't like this little warm-up we did on the maid, if you're just gonna go home—still, I want you to go down to the safe and take something. Even you, Tom.

—Why "even me"? Why do I get singled out?

—Because you were faking it. You weren't changing. Look at you. You're just the same as you always were.

—I was the first one to get my hands on the maid.

—You probably thought she was one of us.

—I knew who it was. I heard Sting. I knew it was happening. I wasn't faking. And, anyway, *you're* the one who said I was changing.

—I was wrong. Take whatever you want and then go.

—To the Peugeot house?

—Just go take something. All of you. Whether you're gonna meet us at the Peugeot house or not.

—You want us to take something because that way you can say we're accessories to the crime.

—No, I want you to take something because that way you *can't* say that I wasn't a good tribal leader.

—There's not going to be anything left for you.

—I already got my wish. I got to see what we all look like as pack.

—Come on.

—What about you, Malcolm?

—I'm gonna wait here until I'm sure you're all out of the house and then I'm going to call 9-1-1 to come get our maid.

—You promise?

—She's gonna be fine. Trust me.

58

Tom and Anquille run into each other while running through the neighborhood.

—Which way you going, Anquille?

   —That way.

   —You're not gonna go to the Peugeot house?

   —Nope. What about you? You wanna come with me?

   —Where to?

   —I don't know. I haven't decided.

   —I'm going to the Peugeot house. I changed for real.

   —I guess so.

   —Look over there. Under the streetlight.

   —I don't see anything.

   —Wait.

   —

   —

   —

   —There.

   —Who was that, Tom?

   —I don't know. I just love that we're all out. Running through the neighborhood like dogs. It must look crazy from a helicopter. If you could see every single one of us going this way and that. Half of us weaving around randomly but slowly headed toward the same little patch of grass by the school, and the other half of us drifting off into the city.

—Do you believe in God?

—I dunno. Who gives a shit? I guess a little.

—I was just thinking, because you said "helicopter," who can see us all? The only answer is God.

—God didn't see the maid. Leastways, he didn't protect her.

—You think Malcolm really called 9-1-1?

—No. Do you?

—My full name is Anquille Alphonse Serron. I was raised Catholic, but now I think God is a werewolf. He's good to us three hundred and fifty-something days out of the year. But twelve nights a year he changes into a monster and makes cancer, makes cars hit us, makes a bunch of kids attack a maid.

—Three hundred and fifty-three. That's the number of days you were looking for, when there isn't a full moon. But the moon's on a twenty-eight-day thing, so there's probably some years when there's maybe thirteen full moons in a year.

—Malcolm's like God. He feels bad about making us attack the maid so he gives us all a bunch of money.

—I guess that tells me what you took.

—You took a gun?

—It seemed cooler.

—You're a fucking idiot, Tom.

—Yeah, I guess, but a gun can get money.

—You're not gonna become a famous bank robber, so give it up.

—You give it up.

—Fuck you, Tom.

—Let me see how much money you took.

—The money was the better choice. I'm gonna be all right for at least a month.

—Unless God changes on you.

—I got two handfuls. Look.

—Why didn't you take the gold? I bet a handful of gold is worth ten times more than a handful of money.

—Think about it, Tom. I can't walk into a hotel tonight and give them a piece of gold for a room. I can't walk into a Speedy Stop and get beer with gold.

—Give it to me.

—Fuck you.

—Set it on the ground and run.

—You're not gonna shoot me.

—You can set it on the ground and run, or you can just run, but I'm gonna shoot you if you don't give me the money.

—Guess this is one of those moments when I'm about to find out if God's moon is full for me or not.

—Anquille Alphonse Serron, you have until the count of three.

—All right.

—One.

—I'm ready.

—Two.

—Let's do this.

—Three.

Fight. Fight. Fight. Fight. Gunshot.

59

The cop and Malcolm talk.

—Did your dog get loose again?

—Yeah. How'd you guess? She's running wild through the neighborhood. I need to get her before someone calls the pound.

—How does that happen? That it gets away from you so often?

—She's an animal. You can only train her so much. She sits and she stays, but if she hears the right sound on the other side of the fence, or if the right smell wafts in through the window, then nature takes over.

—"Wafts," huh?

—You gotta problem with my vocabulary?

—I'm just trying to figure you out.

—I can't wait to read the report. I'm a little confused myself.

—Let's talk about it. Tell me who you are.

—Why would I do that?

—Because you're under arrest.

—For what?

—For running.

—I haven't run yet.

—You're about to.

—You been coppin' a long time, huh? You know everything that's about to happen? You're some kinda prophecy cop? That would make a good TV show.

—I think they already have a show like that. And if they don't—they will soon.

—Yeah. There's nothing new under the sun.

—Your face is healing up pretty nice.

—You catch the guy who did it?

—Not yet. Not yet. I've been watching for someone wandering around the neighborhood, looking suspicious. But you're the only one I find who fits the description. You seem jumpy.

—I am. I got this cop who's been following me.

—You know, you could see this the whole other way. I could be a help to you. I could be your friend.

—Like an angel sent to stop me before I do something I'll regret.

—Sure. If that's what you need right now.

—You wanna see my fifty-dollar bill?

—I assume it's gone. But I wasn't going to hassle you about it.

—It's in here somewhere. Let me see what I've got. Let's see . . .

—That's a lot of money you got there.

—Your bill is in this roll somewhere.

—Why don't you put your hands on the hood of the car and let me count that money for you.

—Naw. You're right. If you get out of the car I'm gonna run.

—All right. Just hang tight for a second. We'll figure out a way to make this all work out.

—You seem good at memorizing addresses. Why don't you put this one in your Rolodex: 67 Crestview Drive.

—Is that where you got that money?

—There's a woman there who wants to see you.

—What did you do?

—I didn't do anything.

—I've been seeing your friends running through the neighborhood all night. Looks like fifty or sixty kids. Did some of them attack this woman?

—What was that?

—That's what a gunshot sounds like. Get in the back of the car.

—I've gotta go now.

—Don't move. Don't move.

—Don't let the gunshot distract you. 67 Crestview Drive. That's where you need go.

—I have to chase you.

—If you chase me, then a woman might die.

—Don't do anything stupid.

—I have to run.

—I'm not talking about that anymore. Who's this woman?

—I have to go now.

—Officer Greggs. If they catch you. If you get caught tonight, ask for me. Greggs.

—I can't be caught.

—You'll be surprised. There's some fast guys on the force.

—I mean, I can't be caught alive.

60

Sitting outside the Peugeot house

—It almost looks like they're expecting us.

—The front door's open. The curtains are drawn back. All the lights are on.

—I dare you to go inside.

—Just walk down the middle of the street, go straight up through the door, and yell, "Come out, come out, wherever you are."

—Fuck that. Come around over here. Look. There's a man in that chair.

—Is he watching TV?

—That's what it looks like.

—That's what it looks like, but watch him for a while. Watch. Watch. Watch. Watch. Watch.

—What? I don't see anything.

—That's it. He never moves.

—You think he's asleep?

—I think it looks like someone's expecting us.

—You think Malcolm set this up as some kind of trap?

—Or Tom?

—Did you see that? A woman just walked by.

—She's naked.

—Cool. Now I double dare you to go inside.

—Come over this way. Over to the other side where we can see her better.

—Is that Angel?

—Holy fuck. It is.

—What's she doing?

—Listen, you can hear it . . .

—She's clipping her nails.

—You can hear that from here?

—She's standing over a sink, trimming her nails. That's disgusting.

—Do you think the man watching TV knows she's in the house?

—Did she pass through his room?

—She walked behind him.

—That's creepy.

—Angel beat us to the Peugeot house.

—And it looks like she's made friends with the Peugeot guy.

—Malcolm's gonna be pissed off.

—Not if she's already beat him into submission.

—Either way. If she made friends with the Peugeot guy that's no good. That means she made friends with our enemies. But if she beat Malcolm to the punch, that means she's stronger than Malcolm.

—It means she's faster.

—It means there's going to be a fight.

—Here comes Malcolm. Right down the middle of the street.

—They're gonna fight.

—How do you know?

—He's taking his clothes off, too.

—They're both gonna die.

—I don't know. Malcolm's smart but Angel's mean.

—When two werewolves fight they both die because every werewolf is the exact same strength and we can only fight to the death.

—But are you sure they're both werewolves?

—I thought it was just a thing we said. Like being cool. You're not literally cool. It's what other people think about you.

—I think it's real.

—I guess we're about to find out.

—He's at the doorway.

—Listen.

61

Malcolm and Angel fight.

—Come in.

—How long have you been here?

—The whole fuckin' time. This is the house of that dick Susan and I met at the party. He took out his keys at the party and I saw he had a Peugeot key chain. I thought, "lucky me. Maybe." I thought, "I'm gonna make this guy my friend one way or another."

—Where's he now?

—In the other room. Watching TV.

—Are you drunk?

—I kinda try to stay that way.

—What's he watching?

—That's how I tamed him. It's just a tape now. But when I did it, it was live and I made him watch it while I did it. You can see how surprised he is. Look.

—This isn't what I had in mind, Angel.

—You wanted to scare him, didn't you?

—I don't know.

—This is what you told us all you wanted.

—I didn't want this.

—Look at the video, he's scared. He's transforming and he's watching it at the same time.

—I just wanted to scare him.

—What you *wanted*—I fucking *did*.

—I was going to make us a home.

—You and Tanya were going to settle down and treat us all like your kids.

—Tanya and I are gonna settle down and treat you however you act.

—She calls us all "baby."

—That's not how she means it.

—You don't get to control how I understand things. That's what I'm fucking talking about! You even want to tell me who means what with their words. You think you're like her interpreter or something. My heart is my fucking interpreter.

—Tanya speaks for herself.

—Yeah, well, she means shit to me.

—Then leave.

—I did. I left and I found us a house. And now you're all here.

—We can't live here.

—We can. No one's going to bother us. The neighbors are terrified.

—We can't even go back to the old place.

—We'll move on.

—Nobody will move with you. They're not gonna like this.

—Where the fuck are they?

—They're out there watching us. Listening.

—Some of them'll like this.

—It's not what they signed up for.

—What did you think you were doing? Norman Rockwell? You don't want to live like normal people. You want to transform. Violently. This is what that looks like.

—We beat someone up at the other house. All together. It didn't feel right. It didn't bring us together. Or it did, some of us. I don't know how many people are out there, but it scattered us. It split us all up.

—The ones who stuck with you are the good ones.

—I don't know about that.

—You hear what he's saying about you? Can you hear him?

—We lost the dog. That doesn't seem like a good omen. Everything's fucked now.

—You hear what he's saying?

—I'm not saying anyone's bad. I'm just saying we can do better.

—I'm not talking to them. I'm saying, listen to the Peugeot guy.

—He's dead, Angel. You can smell it.

—He's trying to say something. Open his mouth.

—No.

—That's our ticket out of here. Open his mouth.

—No.

—I put the keys to his Peugeot in his mouth. I told him if he could swallow them I would let him go. They were on a great big key ring with a metal disc that said "Peugeot."

—We're going to turn you in to the cops.

—Fucking shut up. And listen to what he's saying to you . . . Can you hear it?

—No one is gonna go along with this.

—He's saying we can take his car. He's saying we can take it and drive out to the country. There are homes in the country where there are no neighbors.

—We found guns at the other house.

—You're threatening me with a fucking gun?

—Angel. Stop.

—A gun is just a tool. I know how to kill somebody.

—I can kill, too.

—Then do it.

—No. I'm gonna take everybody away from here and call this cop I know.

—Listen to him.

—He's dead.

—He says you are, too. If you try to leave this house without fighting me.

—Run. Everybody, run.

—They're not going anywhere. They want to see what we're about to do.

Fight. Fight. Fight. Fight. Fight.

Part Three

THE WILD

62

Bobert and Timothy lie in their beds, planning their great escape.

—Robert.

—

—Robert.

—

—Robert!

—What?

—Are you asleep?

—No.

—What're you doing?

—I'm getting ready to crawl out the window and leave this house for good.

—I thought we were going tomorrow night.

—I'm getting ready in my mind. I'm trying to go over everything that's gonna go wrong so when those scenarios come up, we can sidestep 'em. Chess players do it. The night before a big match. Chess players lie in bed like this and they play the game over and over, looking for the quickest way to lose. As soon as a chess player figures out a way to lose, he starts over and avoids that move and looks for the next quickest way and so on and so on, until it's just not possible for him to mess things up.

—I could go tell Mom right now.

—Tell her what?

—Tell her we're leaving tomorrow at midnight.

—Why would you fuckin' do that? You're such a cowardly shit of a little brother.

—Fuck you! I'm just trying to do what you're saying. Telling Mom is the quickest way I can think of to mess this up.

—But you wouldn't go tell Mom unless we were fighting. So calling you a cowardly shit is the quickest way *I* can think of to mess this up.

—You're a jerk.

—Shh. Listen. I love it when the house is quiet like this.

—Do you have the postcard with the address we're going to on it?

—Yeah. It's in the pocket of my jeans.

—Where's your jeans?

—On the floor somewhere.

—That's another way we could fuck up; we could leave the postcard lying around where Mom could find it.

—She wouldn't know what it was. It doesn't have anything but a return address on it.

—It's got blood smeared on it. It looks like they were trying to draw something in blood.

—It's a picture of a wolf. It's code. You have to be one of us to know. And if *you* couldn't figure it out, there's no way Mom's gonna figure it out.

—Mom wouldn't care what your "code" meant. She would see there was blood on the postcard and figure something was up and she'd give it to the cops—

—What if I destroy the postcard so Mom doesn't find it—but then I forget the address, or I remember it wrong, and we end up running away but we never get where we're going.

—Robert.

—What?

—Whose blood do you think it is?

—I don't know.

—Why do you think they were bleeding?

—They might have had a fight.

—Do they fight a lot?

—Not as much as Mom and Donald.

—Mom and Donald don't end up bleeding.

—It's different. It's more honest. They just hit each other. It's like with us. If you hurt my feelings. Or if you cuss too much. Or when you won't stop calling me Bobert 'cause you're trying to hurt my feelings. Then I hit you.

—But I'm not as big as you.

—Everybody is more or less the same size.

—But it's not fair.

—How is it fair the other way? When people yell at each other, or call each other names—not everybody is the same size emotionally. You know what I mean? You might think calling me Bobert is no big deal. You're just teasing your big brother. But you don't know what it does to me.

—I'm scared.

—I'll protect you. If somebody hits you, I'll hit them. It doesn't happen that often. Besides, it's just like a warning. It's how animals talk. We don't hit each other to hurt each other.

—But someone's bleeding.

—They're not bleeding anymore, probably. Besides—besides—besides—it might have just been somebody trying to be cool, like when you become blood brothers with somebody.

—Is that the kind of stuff they think is cool? I don't like blood.

—You sure like talking about it.

—I just can't imagine cutting myself is all.

—I don't wanna talk about it anymore. You weren't alive yet, Tim, but when I was a baby they had just invented those baby monitors and Mom got one 'cause she was nervous about how to be a mom. She was probably feeling the same as we do now—lying awake in bed, trying to figure out all the ways she could mess up. It's hard to sleep when you're a mom, 'cause if the baby stops breathing, the mom won't know it if she's already asleep. So our mom went out and got a baby monitor. She didn't use it on you because by then she was three years into it and she was more relaxed. Who knew she would just keep relaxing to the point that she would let somebody like Donald into the house so he could creep around at night and catch one of us getting up to go to the bathroom and then use that time to make us play with him? But my point is about that baby monitor. She keeps it in the hall closet. And when I came back to get you and the cops started coming around and no one believed my stories—what if Mom got that baby monitor out of the hallway closet and it's under the bed? That would be one way to fuck this up. Sitting up talking about blood and postcards. And Mom could be listening to us right now.

—Then I would say—"I love you, Mom."

—"I love you, Mom, too."

—You want me to check under the bed, Bobert? I mean, Robert.

—No. I know the baby monitor's not under there.

—How?

—Two reasons. First, I saw it in the hall closet today when I was packing us some supplies. The sleeping bags are in the hall closet. And second, we've been sitting in this room talking about what a dick Donald is and how bad he's been to us and what he's done to us and Mom hasn't killed him. I think if she knew, if she heard us talkin' about it in private, she would finally start to believe me, and then she would kill him.

—You think so?

—Donald's the one who started calling me Bobert. That's why I don't like it.

—Let's leave tonight.

—No.

—Why not?

—'Cause that's one of the worst mistakes we could make.

—But we're already packed.

—When I was with the werewolves, we kept our bags packed all the time. And we were always packing 'em and repacking 'em. Each house, if it was a better house, we would unpack what we had and pack better stuff. But we never packed our stupid brains with what was gonna happen next. We never thought about who was gonna be in charge. Or how were we gonna make rules. You know, for a while we let a baseball cap be in charge of us. Everyone wrote stuff down and then just picked ideas out of a hat. How's that for a plan? You wanna do that? Do ya?

—Shhh. You're gonna wake up Mom.

—The plan is we leave tomorrow. Between now and then I'm not gonna sleep. I'm gonna lie here and think up all the ways that this can go wrong. And then, when we're out on the road, I'm gonna only do the things that get us to *happily ever after*.

—You could be such a dick to me that I fuckin' turn you over to the cops and I just go out on my own.

—Well, if you're gonna do it, I would rather know about it now than after two weeks out on the road. So stop cussing at me. You think the cops could hold on to me? No way. If you ever see 'em putting cuffs on me, you better stand back, 'cause that means I'm about to go wild. I'll go so wild they'll be talking about it on the ten o'clock news for weeks. And they're not gonna get you, either. Not while I'm with you.

—You think it's gonna take two weeks to get to the address on that postcard?

—Maybe longer. I think we should walk the whole way. No hitchhiking and no buses. And no stealing cars.

—We should steal Donald's car and roll it off the edge of Glendora Canyon.

—That's not a bad idea.

—You sure? I just said it. I didn't think about it. I just pulled it out of my hat.

—Haha. But I think it *is* a good idea. Especially going down to Glendora.

—I thought you said the address on the postcard was up north? Glendora's the other direction. Down by Fuller.

—That's why it's a good idea. That's what we should spend our time doing tomorrow. All day long we talk to Mom about Glendora and anything we can think of that's down south. Then we steal the car and drive down that way. Then we can trash the car. Or we can give it away to a homeless person. And then we can turn around and head back north and they'll be followin' the wrong trail. Plus it'll be a final goodbye present to Donald.

—I wish we could just leave now.

—I know.

—I have a bad feeling.

—You're nervous.

—I know. I want everything to be over.

—And then what?

—What?

—What does "everything being over" look like to you?

—I don't know.

—Just say it. Like a bedtime story. While I lie here and think. Say it.

—I want you and I to have a place of our own. A house. I want it to be in the woods. And I want all your friends to live nearby. Like in walking distance. You know the way a cul-de-sac is? With all the fronts of the houses facing one another really close, in a circle? But out the back doors we all have big farms, fanning out like a pie chart. And you and I are the hunters for the group. Everyone else, all your friends, farm corn and beets and lettuce. And you and I go out for a couple of weeks at a time and set up a little camp and live off venison jerky and water from some nearby creek. And we sleep on blankets on the ground. Nothing else. We don't need anything but a blanket and a rifle apiece. We probably have a tarp in case it rains, but most nights we lie on a blanket by the fire and we stare up at the stars. And we fall asleep talking. And in the morning when we wake up, we don't say a word. We're as silent as ghosts. It'll be so early, it'll still be dark out. And silently we'll roll up our blankets and go out into the fields and point to where each one of us is gonna sit and wait for the deer. We always know where the other one is, so we don't accidentally shoot each other. We just point at things and we understand each other without talking. And when we hear the gun go off we can tell just by the sound it makes whether it was a hit or not, the way Donald can. If the gunshot sort of goes flat at the end, that's a hit. And then one of us goes to the other one and helps him dress the deer and quarter it and we carry it back to the cul-de-sac we have in the middle of the forest. And when we get back there's a big barbecue and we eat some of the deer right away, roasted over an open fire as we butcher the rest of it to be smoked. And then everybody tells us everything that happened while we were gone. We drink beer by the fire and eat barbecued venison until our faces are just greasy with it. And we have wives. And they tell us what happened with our kids while we were gone. And Mom is there. And she tells us what happened with our wives while we were gone. And we're not gone *that* much. But it's our job to go sometimes. And when we do go, it's just like tomorrow, we wake up in the middle of the night and we leave as quietly as ghosts, so we have a good distance covered by the time the sun comes up.

63

Bobert and Timothy drop fake hints about where they'd go if they ran away throughout the whole next day.

—Can I have a hundred dollars? I want to go to that concert down in Fuller. It's a three-day thing. Come on. You get to see every band in the world. They all come to Fuller, just a few miles south of here. It's the closest I'll ever get to most of the great art in the universe. Please? Please? God! You suck!

—I hate living here. The houses are better down in Glendora. They're bigger. And there's views of nature. Not everything is billboards down there.

—Don't tell me to "go outside and play." I can't. I don't have any friends. All my friends are in Fuller going to the concert.

—If our house burned down and we had to move, would you let me pick the new place? I would pick somewhere farther south. So that we're out of the flight path of the airport and we have less bad traffic all around us.

—How about fifty dollars? I can get a one-day ticket for tomorrow. Please? I'll do all my chores for the next year and a half.

—I don't want to go to Harvard anymore. I wanna go to Fuller State— 'cause I can't get into Harvard. I'm never gonna get into Harvard and you know it. And I'll be lucky to even get into Fuller. I'll have to keep living here and take the bus down there. There's a bus that leaves every day from the Denny's. I know. I've watched the students get on it. I watch 'em get on the bus and I think, "Someday soon that's gonna be me."

—I don't want Domino's. I want Papa John's. Go south on Recoleta. There's lots of Papa John's down there.

—What about you just give me permission to go down to Fuller? I don't need any money. I'll just sneak into the concert somehow. I won't do anything bad. You know, sometimes toward the end of the night they just start letting people in, so that the bands have a full crowd. Or a band from the stage might yell out to the security guards to let everybody in and then they have to. That's what my friend told me. And even if I don't get in, I would be able to hear the music from outside the fence, 'cause music is free. You can come with me. We'll take a blanket and make a picnic outside the fence and get Papa John's pizza on the way. Why not? That's stupid. I hate you.

64

Bobert and Timothy say goodbye to their mother.

—Enough. We're eating Domino's or we're not eating anything.

—Fine. I choose not anything.

—Me too.

—What is with you two today?

—We're just trying to say things could change around here.

—I don't need this.

—We don't need it, either.

—What is it with all this "we" stuff? "We" want this kind of pizza. "We" want to change stuff. It's not you two against me and Donald.

—Then get rid of him. Be on our side.

—I'm not on Donald's side in anything. All of us, all together, are on the same side, about all of this. Even when we disagree. We're a family.

—We're not.

—Your father is the one that isn't part of this family.

—I know. Fuck Dad.

—It's not that we miss Dad. He doesn't call or give you money or anything. We know.

—But Donald is a real asshole.

—I don't want to hear it.

—He is. You just don't want listen.

—If you would tell me the truth, I would listen.

—We are telling you the truth.

—The whole truth.

—We are.

—All right. Where were you the last two months? Where are those people the police are looking for? Let's start with that.

—I ran away because Donald is a pervert, to both me and Timmy.

—All right. All right. Don't stop. Where did you go when you ran away?

—I met these guys who live on the street.

—On the street?

—And they break into people's houses and houses that are for sale and places like that and they live there.

—And what did you do with these guys?

—Nothing.

—Donald attacked and abused you both—right under my nose. But you didn't do anything while you were living with a bunch of fucking homeless thugs?!

—I broke into houses. And I shoplifted. A lot. And I had sex with a girl who I'm in love with. And I drank beer. And I smoked pot. And I vandalized some people's stuff.

—And you burned down somebody's house with those hooligans. Didn't you?

—They're not hooligans. They're werewolves.

—Fucking great!

—And I'm one, too.

—What is that? Is that a gang name?

—And pretty soon, Mom, Robert's gonna take me to them and make me one, too.

—Fucking great. You're both gonna run away again?

—We're not running away because of you, Mom. We're running away because of Donald.

—You want the truth, Mom? That's the truth.

—Oh, yeah? Where are you gonna go? Where are these werewolves you're running away to?

—They're down in Fuller.

—And that's why you wanna go down there so bad?

—Yeah. That's the total and complete truth.

—We love you, Mom. We do. It's Donald who's a bad person.

—I'll talk to him. Maybe we can do counseling or something.

—We'll write to you and let you know we're okay.

—All right. That's great. That's fucking great.

—Are we still getting pizza?

—I thought you weren't hungry.

—We're not.

—You sure?

—We're sure.

—We're both sure.

—Great. Then we can go back home and you can both go to bed hungry.

65

Dawn and Donald have a talk.

—If you want me to, I'll go beat some sense into 'em.

—That's the last thing we need.

—I don't know. You let 'em say anything to you. You let 'em do anything to you. When I was a boy, I got whipped if I didn't end every sentence with "yessir" or "no, sir."

—How'd your mother feel about that?

—I don't know what you mean. But I know you mean it as some sort of put-down.

—I'm just being smart—as if you called your mother "sir."

—You're as bad as those boys.

—We know where they get it from.

—Seriously, Dawn. What's got into you?

—Did you ever touch my boys?

—We already did this.

—Let's do it again.

—I never touched either one of 'em. Unless you knew about it. And then it was only to punish 'em. Usually it was when Bobert sassed off to you. To teach him to respect his mother.

—I don't need a bodyguard.

—You need some kind of help.

—I'm starting to think so.

—Those boys have got you so wound up. It's because Bobert doesn't want to be disciplined that he starts telling stories. He sees it on TV and he thinks he can get out of a jam if he says I attack him. I'm haven't laid a hand on him since he's been back. Now what's he got to say?

—Neither one of 'em says anything.

—Good. I don't know why that worries you.

—Because they should be able to say anything. They should be able to tell me what's happening to 'em. And when they tell me, I should help them deal with it. Instead of running away.

—What did you run away from? Come 'ere.

—Leave me alone.

—That's running away.

—Leave me alone.

—I'm going to bed, Dawn.

—Great. We'll talk some more in the morning.

—What is there to talk about?

—We're gonna keep talking 'til we figure that out.

66

Bobert and Timothy open the window and take off into the night.

—All right. You go first and then I'll hand the bags out to you.
—What?
—You go onto the roof and I'll hand the bags out to you.
—All right.
—Wait.
—What?
—Did you hear that?
—What?
—Shh.
—What is it?
—I thought I heard something.
—What?
—It sounded like an animal.
—I don't see anything out there.
—It sounded like it was coming from inside.
—Don't try to freak me out.
—I'm not. I swear.
—Swear?
—Shhh. There it is again.
—Let's go.

—It sounds like a dog is hurt or something.

—Come on.

—Hold on.

—Hand me your bag.

—Here.

—Give me my bag, too.

—It's heavy.

—I'll figure out what I can do without once we're on our way.

—I told you not to pack any books.

—I'll get rid of them as I read 'em.

—You know you won't.

—Let's go.

—Shh. There it is again.

—Stick to the plan. It's time to go.

—What is it?

—I don't care.

—Hold on.

—Don't. Just step out the window. That's what you promised.

—I'm just going to look down the hall.

—Don't.

—Hold on.

—

—

—

—

—

—All right. Let's go.

—What was it?

—It wasn't anything.

—What was it?

—It was Mom. Standing in the hallway. In her pink robe. Leaning against the wall. Listening to us leave. Crying.

—She knows?

—I looked her right in the eyes.

—If Mom knows we're leaving, then let's go down the stairs and out the front door. I don't want to jump.

—She's knows, but she's not gonna let us walk past her.

—I don't want to jump.

—Trust me. If you try to walk past Mom, she'll grab on to you and she'll start crying. She's already crying. She's going to wake up Donald and then everything'll get fucked up. I shouldn't have left you to see what it was. You were right.

—I told you.

—You did. Now let's go. Jump.

67

Timothy trusts his brother.

Because when Bobert says something—it's true. That's the way I feel about him. For the most part. When he ran away the first time, I tried to follow. I didn't know why he left me behind. Probably 'cause I would have got him caught. I got caught. I didn't know where Bobert went, so I went to the mall, where we used to hang out. That's the first place Mom came looking for me. Just like the hints we spent all day dropping about going down south. Back then I always talked about the mall. So of course Mom would go look for me at the mall. She brought me home. I missed Bobert. I expected him to be waiting for me somewhere. Did you ever feel that about somebody? Even when they're not there, they're just somewhere waiting for you? So I ran away the very next day. I went to the school we go to. It was summer. But some janitor or some teacher who was doing summer work saw me hanging around the school and called Mom and—boom—I was caught again.

I don't know how to go somewhere I've never been. I don't even know how to imagine it. I think you have to get to be a certain age when you can have enough knowledge about the world to think up all the places where people like you don't normally go. I know there are cowboys in the world. I know there are truck drivers. I know there are ballerinas. If I went to one of the places those people go to, then Mom would never find me.

Bobert says there's such a thing as werewolves. We're going to where they are. So I know for sure we're never gonna be caught this time. 'Cause just like I don't have enough experience to go where cowboys go, Mom and the cops don't have enough *belief* to go where werewolves go.

When Bobert came back for me, the first thought I had was "Of course!" He was always coming back for me. All the anger I had for him just disappeared. I thought about how stupid I had been. I decided from then on to trust my brother. No matter. When he ran away, I thought that Bobert was a lie. Not a liar. But, like—if someone *says* he's your brother and he's not, then what he *says* is a lie. But if someone *is* your brother and he doesn't act like it, then *who* he is, is a lie. Does that make sense? Donald is a lie. He says he wants to be a father to me. And I don't like to admit it, but Mom is a lie, too. When she says she wants to be a better mom, that's the truth. That's what she wants. But she can't do it. So it's not who she *is*. I don't even know if she knows she's a lie. When Bobert came back, I knew he was my brother all along. And "all along" means going forward, into the future, too.

"Where were you?" That's what I asked Bobert. And he told everybody else something different. But he told me he ran away to find us a new home. To find us a new way of living. Entirely different from anything that Mom, or any of our relatives, or Child Protective Services could imagine. He told me that he went to a lot of places. To homeless people camps and the way they live together in the woods on the edge of town. And he went to visit some people who were living on an organic farm by the university campus. And he said he talked to a lot of truck drivers when he was thinking about hitchhiking across the U.S. He thought he might have to hitchhike because we wouldn't be able to find a home around here. And at first, talking to these truck drivers, he thought that we, him and me, would make great truck drivers. He thought we would love living in the little cab. There's a bunk bed in back of the driver's seat, and when you have a team of drivers one can sleep while the other one drives. That way you never have to stop except for gas. But we're just kids, he's seventeen and I'm fifteen, so all the stuff we would have to go through to get licenses and not get pulled over every five miles would be too much. Bobert says maybe that's something we can do later in life. I don't think it's going to happen. Like, I don't really think we're going to get to live off the land with farmhouses that face one another and back doors that lead out into the forest. And I don't think we're gonna want to spend all our time together when I'm eighteen and he's twenty-one and we could both be long-haul truck drivers.

Why can't you do the things you wanna do *when* you wanna do them? That's the fundamental problem with the world. By the time he's twenty-one, Bobert will want to be married, or in a college, or in jail for fucking killing Donald. That's what's gonna happen if we get caught and we get taken back. But why can't we be long haul truckers at the age when we want to be? The stereotype of a bunch of grisly, old, dirty truckers who hate their lives and take speed to get through the long drives wouldn't have to be the case. A bunch of dirty old truckers who want to fuck little boys. Because how else did Bobert get to see the bunk beds in the cab? You think he met the world's nicest trucker? That's harder to believe than werewolves. You might as well believe that the rules are gonna be changed so that all the young pairs of brothers in America are going to be allowed to drive all the trucks back and forth. They're gonna open up big schools to teach driving to all of us. And they're gonna assure the American public by putting GPS things in the trucks so that if we go over a certain speed limit or start weaving from our lane, then the engine shuts off.

It's stupid, isn't it? In the details it becomes just a kind of dumb joke to imagine. I know. But I also know that wanting it, or something like it—that's *not* stupid. Feeling like you want something is never stupid. I'm fifteen and I want to leave my life. So that's what I did. Bobert says he knows a way we can do it and I trust him.

68

Do you even know how to drive?

—How did you get his keys, Robert?

    —I found an extra set in a drawer in the kitchen.

    —How did you even know they were there?

    —If I learned one thing while I was squatting in houses, it's that normal people are super paranoid about being locked out of their own lives. In every house in America there's extra sets of keys to everything. And in most houses, the extra set of keys is in a kitchen drawer with the manuals to all the appliances.

    —Cool.

    —You wanna drive?

    —Really?

    —Yeah. Why not? You can do it, right?

    —Yes.

    —I mean, you don't hafta if you don't wanna, Tim.

    —I'm just scared. What if I crash it and we get caught right off the bat?

    —I think we have more to worry about if I don't let you do anything. If I try to keep us extra safe and we never take any risks or have any fun, then we're in serious trouble. I mean, I'm not a great driver, anyway. I could have a wreck probably as likely as you.

    —All right. Let's go.

—Wait. Let's do this like we own it. Let's do this like we got all the time in the world.

—What do you mean, Robert?

—Put the bags in the trunk. Not the backseat.

—Let's go.

—Put the bags in the trunk. That way if get pulled over by a cop, we can say we're out for a joyride and we're sorry and try to get him to let us go. But if he sees our backpacks, he's gonna know we're runaways.

—Really?

—Yeah. When we get with everybody else, you're not allowed to go out with a backpack unless we're moving house. Once we get dirty and we look like homeless people, a backpack will get you busted faster than almost anything.

—You're not a runaway anymore. You're seventeen.

—They're looking for us. If not tonight. By tomorrow.

—All right. Trunk's open. Put the bags in. Let's go.

—This is awesome.

—You sure we can't drive there, Robert?

—We'd be caught in a day. They'd put out an Amber Alert and every electronic sign on the highway would be flashing our license plate number and there's nowhere we could run to.

—How far away is it?

—It'll probably take us about two weeks. It's about five hundred miles away.

—Goddamn.

—All right.

—Here we go.

Drive. Drive. Drive. Drive. Drive.

—You can go faster than this.

—The speed limit's thirty.

—And you're going, like, twelve.

—I'm nervous.

—There's no one out. No one can see us.

—It's a little weird.

—Isn't it?

—It's like the whole world is pretty empty at night.

—More than it seems like it should be, right?

—And it's pretty.

—The moon is out.

—It smells good, too. Roll the windows down. See?

—Why is that?

—I think 'cause it's cooler at night and it's quiet. You can notice more at night.

—You'd think more people would be out walking the dog.

—Especially with how hot it is during the day.

—I could get used to this, Bobert.

—Well, get used to calling me "Robert," too.

—Sorry. Sorry. I'm trying.

—That's all right. This is how we're gonna live for the next two weeks. We'll only move at night and everything will be relaxed like this.

—Which way should I go?

—Take Wicklow Creek. We'll go on back roads to Glendora Canyon and then give the car to the first homeless person we find in Fuller.

—Haha. This is awesome.

69

Timothy and Bobert try to give Donald's car away.

—What do I want with a car, kid?

—You can live in it.

—*You* live in it. If I lived in a car I wouldn't be able to see the stars. Get me a convertible. I'll live in that shit.

—Let's just go find somebody else, Robert.

—Wait. Come on, kid. Why can't this be simple? Give me five bucks.

—We're trying to give you a car!

—But why? It's stolen, right?

—We're rich. Our family is like, superrich.

—This is just a Honda. You ain't all that "superrich," kid.

—This is the shittiest car we own.

—How many cars does your family have?

—Including the ones at the lake house?

—Haha. All right. That's clever. I'm listening.

—We superrich, but we're trying to get away from all that. We're running away. We're going to the concert here in Fuller, and then we're gonna follow it down south for the next couple of weeks, and we don't want to be followed by our parents.

—You wanna make it look like I killed you and stole the car so you can have a few extra days.

—Shit, dude. If you just go through the cushions in the backseat you're gonna find five dollars. Then you can take your five dollars and leave the car where it is and we both think we've got what we want.

—You're a good salesman.

—I'm trying. I got a customer who's making me work too hard.

—Then you're gonna be real disappointed when I tell you no.

—Why not?

—You ran over somebody or something. There's probably a body in the trunk. You just want my fingerprints on the motherfucker. There's something weird. People don't just give you cars.

—People don't just live on the street.

—Fuck off.

—Come on, Robert.

—Wait. This is my last try, and then we're gonna get back in it and go somewhere else.

—All right, let's hear it, kid.

—We have a nice family and we have a nice house and we have a lake house, too—but in a year I'm supposed to go to college. To Fuller State. And I don't want that.

—You're superrich and you're going to go to Fuller State?

—I can't stay in school. I keep running away.

—That's true, dude. He runs away every other month for as long as he can.

—And this month he's taking his little brother with him.

—Yep.

—Why would two kids like you choose to leave their house and live out on their own with no support?

—Why do you do it?

—I just had a run of bad luck. I couldn't get ahead. But now I manage. I get by.

—It's the same for us. Only our bad luck is in people. I don't know if yours was bad luck with money or health. I don't know. Don't tell me. I'm not asking. What I'm saying is, along with this car and all our houses and all our money and clothes and everything, we also have this asshole that comes with it—I wasn't gonna say his name. But all right. We got Donald.

And he's our run of bad luck. So we decided to run away. But first, we thought, why not take some of our luck and give it away?

—Make Donald's bad luck good luck to somebody else, huh?

—That's the whole thing. So I'm just gonna drop the key here. And walk off. I don't even care if you take the car. Give it to someone else. But if anyone asks who gave you the car, my name is Robert DeShaw.

—And I'm Timothy DeShaw.

—But don't tell anybody we're headed south following the music festival. Tell them whatever you want. But don't tell them our plans.

—All right. We have a deal. Drop the keys.

70

Bobert and Timothy realize their first mistake.

—We have to go back.

    —We're not even three blocks away.

    —Fucking dude drove off with our backpacks.

    —Oh, no. I forgot.

    —Yeah. I fucking forgot, too.

    —All right. That's enough.

    —What are we gonna fucking do?

    —That's enough! We'll figure something out.

    —Should we go home?

    —No. We're not going back.

    —I don't want to go back, either. But it just seems like all the fun is gone. I was looking forward to using our packs. And making a tent with the tarp. Shit like that. I packed *War and Peace*. I was going to read it out loud at night like TV. So we'd have something to think about for two weeks. Now we're not even gonna make it.

    —It was my fault. I was just stupid.

    —I forgot, too.

    —Now we have to find a way to get our supplies day to day. We need to get started now.

    —What time is it?

—About three a.m. We should try to be someplace where we can sleep by six, before people wake up and start looking for us.

—All right, what do we need?

—We should get some food and some sort of basic way to stay out of the weather and something to do tomorrow during the day.

—We could try to find the car.

—It's a car. It's probably out on the road, twenty miles away from here already.

—Even half a mile is too far for us to find on foot by now. I feel sort of sorry for the guy. You know the cops are gonna find him. They're gonna arrest him for stealing the car we gave him.

—Tim, I bet you a hundred dollars he doesn't even have the car anymore. I bet he sold it for a week's supply of malt liquor and he's already forty ounces into the night.

—Oh, shit. When the cops find the car, they're gonna find our backpacks, and then they're gonna find the postcard, and then they're gonna find the werewolves.

—Well, that's one thing I didn't fuck up.

—Let me see it.

—See? But all the road maps are in the backpacks so that's another thing we're gonna want to get our hands on.

—Let's get started.

—All right. There's a 7-Eleven right over there.

71

Bobert convinces the guy at 7-Eleven to let him use the bathroom.

—How do *you* go to the bathroom when *you* need to?

—There's a bathroom for 7-Eleven employees. There's just not one for you.

—Come on. Be cool. Where else am I gonna go?

—Go home. That's my point. You don't need to be out at all hours.

—I'm not gonna make it home. Home is like twenty miles away. If I start running now, my pants will be full of shit before I reach the chip aisle.

—It's not my problem.

—Where else am I gonna go?

—I told you.

—No, I mean, seriously, where else in the neighborhood do you recommend?

—Try the chicken place.

—They let customers use the bathroom?

—No.

—Then what?

—There's a construction site on Wicklow. Break in and use their little port-a-let.

—How far is Wicklow?

—Where are you from?

—We're down to see the music festival.

—You and everybody else.

—Please. You can keep my little brother for ransom.

—Please. He's a nice guy. Please.

—Awwwwrrrgh. All right. Go fast, dude. And don't do anything bad in there.

—I won't. I promise. Watch my little brother for me, all right?

Watching. Watching. Watching. Watching. Watching.

—Seriously. Where are you two guys gonna sleep tonight?

—I dunno. He's in charge.

—Well, be careful. And don't try to sleep here. Or out back. I get in trouble for that shit. I was nice to you. Don't push it.

—I'll tell him.

—You do that.

—Do you have trouble staying awake when you work the night shift?

—No. The fluorescent lights are made to make it bright in a kind of way that makes it impossible for people to fall asleep.

—Yeah, it is a weird kind of light in here.

—And I get as much coffee as I can drink.

—The coffee is the first thing I smelled when I walked in.

—I just made a new pot. It's 7-Eleven policy that we have to make a new pot every hour. If I'm feeling sleepy I tell myself I have to drink everything that's left over before the next pot. I do that every hour.

—That sounds like a lot of coffee.

—What bands did y'all see today?

—We just got here. We're gonna see the bands tomorrow.

—Is that why you're not inside the gate? You showed up too late?

—I guess. He knows. He's in charge.

—Well, once you get inside tomorrow you'll be able to crash at somebody's campsite at the festival. I'm sure. I heard the Clash was playing.

—Joe Strummer's dead.

—Mick Jones is singing all the songs. As a tribute.

—Weird tribute for the guy who got kicked out of the band to take over as the lead—

—Come back here! Please! I cut myself! Help!

—I can't leave the register. What did you do?

—The paper towel dispenser has a jagged edge. I'm bleeding on everything.

—Put pressure on it. Grab a bunch of paper towels.

—That's how I got cut in the first place.

—Come out to the front and let me see.

—All right. What do you think?

—Oh, Jesus. You're bleeding on everything.

—I told you.

—Did you cut open your whole arm?

—Just my hand, but it's bleeding bad; it's dripping over everything.

—Oh, Jesus. This is what I get for being nice.

—Don't worry. I'm not gonna sue.

—Who said anything about suing?

—Do you have a first-aid kit?

—It's back in the office. Hold it up. Stop dripping on everything. Put some napkins on it. Come here.

—Timothy, you come, too.

—No. Neither one of you is supposed to be back here.

—I have to keep an eye on my little brother.

—For all I know you two are gonna jump me!

—We're not gonna jump you.

—It wouldn't do you any good. Night managers aren't given the combination to the safe. They don't fucking trust us.

—You don't have to curse at me. I just wanna make sure some pervert doesn't come in here and snatch my little brother.

—He can take care of himself.

—See, Robert, even the 7-Eleven dude knows I can take care of myself. I'm fifteen!

—Come here. It's just right here. This door is the office. Come here. Your brother will be able to hear you the whole time. Little brother, make some noise, so big brother knows you're all right.

—I'm all right . . . I'm just standing here . . . waiting for you to stop bleeding . . .

—All right, Timothy, I'm just behind this door, getting doctored. Oww.

—Hold still.

—It stings.

—I'm just standing here . . . waiting for you to stop being such a big baby . . . waiting to get on with our lives . . . waiting to get out of this place . . .

72

Timothy lists everything he stole so that Robert can get a sense of their supplies as they walk to the construction site.

—I got all the Lunchables and all the sandwiches I could.

    —The ones with mayo aren't gonna keep. We should eat those first.

    —Like pimento cheese?

    —Yeah.

    —What's the deal with pimento cheese?

    —It's a Southern thing.

    —Like poor people food?

    —No. They also serve pimento cheese at, like, the Masters Tournament. It's a big deal.

    —Is that a golf thing?

    —Yeah.

    —What's the deal with golf?

    —You got me.

    —I got Gatorades. Just two. I figured we could use the bottles over and over again.

    —Cool.

    —I got all the granola-type bars.

    —Cool.

—I grabbed what I could off the medicine shelf.

—Let me see.

—What do you think?

—I think it looks like you're expecting a hemorrhoid.

—I just grabbed whatever.

—Well, who knows? With all the pimento cheese. It's not impossible.

—What is a hemorrhoid?

—It's when part of the inside of your intestine, like, gets squeezed out and it fills with blood and hangs outside your asshole. You get 'em from trying to force yourself to shit.

—Why would you do that?

—Look at all this shit that passes for food. All the chemicals and shit. Pimento cheese. That's what I'm talking about. This stuff'll give you hemorrhoids the size of golf balls.

—Haha.

—What else did you get?

—I was scared, Robert.

—Yeah, I bet.

—I thought he was gonna come out any second.

—You did a good job.

—I thought he was going to peek his head out around the corner and catch me.

—And then what?

—I don't know. Call the cops.

—What are the cops gonna do? It takes 'em ten minutes to get anywhere. If that convenience store clerk caught you, I would have just punched him in the face and we would have run.

—Did it hurt?

—What?

—Cutting your hand?

—No. I just thought about how much I fucked up leaving those bags in the car—

—You didn't fuck up.

—Insisting that we put them in the trunk in the first place—

—It was as much my fault as it was yours.

—Overplanning. That's what's gonna get us caught. We have to be wild animals. So it's a good thing that happened. As a reminder: We have to be wild animals.

—So far it hasn't been too bad.

—That's a real vote of confidence, Tim.

—Look there's Wicklow. Take a left.

—Just before I cut my hand, I thought about how mad I was at myself, for letting you down—

—You didn't let me down.

—And then it was no big deal. It didn't even hurt, really. It was like my emotions were a gun. And I just picked up my anger and I pointed it at myself, and then . . . I let me have it.

—I also got us a couple of newspapers. I figure tonight we can spread the papers out and sleep on 'em. Then tomorrow, while we're waiting for the sun to go down, we can read 'em. And I got us a new map. And I got us a few scratch-off tickets.

—I don't think those work if they're not sold to you.

—What do you mean? The tickets don't know if they were bought or stolen.

—The code on the back. When you buy it, they scan it in at the cash register. That puts it in the computer system. Then when you win and you go to cash it in, they scan it again. That way they know where it was bought. But if you didn't do the first scan, the one that puts it in the system that you bought it, then the second scan won't work. They'll know it was stolen.

—Are you sure?

—No. But that's the way I think it works. I'm pretty sure they must do something to keep you from stealing lottery tickets. Otherwise people would steal lottery tickets all the time.

—That sucks.

—We can still scratch 'em. We'll divide the cards in half and whoever has the most winnings, they get something.

—Whoever has the least winning cards has to do the shoplifting next time.

—You really didn't like it, Tim, did you?

—No.

—All right. I have a fifty-dollar bill in my pocket—

—Are you fucking kidding me?!

—It's special. I was saving it for emergencies.

—This is an emergency.

—It's not like it's gonna last us more than two or three days—then what are we gonna do?

—I don't care if we have to steal. If it's the only way, then it's the only way.

—All right. We'll use up the money first. Then we'll try to find another way when we can. But you aren't the only one who took shit. I took what I could squeeze into my pockets. I got a bunch of trash bags.

—What for?

—To sleep on. To wear when it rains. To hold a bunch of potatoes and shit when we get out of the city and can start living off people's farms so we don't have to shoplift.

—Cool.

—And I got little soaps and some toilet paper.

—It looks like we're here. Does this look like a construction site to you?

—I guess. I thought there'd be a structure or something, though.

—I guess you have to start somewhere.

—There's nothing but a port-a-let surrounded by a barbed wire fence.

—What do you wanna do?

—Let's figure out a way in. 'Cause I really do have to go to the bathroom.

73

The newspaper

—What do you think, Tim? You think this'll do for our little daytime hide out?

—We got sunlight coming in through the trees. And I think we'll be safe here. I don't think anybody'll bother us.

—Still. Sitting in a dried-up drainage pipe for twelve hours sure is gonna be interesting.

—I just hope it doesn't rain. Then where would we go?

—I guess we'd put the garbage bags over our heads and head for higher ground.

—Odds are it's gonna rain *sometime* in the next two weeks. Right?

—Take out the paper. Let's see what the forecast is.

—How'd you sleep last night?

—Not good. How about you?

—It's gonna take some getting used to.

—We can take turns napping today, while the other one keeps watch. I'll go first. I'm older.

—Go first what—nap or watch?

—Whatever I want. I'm older.

—Yeah, I guess. Hey, are these your friends on the front page?

—What's it say?

—That housekeeper who got assaulted came out of her coma. She said some friends of the daughter of the people she worked for attacked her. She was cleaning the house and they busted in and beat her up and stole a bunch of shit.

—That doesn't sound like my friends.

—Police think there might be a connection between this attack and the two dead bodies they found in that burned-down house near Colston.

—I guess they found the Peugeot house.

—What's that mean?

—Malcolm was looking for somebody in that neighborhood who owned a Peugeot.

—That's a car?

—Yeah. And I just happened to see that car at a house over by Colston. So maybe that *is* some of the people I was staying with.

—So some of your friends killed the people who owned the car?

—Whoever owned that car tried to run Malcolm over. They tried to kill him first.

—So he killed them?

—I don't think so.

—And then he burned the house down?

—I don't think so.

—That's what the newspaper says.

—Maybe.

—Still.

—I don't think the others would let Malcolm kill anybody.

—Really?

—Yeah. Sure. I don't know. What do you want me to say?

—Whose bodies do you think they found in this house?

—I don't know, Tim. Leave me alone. Who cares? For all I know it's complete strangers. The police can't solve a murder so they try to pin it on a bunch of homeless people. Hell, it could be Malcolm and Angel.

—Who's Angel?

—She's someone who was sort of challenging Malcolm to be the leader just before I left.

—But she didn't win?

—It was a tie. You know, they always said, "When two werewolves fight each other, they both die because every werewolf is the exact same strength as every other and werewolves can only fight to the death."

—I thought you said you didn't have a leader. You said we would all decide *together* what to do next or we would pull our ideas out of a hat.

—Sometimes. But Malcolm was trying to organize things more. Like train us and give us more discipline.

—They killed somebody.

—You don't know that. And it was probably each other if they did.

—And they beat up some poor maid.

—Just because the police say it's all connected doesn't mean it is.

—And they burned somebody's house down.

—That's something Malcolm's into. I don't think it'll happen anymore now that he's dead.

—You don't know that he's dead.

—It was his idea of the best way to get rid of evidence.

—There was blood on the postcard they sent us.

—So?

—I didn't know we were hitchhiking our way into all this fucked-up trouble.

—We're not hitchhiking.

—Why? Because it's not safe?

—Yeah.

—That's the dumbest fucking thing I ever heard. You know what's not safe?

Newspaper. Newspaper. Newspaper. Newspaper. Newspaper.

—Why would they send us a postcard and tell us where they were if they wanted to hurt us?

—Because you're evidence. And apparently your leader is *into* getting rid of it.

—He's not my leader. And he's probably not even around anymore.

—You don't know.

—You don't know, either. You don't know anything.

—Why are we going to be with these people?

—Because we can't go home. We stole Donald's car. We stole money from Mom.

—I didn't steal any money.

—I did.

—Then why did you make me shoplift?

—It was in my backpack.

—So now some homeless guy has a bunch of Mom's money.

—I was trying to take care of you.

—Donald never touched me.

—What do you mean?

—

—

—

—What do you mean, Tim?

—I mean—what you say Donald did to you—he never did that shit
to me.

—What do you mean, "what I *say* Donald did to me"?

—I believe you about you. But you have to believe me about me, too.

—Why would he only fuck with me?

—Maybe he was in love with you.

—That's fucking sick, Tim. That's fucking sick.

—He was a dick and he had a shitty temper, and he was definitely a
pervert in the way he talked, but he never actually did anything perverted
to me or around me.

—He would have eventually.

—Listen, Robert—he didn't. I'm telling you the truth. I'm sorry he
didn't touch me. But he didn't.

—Don't say that. I didn't want it to be true for you. I just don't know
why he would get me and leave you alone.

—Now you tell me.

—What?

—Robert, tell me the truth.

—I did. I swear. Everything I told you about Donald was true.

—I know. I know. I mean, tell me the truth about your friends.

—I did.

—Some of it. But you didn't tell me about burning down houses. Or
killing each other.

—Maybe that's not them in the paper, Tim.

—You don't think so?

—Maybe the police are just trying to scare people.

—Tell me the truth, Robert.

—Let me see the paper.

—There. Take a good fucking look at it. And then tell me. Tell me everything.

74

Detective Raphael interviews the housekeeper in the hospital.

—Thank you for agreeing to talk to me.

—I already told those other police everything I know.

—I know. They told me what you told them. They let me read their notes.

—So then what am I supposed to fill you in on?

—What I do is: I let a few days pass after I read a file, and I do other work. It's a demanding job. The average detective around here is working maybe fifteen or twenty cases at a time. And each case has a certain amount of paperwork. And we have to go to court every once in a while—and parole hearings. So what I do is, after a couple of days of that sort of thing, I sit down and I type up everything I remember from the file in question. I do it all from memory. I try to be as specific as I can be. Ideally what I type up would be the same length as the original file and contain all the same facts. It never does. As soon as I finish typing up what I remember, I compare it to the original file. You'd be surprised at the sort of important details that slip your mind. And you'd be equally surprised at the sort of assumptions you make about a situation that are in no way based on fact. It's these lapses and assumptions that I want to talk to you about.

—I didn't do anything wrong.

—You're not under investigation. You're in a hospital. The people under investigation are the ones who put you here.

—They're animals.

—I don't understand it myself. When I see what people do to one another. How do they continue to call themselves people? And why do we want to hang on to the title ourselves, when it's used by so many monsters?

—They attacked me for no reason.

—I remember you saying you just opened the closet in the master bedroom and someone jumped out and started attacking you.

—And then they rushed in from everywhere. From the bathroom. From out in the hall. While the first few were attacking me I could hear more of them coming up the stairs. While the first few were holding me down I watched one crawl out from under the bed.

—They were waiting for you.

—That's what it seemed like.

—You're the housekeeper for the Baxters?

—Who are the Baxters?

—I'm sorry. I read so many files. I get the little facts mixed up. You're the housekeeper for the Yorks.

—That's right. I normally work Tuesday, Thursday, and Saturday, but they're in Israel—

—They're back.

—Excuse me?

—The Yorks have been back for some time. They heard what happened and they came back. They haven't been in to see you?

—I don't think so. I don't remember.

—They may not know you're talking. They probably do. But they may not. They may have come while you were unconscious and they haven't had time since you started talking.

—I don't remember.

—But you were saying—when the Yorks were in Israel—what was your schedule then?

—I didn't have a schedule. I just stopped by at random times and checked on the place.

—But the plants had to be watered.

—Yessir.

—So that means you were still probably stopping by about—what?—three times a week?

—Oh, no. That'd kill a plant to get that much water. I imagine I stopped by once a week.

—But on different days.

—Sure, because if there were burglars casing the joint, or something, I wouldn't want them to know my pattern. So I would randomly stop by.

—And you would water the plants and do some laundry—that sort of thing.

—There wasn't any laundry to be done. There wasn't anybody home.

—Well, maybe you would dust or something?

—No sense in dusting until the day before they return. That's what I had planned. A big cleaning day the day before they return. Dust everything. Do windows. Fresh sheets. So that everything would seem fresh.

—That's today.

—What?

—Well, if everything had gone as planned they would have been returning from Israel tomorrow and you would be doing the big clean today.

—I guess so.

—But the house got broken into and you got attacked and the Baxters came back early.

—The Yorks.

—That's right. The Yorks. The reason I keep saying "the Baxters" is I have this other case where this house got burned down maybe a month ago. And I keep wondering if maybe the two cases are related.

—Why?

—Well, the arson investigator said there was evidence that some homeless people had been living in the Baxters' house, because there were blankets and mattresses all over the place—and trash and food.

—And you think these are the same people?

—But you didn't see any blankets lying around all over, did you?

—No.

—Where do the Yorks keep their blankets?

—You know, in drawers and closets.

—And where do they keep their plants?

—What do you mean?

—Where are the plants in the Yorks' house? I got that right that time, see?

—Yeah. I see. The Yorks keep their plants all over.

—Are there any plants in the closet in the master bedroom?

—I see. Yeah. There's no plants in there.

—Just blankets and clothes?

—Yessir.

—And you weren't doing any laundry or putting away any blankets you saw lying around in weird places all over the house?

—No, sir.

—Then why did you open the closet?

—I don't remember.

—What *do* you remember?

—They were in there, waiting for me.

—You were looking for them. Weren't you?

—I must have heard something.

—Probably Sting. That's what was playing on the stereo when the EMS got there. On repeat.

—Did you tell the Yorks all this? Is that why they haven't come to visit?

—I haven't told the Yorks anything. I don't know why they haven't come to visit. I'm not really interested in the Yorks. And I'm not really interested in you. You're not under investigation.

—What do you want to know?

—The other police that you spoke with told me you were the Yorks' housekeeper. And when I wrote down what I could remember, I wrote that you were there, at the Yorks' house that night, working. But when I looked back at the file I saw that that was only an assumption I was making. So what I want to ask you about is: Why were you up in the master bedroom? Why did you open that closet door where someone was waiting to attack you?

—I was looking for them.

—You knew they were in the house. You had spoken with them before. And you had struck some kind of deal.

—And I was looking for them to tell them the deal was off.

—And what did they say?

—They attacked me before I could say anything.

—I guess they had made some assumptions of their own.

—Yessir.

—But you spoke with them before. You made some kind of arrangement. You can tell me. I'm not going to tell the Yorks.

—Thank you.

—I want you to tell me everything. How many there were. What size, shape, and color they appeared to be. How long you think they were there. How long you had agreed to let them stay. And I'm gonna need you to tell me *why* you agreed to let them stay. But first I want you to tell me what they were like.

—They were stupid.

—Go on.

—They didn't really have a plan. I mean, they figured out how to manipulate me for a day or so. But after I thought about it, I decided I could get rid of them.

—But they attacked you.

—Even then. They didn't know what to do. They were just as surprised and as scared as I was. I mean, the first one hit me pretty hard. But then after that, the rest of them, they just held me down. That's why I could hear them coming up the stairs and out from under the bed. They weren't doing anything. They were just holding me and calling out for Malcolm.

—And Malcolm is the one that did all this to you.

—Malcolm did some of it. At first. Like he was teaching a lesson. And then slowly, the others learned how to do it, too.

75

Timothy wants to stop walking.

—We gotta stop, Robert. My feet are tired.

—You still have feet? I wore mine away a couple nights ago. Now I just have nubs I balance on. If I stop I'll fall over.

—Give me five minutes to take off my shoes and rub my feet.

—Are you crazy? If you take off your shoes now your feet'll swell up and they won't fit back in your shoes for at least six hours.

—How do you know?

—The hard way. I ran away from home before—remember?

—Well, just let me stop and sit.

—No.

—Five minutes. Please.

—It's the same thing. You try to rest for five minutes and your legs'll cramp up and it'll be two hours of me feeding you water and massaging your calves.

—That sounds nice.

—Yeah?

—Yeah.

—All right. If you keep walking 'til the moon goes down, I'll massage your calves until you fall asleep.

—That sounds like a good deal, but it's just the reverse of what you were saying about time. I agree to it, imagining you're gonna give me a two-hour massage, but after I walk all night, I'll fall asleep in five minutes. Less than five minutes. You think it's possible to sleep while you walk?

—It's called sleepwalking.

—But sleepwalkers normally start out lying down. I'm asking: Do you think it's possible to fall asleep *while* you're walking?

—I think I've read about soldiers doing it. Like during the Civil War and the American Revolution and stuff.

—I wish I could do it.

—Try it.

Walk. Walk. Walk. Walk. Walk.

—It hurts too much to fall asleep.

—You have to get past that.

—Then let me rest.

—No.

—Please, Robert. Please!

—Stop it.

—Please! Just five minutes!

—No. We have to keep going.

—Please! I'm begging you! I'll do anything!

—Fine. Rest if you wanna.

—All right . . . Wait. Where are you going?

—I told you. It's a bad idea.

—You're gonna leave me if I stop to rest?

—Yeah. I'm not resting. I'm walking. I'm walking all night. Then I'm gonna sleep all day. Then I'm gonna walk all night again.

—Aren't you sore?

—It doesn't make any difference. The trip only gets longer if I stop and rest. I don't have any less steps to take.

—But what about enjoyment? What about fun? I thought this trip was gonna be fun.

—What did you think would be fun about it?

—Being out in the wild. With you.

—That's exactly what you got.

—I just didn't think I'd be so tired.

—We just started. In a couple more days you'll be used to it. Then it'll be fun again.

—I'm hungry.

—We'll eat when we stop.

—What are we gonna eat tonight?

—I think we have one more can of sardines. But tomorrow we're gonna have to find some more food. And that fifty-dollar bill is just change now.

—You know what I want? Sugar cereal in cold milk.

—Yeah. I can imagine it perfectly.

—Next time we shoplift, let's get that.

—We can try. It just depends on what kind of store it is and where the cameras are and all that.

—Please.

—I said we could try.

—No. I want to stop for ten seconds.

—You can stop if you wanna. I'm not gonna stop until it's time to go to sleep.

—I'm gonna stop for ten seconds and just relax and listen to everything and take it in then I'll run to catch up with you.

—All right, but I'm not coming back for you.

—All right.

—

—

—

—

—

—

—

—

—

—Wait. Wait up. I'm coming. I'm coming. Wait. Slow down. You're not walking the same pace. You're walking faster. Slow down.

—How was it?

—It was awesome.

—What did you hear?

—The stars. They make a whirring sound. Like they're spinning in their sockets. And you can hear the highway over there. You can hear the tires smoothing out the pavement. Eventually the whole thing is gonna be smooth, like a long strip of polished black marble. And there's a cloud that's following us. It's asking questions at all the places we've been. It's asking the tree how long we slept under it. And it's asking the creek how long we drank from it. And it's asking the bush how long ago we shat in it. I heard a dog bark. It was barking at the cloud. Telling the cloud to leave us alone.

—That sounds pretty awesome.

—You can do it, too. Whenever you want.

—Just ten seconds. Then we keep walking again.

—Just ten seconds.

—This isn't some trick you're trying to get me to stop 'cause you think if you can get me to stop I'll stay stopped and wait for you—'cause I won't.

—Just ten seconds.

—All right.

—

—

—

—

—

—

—

—

—

—

Walk. Walk. Walk. Walk. Walk.

—So?

—What?

—What did you think?

—I thought it was beautiful. We're in a beautiful place. The night covering everything as far as we can see. And you breathing. I could hear you smiling by the way that you were breathing. Just ten seconds. Finding a way to capture ten seconds of our lives. Knowing it was all about to end. And then we'd keep walking together through the rest of the night.

—Yeah.

76

Detective Raphael interviews the man who was found in Donald's car.

—How many days ago did they give you the car?

    —I dunno. What day is it today?

    —It's the twenty-eighth.

    —No, I mean, what day of the week is it? I don't know any numbers.

    —Do you know what month it is?

    —Yeah.

    —It's Wednesday, the twenty-eighth.

    —Then this was Sunday. Night.

    —Sunday night or Monday morning?

    —Yeah, those two are the same. One turns into the other.

    —And you didn't give those young men anything in return?

    —What do I have to give?

    —They didn't wanna get high? They didn't ask you to go buy beer for them? Anything like that?

    —Nope.

    —Why are two boys gonna walk up and hand you the keys to a perfectly good Honda?

    —It wasn't theirs.

    —You should be a cop. Go undercover. We'll get you a badge and a gun. You can be like the first homeless-man cop. 'Cause that's fucking brilliant. "It wasn't theirs." No shit, Sherlock.

—I thought maybe they'd done something bad with it. Like hit somebody and they wanted me to be in the car so they could say I'd done it.

—Why did you think that?

—Because of what you said. Why are two boys gonna walk up and hand me a car?

—Did they say anything about an accident?

—No.

—Did they seem nervous or panicked?

—No more than the situation called for.

—So you decided to go ahead and take the car?

—Yeah. The kid was good. The older kid. He said he would just give it to someone else.

—And you didn't want to miss out on that kind of deal.

—No, sir.

—What did he look like?

—The older kid.

—Yeah. That's who we're talking about. Unless you feel more comfortable talking about the little kid and working your way up? Is that the way you normally do things in your precinct?

—They were both pretty close to the same height.

—Yeah?

—Yeah, but you're right. The older kid was just a little bit taller. Maybe my height.

—How tall are you?

—Five-nine.

—And what color would you say your eyes are?

—They're hazel.

—Oh, hazel. That's nice. And would you say this older kid's eyes were darker or lighter than yours? 'Cause if we're gonna base everything off the standard which you set for humanity, I'm gonna have to get to know a lot more about you. We might have to keep you for a while and study you.

—He wasn't nervous.

—What do you mean?

—I still get nervous when I try to talk to other people. If I'm panhandling. Or if I'm walking up to a group of hoboes I don't know.

—"Hoboes" is nice. Is that what you call one another? It's very midcentury.

—But this kid was cool. He wasn't afraid of me at all.

—Maybe he should have been.

—I don't think so.

—Where did you drop him off?

—I didn't drop him off anywhere. He didn't get back in the car. He just set the keys on the pavement and backed away. And then, right then, one of you guys showed up and started shining a light on us, and the kids took off and I just walked over and picked up the keys and drove away calmly.

—Wait, wait, wait. I thought you said you were nervous. And I thought you said the kid was calm. But now you have the kids running and you just picking up the keys like nothing.

—The younger kid ran. He was about your height—if you want a different standard of measure. And the older kid went after him.

—And the officer didn't say anything to you?

—You call one another "officers." That's very Turgenev.

—Where'd you go to school?

—Fuller State.

—I'm sorry to hear that.

—It's a good school.

—A state school.

—So?

—I probably paid for your education and this is what you do with it—

—I taught myself to act calm, even when I'm scared, especially when I'm scared. I've been out on the street long enough I can do it so the officers I meet have no idea what I might be nervous about.

—So what would your reaction be if I told you you weren't here because you were in possession of a stolen car, but that I wanted to hold you on suspicion of murder?

—Oh, Jesus.

—That's good. Did you study acting at Fuller State?

—Did you find those boys dead?

—We found that you forgot to dump their backpacks with their bodies.

—I didn't dump their bodies anywhere.

—Their backpacks were in the trunk of your car.

—I never opened the trunk.

—Why would two boys pack their bags to run away from home and then give away their father's car and leave behind everything they packed?

—They said they were heading down south.

—Did they?

—The younger kid said it. He was about five-five or five-seven maybe. And he was wearing a Windbreaker and shorts. Which I thought was weird.

—Like he didn't know what the weather was gonna be.

—And he had at least two T-shirts on because I could see the different-color collars underneath one another. I remember thinking he was dressed the way homeless people dress. Wearing his suitcase, sort of.

—You were paying a lot of attention to the younger kid, weren't you?

—No. I just didn't know why you were asking all these questions. I thought it was about the car. But now I understand. The boys are missing.

—You seem nervous.

—I'm trying to be cooperative.

—Well, if that's the case, I'd like to start all over at the beginning, if you don't mind.

—That's fine.

—How many days ago did they give you the car?

—It was the twenty-sixth, about three in the morning.

—You know the date.

—Today's the twenty-eighth, right? It was three days ago. I'm sure.

77

Your hand is infected.

—You're walking too fast, Robert.

   —You're complaining too much.

   —At least the moon's out, I guess.

   —Yeah, it's pretty, isn't it?

   —It makes it easier to see what we're doing.

   —But we gotta be careful. It also makes it easier for people to see us.

   —I don't think anyone cares.

   —As long as we keep moving, they won't. We stay on private property, about ten feet inside the fence line like this. If the property owners look out their windows, they'll assume we're walking along the road. If a cop comes down the road, he'll assume we're the property owners or their kids.

   —The trees are nice.

   —That's more like it. I don't wanna hear any more complaints for the rest of the night.

   —You're complaining about my complaining.

   —That's not true.

   —How is that not true, Robert?

   —All I'm doing is asking you to stop. That's a little bit different than a straightforward complaint.

—It sounds a little bit like bullshit to me.

—Yeah, well.

—How come you don't care if I cuss anymore?

—We're about hundred miles or so away, from what I figure. We can do twenty miles a day easy, it seems. So we'll be there in five days. And when we get there, I'm not gonna tell you to do anything. You can cuss if you want to. You can go upstairs with a girl. You can go upstairs with a *guy* if you want to.

—Ewww.

—Don't act all put out by that. There might be some gay guys still. And the ones there when I was there last will kick your ass if you make that face at them.

—It's cold.

—You wanna put a trash bag over your clothes?

—No.

—You want me to put my arm around you?

—No. I'm just saying.

—You're getting tougher.

—I'm scared.

—I know it.

—What's it going to be like?

—I don't know. I don't know who's in charge. If they found a man and a woman in that house, it could be that both Malcolm and Angel are dead. Maybe nobody's in charge?

—Maybe you're in charge?

—Watch out for that ditch.

—Why do they have to put all these fucking ditches everywhere?

—'Cause it's a farm.

—So?

—Stop fucking complaining.

—Are you gonna jump it?

—No. Look. There's a two-by-four across it down there.

—Thank you, moon.

—That's more like it.

—Give me your hand.

—Ow.

—What's the matter?

—That cut from the 7-Eleven. I guess that's what I get for opening my hand in a convenience store bathroom.

—Let me see it.

—You can't see it good out here.

—I can see it's bad, Robert.

—I could've told you that.

—Why didn't you?

—What are you gonna do about it?

—What's your big problem with complaining?

—If you can't do anything about a situation, then there's no point in complaining about it. And if you can do something about it, then shut the fuck up and do it.

—Robert, the walking proverb.

—You can call me Bobert. That's what everybody else is gonna call me when we get there. If there's anybody else who remembers me.

—Somebody sent you the postcard.

—Yeah.

—You told me everybody called you Rob.

—I wish everybody would call me Rob or Robert.

—How did they even find out anybody ever called you Bobert?

—I told them.

—Why?

—'Cause they wanted to nickname me "Titties."

—Haha. Why'd they wanna call you "Titties"?

—The first day I was with them there were these two girls who weren't wearing shirts, and I swear, I tried, but I couldn't look at them. I was embarrassed. Then all the girls started taking off their shirts whenever I came into the room. To make me blush.

—Titties DeShaw. It has a nice ring to it.

—It's better than Bobert. I wish I hadn't been so embarrassed.

—Hey, just so you know—I like Bobert. I don't care that Donald gave it to you. It makes me think of you when we were kids. Fuck Donald. He doesn't get to say what your name means.

—It's getting light out.
—What about that shed over there?
—It's pretty close to that house.
—The house looks abandoned.

78

Detective Raphael interviews the owner of the garage.

—I told 'em to wake up. I told 'em to get outta here. I didn't need any trouble. I beat on this barrel with this stick to wake 'em up. And then I held on to the stick in case they came after me.

 —Did they come after you?

 —No. The little one, he started telling me to calm down—

 —Were you angry?

 —I musta been a little frightened.

 —And what did the older boy do?

 —He just set about his business. Putting on his boots. Picking up his things and putting them inside the trash bag he had been sleeping on top of to stay dry. Then he checked it for holes and twisted the neck. Then he told the little one to get ready, and the little one stopped talking to me and did what the bigger one said. The little one had been asking me for food and telling me to calm down. I thought the bigger one was going to ignore me altogether, but as soon as he saw the little one was doing as he was told, putting his stuff in his own trash bag, then the bigger one turned to me and asked for medicine.

 —What kind of medicine?

 —For his hand. He stuck out his hand palm up and asked if I had any Neosporin. His palm was deep infected.

—What else did you notice? About the way they looked?

—They were dirty. They looked kind of thin. But maybe I say that because the little one was asking for food. They had a lot of layers of clothes on and the top layers didn't seem like they fit. The little one was wearing a Carhartt that must be twice as big as he is.

—It's probably stolen.

—Well, I didn't see him take it. So I couldn't say.

—What about the older one?

—His hand is what I remember most. It was infected, and the wound was weeping a little bit. It seemed like to make a fist would be like squeezing a sponge. And I remember his hair was greasy.

—His hair was greasy?

—Like Elvis. I remember only 'cause I had the strange thought he might be slicking it back with the bad hand. I get thoughts like that and I can't get rid of them. That hand is going to be stuck in my mind for years, if I still have years. Every time I reach to pick up a knife, I'm gonna think about that cut. Probably until I see something worse that can replace it. I bet you see a lot of bad stuff as a policeman.

—I'm trying not to see anything bad with these boys.

—Me, too.

—Did you give him the Neosporin?

—I had them both in the kitchen. I cleaned out his wound as good as I could. I think that part of my mind that fixates on that kind of thing really just wanted to get a good look at it. But while it did, I was able to clean it out real good. The little one ate cornbread and milk. I hardly have anything.

—So you really helped them out.

—I did. I had half a mind not to call you.

—You didn't call me. You called local and it all got sent around, and I'm the one working it so it got to me.

—Where are they headed?

—I was about to ask you the same thing.

—Half of me wants to lie to you. To walk over to that window and point in the wrong direction. But then that same half of me wants to break the window and take a piece of glass and cut open my hand and just wait for it to get infected.

—He cut it on some metal in a gas station bathroom. I think if you want to get an infection that bad you're gonna have to use something worse than this windowpane.

—I wish you hadn't told me that.

—I bet you only half wish it.

—They're walking west along County Road 92 at night, from what I gather.

—Are you sure?

—Yessir.

—I know what it's like to want to see those boys get away. But that's a fantasy. You know that? To imagine they're just going to walk until they find some version of you with plenty of food and an extra bedroom. You know that. It's a fantasy that I can't indulge in. You keep calling them big and little. And I keep calling them younger and older. And in your system, the big one might be bigger than you and you can think that he's strong and he can take care of himself and the little one. But in my system, no matter how much he grows up, he's always gonna be younger than me. They're both younger than us and we know better 'cause we're older. We have to know better. And what's best is for them to be back with their mom and their stepdad.

—Is that what you think?

—That's what I know.

—I'm not so sure.

—Well, I am.

—Yeah, well, I'm older than you and it doesn't seem as clear to me.

—Is there anything else you wanna tell me?

—Be careful. The bigger one is bigger than you and he looks like he's goin' wild.

—What makes you say that?

—He cut his own hand. He told me, and you seem to know, too.

—Yeah, I guess that's pretty tough.

—When I was young, if we were gonna have a big fight, we'd slick our hair back with grease so people couldn't get a grip on it and pull it. That's what the big one looked like to me. Like somebody slicked back and ready for a fight.

—West on 92.

—As far as I could tell. Although they may have waited until I stopped watching and then went another way.

—How long did you watch?

—Until I couldn't see 'em no more.

79

At the address on the postcard, there's a scarecrow in the front yard that Robert kind of recognizes.

—All right. This should be it.

—Are you sure?

—Look at the postcard. Now look at the dumb wooden sign on the fence. Do they match?

—Yeah.

—

—So what should we do?

—What do you mean?

—Like, knock?

—When you're out in the country you just open the fence and go in.

—I thought that was how you got shot out in the country.

—Look. You can see the house over there. Let's cut through the woods.

—You don't want to stay on the road?

—I'm not a car. I can do what I want.

—All right.

—Let's go.

—

—

—

—

—Well?

—Well, what?

—Does this look right to you?

—What?

—It just looks like a normal farmhouse.

—So?

—It seems like nothing's happening?

—What did you expect?

—I guess I thought we'd see people out walking around.

—Let's lay up in the grass over there and wait.

—What are we waiting for?

—Just to see what's going to happen.

—What's going to happen?

—I have no idea.

—All right. Sounds like the rest of the trip.

—Don't complain.

—I'm not complaining.

—You think it's weird?

—I do. We do all this hiking. We're sick. Your hand is about to fall off. I've never been this dirty in my whole life. My head itches like it's full of bugs and my hair is so slimy I couldn't even keep a hat on. I'm tired. My feet are throbbing. We finally get here. This is everything we want, and you want to sit at the edge of it.

—I like doing that. Up here under these trees. In about an hour, we'll walk down this hill and go into that house and take showers and eat hot food and sleep in clean sheets.

—An hour?!

—It took us two weeks to get here. You can wait an hour.

—Yeah. I can. But why?

—All my friends are down there.

—What are you afraid of?

—It's not fear.

—Then what? You wanna be safe?

—That's part of it. I wanna see what's happening down there before I go running into it.

—They're probably all sleeping.

—It's five thirty in the evening.

—They're probably all just waking up. I bet they sleep all day, and then at night, when the moon comes up, they do their chores and then go out and go fishing.

—Night fishing?

—Yeah. Why not.

—Can you fish at night?

—Yeah. Why couldn't you?

—Are the fish even awake?

—We'll find out tonight when your friends wake up.

—Take a nap if you want. I'll wake you up if I see anything.

—What is there to see? There's an old-timey farmhouse surrounded by fields and way over there is a scarecrow watching over everything.

—Yeah. Me and the scarecrow'll watch over you. Go to sleep. I'll wake you up.

—You're seriously gonna sit here and just watch nothing happen.

—Yeah. This is what I like to do. When I finish something. When I get right to the edge of completing something, I like to take a look at it. In school when I would finish an exam in class, I would just sit with it for a minute before I would turn it in. Or when I'm with a girl. Just to give it a moment.

—Yeah?

—We're here.

—Yeah.

—It feels good, doesn't it?

—Yeah.

—I didn't think we'd make it.

—Seriously?

—Yeah. I thought we'd get taken back. I kept giving myself pep talks about what I was going to do if they tried to take us back.

—What were you going to do?

—I don't wanna talk about it.

—All right. I am gonna rest my eyes a little bit while you just sit there and look at things. Let me know if you see anything funny.

—I will.

—I hope they have canned peaches.

—After two weeks on the road on the way to a farm where they probably grow fresh food, you wanna eat canned peaches?!

—Yeah.

—Why?

—Because that's what I want. I want to pull the top off a can and fish the little peach slices out with my dirty fingers, and when I'm done I wanna drink the juice.

—That's not juice. That's chemicals.

—It's robot fruit . . . The peaches are the fruit . . . The can is the peel . . . And the chemicals are the juice . . .

—Hey!

—What?

—Wake up.

—I was just drifting off. I didn't even barely close my eyes.

—That scarecrow is wearing our hat.

—Whose hat?

—That hat is a god.

—That's the hat?

—We have to do whatever that hat says.

—So this is it?

—Yeah. This is definitely it. Let's go.

—Wait. What happened to waiting? Wait for me.

80

**Bobert and Tim knock on the door and
a little old lady answers.**

—May I help you?

 —Oh. I'm sorry.

 —Are you lost?

 —We're looking for our friends.

 —Well, they're not here now. But you're welcome to come in and wait for them.

 —Are you expecting them back?

 —Who?

 —Our friends.

 —I'm not sure I know who you're talking about. But I just took a fresh pot of chili off the stove. Why don't you and your brother come inside and have a bite?

 —How did you know he's my brother?

 —You have the same eyes. Identical eyes. You both look like you think I'm going to bite you. But I'm not. I'm not. Come inside and eat and we'll get this all sorted out.

 —This is a nice house.

 —Shut the door behind you.

 —Do you live here alone?

 —Yes. Ever since Justin died. Must be seven years ago.

—I'm sorry to hear that.

—No. No. I'm going to meet him by and by. Now sit down and eat some chili. No. Wait. You're filthy. Don't sit there.

—We've been traveling.

—You look like you've been hitchhiking.

—Walking.

—You look like you've been hitchhiking on garbage trucks. Let's all take a shower, shall we? You go first. And while you do I'll look to your brother's hand. The shower is upstairs on the left. Use the gray towel on the back of the door. Don't you dare use the yellow towel on the towel rack or there'll be hell to pay. I'll lay out some of Justin's old clothes.

—Uh . . .

—He's waiting for you to tell him it's all right.

—It's all right, Timothy. We're gonna be all right.

—Good, good. Now go on, Timothy. I want to talk to your brother alone while I clean his hand. Go on.

—Thanks.

—I'll set Justin's clothes on the chair outside the door.

—Thanks.

—You're welcome . . . He's very polite.

—Yeah. And so are you. Or, not "polite." You're very *kind*.

—It's the Christian thing to do. There's a Bible verse directing us to treat everyone we meet as if he or she were Christ himself. Can you imagine?

—Imagine what?

—If Christ knocked on my door and looked like you?

—I guess I can't.

—Well, I suppose you're supposed to imagine that you knocked on that door and Christ answered looking like me. What would *that* be like? What would that mean? You would have to treat him very nice and respect all his things.

—We will. We don't want to impose. But I was wondering. I think my friends may have visited you and I need to find them.

—Come over here into the kitchen where I can get to work on that hand. What did you do? The cut isn't that big, but it's just full of pus, isn't it? I'm going to get some hydrogen peroxide to pour on it, but first I'm going to have to milk it.

—Milk it?

—I'm going to squeeze on it until no more pus comes out. Now just stand there while I look up here for that hydrogen peroxide.

—Let me help you.

—Nonsense. I've been making do without Justin for seven years. I can stand on a chair and look in the high cupboard without any help. All right. Here we are.

—What about my friends?

—What friends?

—Did a big group of people about my age, some older, come through here in the last month or so?

—Those were your friends?

—Why, what did they do?

—I let them camp on my lawn overnight. A regular tent city.

—Were they polite?

—They were not.

—Where did they go?

—After they took what they wanted from me, they left in the middle of the night. It taught me a very valuable lesson.

—Do you know where they went?

—I think your friends are ne'er-do-wells. I think they were happy to live hand-to-mouth for as long as they could. No ambition. And no kindness.

—Maybe those weren't my friends.

—I hope not. But they taught me a very valuable lesson. Now, tell me if this water is too hot.

—No. It's all right.

—Okay. Does pain bother you very much?

—It bothers everyone, doesn't it?

—Oh, no. It doesn't. It doesn't bother me at all. Once Justin was hanging a portrait for me. And I was holding the nail for him. And something happened. I must've moved. Although I swear I didn't. I think he mis-hit the nail. But however it happened, Justin ended up hammering the nail through the middle of the tip of this finger.

—It sounds like it must've hurt quite a bit.

—Justin nearly passed out. But I just looked at it. I lifted it up in front of my face like this. I can still see it there. A nail driven clean through my finger. There wasn't a single drop of blood. And I didn't cry at all. I didn't make any noise of pain. What I felt was wonder. I thought, "Oh, my God, I have a nail through my finger." And then I picked up Justin's hammer from the floor. Justin was panicked. He was not a calm man. He kept asking me if I was all right. I had a nail through this finger. And I set my hand on the dresser there. And I hooked the claw of the hammer around that nail and I levered it to pull that nail out. Boy howdy, was that ever a mistake. That's when it started bleeding. That's how my finger got so mangled. You think a nail gets pulled out straight, but if board could talk they'd tell us that it's not so much the nails that hurt. They go straight in. It's pulling them out with that lever action that drags the nails sideways. Just think about it. It's enough to bend most nails and most nails are made of steel. Once I pulled that nail out, then I started bleeding something terrible. But I never screamed. Justin did all the screaming. I never made one noise of pain. I don't think I feel it like other people. My face stays as calm and serene as a picture. We were hanging that picture there.

—Is that you?

—It is.

—You're very beautiful.

—It was my wedding day. I was about your age.

—You look very calm about it.

—I was terrified on the inside. I was about to be changed forever.

—But it sounds like Justin was a good man.

—He was what the Lord provided. He was never cruel. Except the day he put a nail through my finger. Although that was an accident. And he was never good in an emergency. Some people put on a countenance in an emergency. Do you know what that means?

—Like you remaining calm about your finger?

—Exactly. It means you put on a face that says you can tolerate a situation. No matter how painful or dirty or filthy it might be. After I pulled that nail from my finger and it really started bleeding, Justin panicked. He started running around talking about going to get the doctor. So I had to walk over to this sink and clean myself up. Just the way I'm going to do you.

—All right.

—Now, I'm going to squeeze and open this up and squeeze until all the pus comes out. And then I'm going to hold it under the tap for a while. Then I'm going to squeeze again and we're going to keep doing this for a while.

—All right. Thank you very much.

—That's it. You've got your countenance on. Very good.

—I'm ready. I appreciate this.

—But wait. Even after I turn the water off, we're not done.

—All right.

—Because then I'm going to pour the peroxide on it and that's when I want you to be the most calm.

—All right. Thank you.

—Thank me when it's over. If you thank me then, then I'll say, "You're welcome."

81

Tim and the old lady eat dinner alone.

—That smells good! Oh, I'm sorry, I didn't know you were on the phone.

—That's all right. All right, then. Just as soon as you can. Goodbye. And hello to you. You look very nice, young man.

—Thank you. It feels pretty good to be clean.

—I would imagine so. Sit down. I'll get you something to eat.

—It smells good. I could smell it in the shower. I almost didn't wash my hair so I could come eat sooner. But the shower felt so good. I hope I didn't use up all your hot water.

—You can have as much as you want.

—Where's my brother?

—He went out for a walk.

—Why?

—I think he wanted to get his head together after we cleaned out his wound. The cut was deeper than he thought. And the infection was pretty far gone. I had to milk it a long time. And then I held it open and poured in hydrogen peroxide, and the wound was so deep it held it like a cup. But I shouldn't say that before we eat.

—Is he all right?

—I think he should go to the hospital.

—He's not going to.

—You never know what he might do.

—He might miss dinner if he doesn't come back soon. 'Cause I'm gonna eat it all. It all looks so good.

—Justin's clothes fit you pretty good.

—Can I wash my own clothes?

—There's no need for that. You just give them to me, and I'll do it tonight while you sleep.

—I can do it.

—It's no trouble.

—There's more than just the clothes I was wearing. We've been on the road for two weeks.

—And your brother has clothes, too, no doubt.

—But we can wash 'em tonight before we go to bed.

—Is there something in the pockets you don't want me to see?

—No, ma'am.

—What's the rush?

—I don't know when we're leaving and I don't wanna take your husband's clothes from you.

—Nonsense. He doesn't need them anymore. And they fit you reasonably well. But I don't want to think about you sneaking off in the night. For some reason that scares me. You sneaking around in the night. It's not a safe thing to do in this house. Once you go to bed, I expect you to stay in bed until I wake you up with eggs and bacon and coffee.

—That sounds too good to be true.

—Well, it isn't if you'll just stay in bed until I come and get you in the morning. And I'll wash your clothes and you can add my husband's to your pack. I imagine that's all you have in the world.

—It's true.

—When you meet someone with less than you, you should give to them until you're equal. If everyone did that, there'd be a lot less trouble in the world.

—The trouble is there's fewer ten thousand–dollar bills in the world than there are people. Not everybody can have one.

—Then we probably don't need them.

—I guess not. I never needed one.

—You need food. And blue jeans and a T-shirt and a bed.

—And I'm getting all that from you.

—And I'm happy to share them with you.

—You have a nice house.

—Thank you.

—I like all the wood, on the walls and the table and the chairs. You didn't cover everything in paint or wallpaper. Everything seems . . . authentic.

—It's old. That's what makes it authentic. Like me.

—Maybe there's something around here that my brother and I could do for you?

—What do you have in mind?

—Chores. Is there anything you need done around here? Do you need something painted or your lawn mowed?

—My lawn is one hundred and forty-eight acres. It's a ten-minute walk to the scarecrow.

—Well, we might have to sharpen the scissors a few times, but we could get it cut. I'm serious. We'll do something for you.

—That's very sweet. I'll think about it tonight.

—You think about it. 'Cause what you said is true. If you meet someone with less than you, you give to them. And there must be something my brother and I have more of . . .

—You have more of an appetite than I do.

—I'm sorry. Am I bolting my food?

—Don't be sorry. There was a time when it was a compliment to a woman if you asked for more of what she was making.

—Well, I might want to give you two or three compliments.

—I appreciate it.

—Is there gonna be enough left over for my brother?

—If we run out of chili, I think he'll find a valuable lesson at the bottom of the pot.

—You're funny.

—I'm just the way I am and as times have changed I've turned out to be funny.

—Why don't you come with my brother and me?

—Where is it you think you're going?

—I think we're going to go live the way things used to be.

—And what do you know about the way things used to be?

—That's why we need you. You can be our queen. If we have an idea for a barn raising or a barn dance, we'll come to you and ask if it's authentic.

—You and your brother are going to have a barn dance.

—We're going to meet those friends of his.

—And where is it you think they are?

—I don't know. We were hoping they were here.

—They were.

—Do you know where they went?

—There was a time when children your age didn't wander around the countryside. There was a time when there was work to be done.

—You tell us what to do and my brother and I will do it for a day or two.

—For a day or two?

—I guarantee that we'll work for at least one day. I don't know what my brother wants to do, but if I tell him I promised you a day, he'll let us stay and work it off.

—If he comes back.

—Why wouldn't he come back?

—I don't know. But his friends didn't. A single night was too long for them to stay. When I woke up in the morning, they were gone. And so were some of my things.

—I'll ask my brother if we can stay and work until you're paid back.

—We'll talk about it in the morning. Let me show you where your room is.

—Do you mind if I wait up for my brother?

—I'll show you where your room is and I'll start your things washing, and then if you want we can sit in the living room and talk until your brother comes back.

—He's gonna come back.

—I hope he does.

82

Bobert's conversation with the scarecrow.

—Funny meeting you here, Mr. Hat. Is the scarecrow a good boss?

—

—Yeah, well, it could be worse. You could be left with nobody, like me.

—

—My brother can't help me. He doesn't know where the others are. He's never even met the others. You know them better than he does. You're wearing a hat that belongs to one of them.

—

—Why do you think they left us here with this old lady?

—

—She's being cagey. She knows something. But she's not telling. And I'm not smart enough to trick her into giving me a hint. But we're close, aren't we?

—

—What should we do?

—

—Answer me.

—

—If you don't answer me, I'm gonna punch you in the fucking face.

—

—All right. You asked for it.

Punch. Punch. Punch. Punch. Punch.

—Oh, look, I knocked your fucking hat off. And it looks like there's one last little instruction inside. Maybe this is your way of saying what we should do.

—*Run. The old lady called the cops on us in the middle of the night. We sent the postcard earlier in the day. We all got away, but she's gonna do the same to you. Meet us at these coordinates: 34° 2′ 29″, 102° 38′ 41″*

—Fuck.

83

Detective Raphael and the little old lady talk.

—Where is the little boy? What did you do to him?

    —He's all right. He's under arrest.

    —Where?

    —He's in my car. Out behind your barn. I don't want to scare off his older brother.

    —I didn't call for you. I called for the sheriff.

    —Sheriff Hanson's here. He's out by the road. He's going to make sure no one gets away like last time.

    —I changed my mind last time. I told them they could stay here and camp in exchange for some work, and then I changed my mind.

    —Minds are like that.

    —I gave them dinner and showed them the place on the lawn where they were allowed to camp. But I couldn't sleep with them out there. I was afraid one of them was going to wander in to use the bathroom and scare me. I was afraid I might end up shooting one of them.

    —You did the right thing.

    —I started thinking, "What would Justin think about all this?"

    —He'd be glad you called the sheriff.

    —I don't know. He wasn't the sort to call the sheriff about his troubles.

    —You don't think so?

—No, sir. He would've got the shotgun out from under the bed and cleared those hooligans out himself. Screaming and hollering. The least calm man in an emergency.

—These kids are dangerous.

—So was Justin with a shotgun.

—Mrs. Thomas, with all due respect, it's not just kids we're looking for. It's grown men and women, too. We think they might be armed. And we know for certain they're dangerous. They burn down houses. They vandalize homes. And it's possible they're responsible for more than one murder.

—These boys wouldn't hurt anybody.

—Maybe not these boys. But the people these boys are trying to find.

—They just wanted somewhere to camp.

—Well, somebody's dangerous. Somewhere. So we have to be careful how we deal with strangers.

—You're the stranger here. I fed that boy. I ate a meal with him.

—He's going to be fine.

—I promised him dessert.

—Maybe you can bring it to him at the station.

—What if he gets out of the car and leaves?

—It's a police car. There's no way out of the backseat unless you have these keys on my belt. And besides. He's in handcuffs. Where's he going to go wearing handcuffs?

—I don't know. If he got away and he hid out in the forest and then he came back here in handcuffs, I'd free him.

—So now you've changed your mind again. Have you?

—I called Sheriff Hanson.

—You wanted the same thing to happen, didn't you? You wanted him to wheel up here with his lights on and scare the boys off and make them someone else's problem.

—I trust Sheriff Hanson. That's why I called him.

—I was with Sheriff Hanson when you called. I figured the boys were headed up this way. Someone else got suckered into their story, just like you, and tried to set me off in the wrong direction. But I figured the boys were headed north. Now I'm going to ask those boys to lead me to the others.

—Is that how you think this is gonna work?

—I don't think the older brother will leave his kid brother behind. But you never know. So I asked Sheriff Hanson to watch the road.

—He's probably out in the woods and never coming back.

—Well, like I said. I don't think Robert will abandon his brother. I think he'll come back, and when he does, I'll be sitting here, waiting for him. You can go to bed if you want to.

—I couldn't sleep.

—I guess not. How long ago did Robert leave?

—Before dinner.

—I bet he'll be back soon.

—What if I let the boys stay with me? If I say I don't mind and they can sleep in the upstairs room and do work around here?

—I know you're nervous. It always happens before an arrest. I'm nervous, too. But Robert's a good kid. Just as you suspect. And I'll tell him he's under arrest and he'll walk out to the car with me like his little brother.

—And you think they'll tell you where the others are hiding out?

—I do. And then we'll put the bad ones in jail and let the good kids go. Just like the old days. And then you'll be able to sleep at night.

—You're making a mistake.

—Shh. What was that?

—I said, "You're making a mistake."

—I thought I heard something. Like somebody at the window.

—I said, "YOU'RE MAKING A MISTAKE!"

—Shhh! Don't try to warn him. You can become an accessory.

—I'll be quiet. You tell me when I can talk.

—Robert! If you can hear me—it's all right. I have your brother. And he needs you. He needs you to come in to the station with him and answer a few questions.

Listen. Listen. Listen. Listen. Listen.

—He's not there.

—I guess not.

—Can I finish what I was saying now?

—Please.

—You're making a mistake.

—What's that?

—When you say things are gonna be just like the old days. And I'll be able to sleep.

—You couldn't sleep in the old days?

—You have no idea what the old days were like.

—I read a lot.

—There were people camped out in people's lawns quite often in the old days. And if someone needed a little work it was quite common for them to go around knocking on people's doors. That's how you started a new life. You just headed out into the world. That's how it was in the old days. That's why it was hard to sleep. Not because I was afraid of all the people traveling back and forth at night. But because I thought that maybe I should get up and join them.

—But you never did.

—Like I said. Justin was quite dangerous with his shotgun.

84

Timothy talks to Bobert from the back of the police cruiser.

—Timothy.

　—Bobert? Is that you?

　—Yeah. I'm over here.

　—Get out of here. She called the cops.

　—I know.

　—I guess it's pretty obvious, huh? Me sitting in the back of a cop car in handcuffs. Where are you?

　—I don't wanna step into the light in case he's got some sort of a trap set up.

　—I was just talking to the old lady, sitting there, and there was a knock at the door. I thought it was you.

　—But it was that asshole in the tweed jacket.

　—How do you know what he's wearing?

　—I just crept up to the window and watched him talking to her. That's how I found out where you were, where he parked his car.

　—You weren't scared he could see you then?

　—When people are sitting in a house with the lights on, it makes the window into a mirror. We used to sit and watch different houses like TV. I'm just being careful in case he comes outside.

—But how did you know not to just go through the front door?

—The scarecrow told me the old lady called the cops before. That's why everybody else isn't here. But they left us a new address.

—Tell me.

—No.

—Tell me and I'll come meet you there after I get out of this.

—They're gonna try to use us to find the others.

—I won't tell them anything. I'll just keep my mouth shut and after they send me back home I'll run away again and meet you.

—They would let you go and they would follow you.

—I'll lose them. We didn't know they were onto us this time. But now I'll know, so I can be trickier about how I move.

—Shut up.

—Fuck you.

—Shut the fuck up and listen to me, Timothy.

—What?

—Did you see anyone else?

—Just the guy in the tweed jacket.

—And he didn't talk about anyone else?

—He radioed someone that I was in custody.

—Probably the sheriff who's up watching the road.

—So there's just two of them?

—I don't know. I think so. What else happened?

—What do you mean?

—When the old lady let him in the house, did he draw his gun?

—No.

—What did he do?

—He asked me how I was feeling. He asked me where you were. He asked about your hand.

—How does he know about my hand?

—Maybe the old lady told him?

—When did she call the cops?

—Maybe while you were out and I was in the shower.

—What else do you remember?

—He just sat down, like it was no big deal.

—Did he say he was a cop?

—He asked about the others. He asked if I knew where they were. If they were coming here. And then he said I was under arrest.

—And that's it?

—He asked if he could put the cuffs on me. He called it a formality. I didn't even know what was happening. He was so calm. I just went along with everything. And then he said I should wait in the car and this would all be taken care of in a little while.

—All right. Wait here.

—Do I really have a choice?

—I'm gonna go take care of this and then come back and get you, and we're going to get out of here.

—You sound like him.

—I am. I'm calm. But there's one big difference between me and him.

—What are you gonna do?

—I'm gonna change.

85

The old lady tells Sheriff Hanson what happened.

—What happened in here?

    —I'm all right.

    —You're hurt. Don't move. Stay there.

    —I'm all right, John. It's not my blood.

    —Is he still in the house?

    —Put away your gun. The young man's gone.

    —There were two boys.

    —I know that. I'm the one that called you, John. I wish I hadn't, but I did.

    —So you think they're both gone?

    —Yes. That's what I think.

    —Where's Detective Raphael?

    —The detective's locked up in my front closet.

    —What happened in here?

    —They had a fight.

    —I'll say. Every last fucking thing in your house is broken or covered in blood, Ellie.

    —Don't open that door.

    —I thought you said the detective was in there?

    —I did. But I think the young man may have rigged it so that if you open the door the shotgun goes off and the detective's head gets blown off.

—What shotgun?

—The young man must've overheard me telling the detective about Justin's shotgun.

—Well, there's plenty of evidence—handprints on the door. Pretty small. How old is this kid?

—You'll have to ask the detective. He knew who they were.

—EMS is on the way. Can you hear me, detective? EMS is on the way! Don't worry. We'll get you out of there.

—I don't know that he's conscious.

—Oh, Jesus, Ellie. How bad is he hurt?

—He'll be all right. He's bleeding. But he hasn't been shot or stabbed or anything. The young man just gave him an old fashioned beating.

—What for?

—I guess the young man didn't like the detective's tone of voice, John.

—So he flipped over the dining room table and broke your dishes?

—The detective was condescending.

—What's that?

—He was talking down to the young man.

—Kinda like the way you're talking to me, Ellie?

—You were supposed to come, John. Not some impolite detective.

—He said he knew these boys. He talked big about how he knew how to handle 'em. And he sure did treat me like shit for letting the whole tent city get away three weeks ago.

—Well, now he's cuffed to the rod in my closet.

—I could kick the door down.

—I think that would set the shotgun off.

—How has he got it rigged?

—I have no idea, John.

—What happened?

—We were sitting here. The detective had already arrested the little one and taken him out to his car behind the barn—

—We should go get him.

—Let me finish. The young men are gone. If you let me finish, you'd know that.

—You want me to get you a warm rag or anything to wipe the blood off you?

—That'd be nice.

—Where are your towels?

—I don't know where the kitchen rag is. You'll have to get a towel from the bathroom upstairs.

—Go on. I'm listening.

—We were waiting for the older one to come home. And he did. He didn't knock on the door or make any kind of announcement. The young man simply walked in and went straight up to the detective. The young man knew what was going on. The detective started talking, and the young man just stuck his hands out in front on him about waist-high, his hands in fists, as if to say, "Shut up and put the handcuffs on me." The young man didn't look right. But then I don't know what a young man who's being arrested is supposed to look like—

—Here you go, Ellie.

—Not the good yellow towels, John. Although I'm glad to see they're still clean. There should be a wet gray towel on the back of the door.

—There's blood on the lampshade, too. It musta been a hell of a beating.

—The detective cuffed one of the young man's wrists, and then it happened so fast. That was what the young man was waiting for. As soon as that cuff was on one of his wrists, the young man started swinging that hand around, using the handcuff as a whip. He drew blood immediately. He hit the detective in the face. Maybe the eyes. Around the eyes. He drew blood and the detective couldn't see what was happening and I don't know that it would have mattered. The young man wasn't fighting the detective, he was attacking. Screaming. Flailing. Biting. Smashing everything. At one point the young man picked the detective up by the neck and threw him. He was so angry he didn't know what was possible and what was not. He whipped the detective to ribbons with his own handcuffs. When the detective covered his face, the boy kicked him in the stomach. When the detective protected his body, the boy hit him in the face.

—What did you do?

—Everything I just described happened in five seconds. I stood there.

—The boy didn't attack you?

—He never lifted a hand to me.

—But you're covered in blood.

—It was a hell of a beating.

—The kid picked him up by the neck?

—He went wild.

—All right, Ellie.

—Don't open the door.

—I don't think a wild child is gonna rig up a shotgun trap. I think you're lying to me, Ellie. I could be wrong. But I'm going to risk it.

—I wish you wouldn't.

—Oh, Jesus, Ellie.

—I told you. The young man beat him to ribbons. But he'll live.

—How do you know?

—Trust me. I've seen worse.

—And you watched this happen.

—To tell you the truth, John, I rooted for it.

—And then you stalled for time. You waited while this detective was bleeding like this. You waited for me to finally get bored out on the road and come wandering in to find out what was going on.

—I did more than wait.

—You probably spent a good hour making up what you were gonna tell me.

—Everything I told you about the young man was true.

—Except using the shotgun to booby-trap the closet. You probably gave it to the boy as a parting gift.

—I did.

—You know I am called on to do some detective work of my own, from time to time, Ellie.

—I know that.

—Don't treat me like a complete idiot.

—I'm sorry. Everything I told you about the attack was true.

—And then, after the boy left, you dragged the detective to this closet. That's how you got so bloody.

—You can believe what you want, John.

—What I believe, Ellie, is that the handprint on the door is too small to pick this detective up by the neck. I believe the boy beat up the detective and then you dragged the detective into the closet and hung him up by the wrist, with his own cuffs, to the closet rod.

—You can believe what you want.

—Jesus, Ellie. Jesus, Jesus, Jesus! That's your kitchen rag in his mouth.

—I want the young men to be free.

—Then why did you call me in the first place?

—I called *you*. Not this asshole.

—All right. Where are the keys?

—The young man took 'em to set his brother free.

—All right. I'm gonna pull the rod out and let him down. Then I'm gonna take the dish towel out his mouth, and I want you to use it to smear out your handprints on the other side of the door.

—All right, John.

—Jesus, Ellie. You're one step away from living the rest of your life in jail. You know that? It's a good thing it's me standing here before you.

—That's why I called you.

86

Timothy won't let Robert stop walking.

—Oh, no, you don't. Keep walking. We're getting away. I'm not gonna let whatever you had to go through go to waste 'cause you got tired. Put your arm around me. Don't fucking fight me. Sorry. Don't fight me. I can change, too. I'm helping you. You helped me. I'm gonna help you. We're gonna walk into these woods until they never find us. They're gonna have helicopters with searchlights looking for us soon. So we have to go farther than they think we could possibly go. We have to be outside their search radiuses or whatever. They're gonna draw a circle on a map and everything inside that circle is what they believe we're capable of. But you're outside that circle. Aren't you? And they're gonna have dogs that can find us by smell. So we have to wash in the next pond we come across. I might make you wash in every pond we come across. I might make you rub sage all over your body. So don't tire yourself out trying to fight me now, when I'm just trying to hold you up and keep you walking. You're gonna wanna save some fight for when I'm holding you down trying to change your smell. They have dogs that can get a perfect image of us from a shit we took last week. Think about that for a while. What item that you left behind at home most smells like you? I think if they were smart they would give the dogs my pillow. It's got sweat on it. And drool. And little bits of skin and hair. But they'll probably dig up my gym shorts or something. And for you, they'll probably dig up your old baseball glove. That's got five or six years of sweat. Remember when you used to play ball? Remember that? Dad played with you, didn't he? All right. Now you're walking a little better. Maybe that's who they should dig up. Give the dogs a little bit of Dad's smell and a little bit of Mom's smell and I bet those dogs could mix them together perfect into you and me. Step bigger now, we're starting to head uphill. I don't want you to trip. I bet you're trying to fall down. You think if you fall down in this cedar and brush it'll feel like a bed. You think if you fall down I'll let you lay there and sleep. You've got used to our schedule of sleeping through the day, but we're gonna keep walking. And if you fall down, I'm just gonna pick you up and carry you. So if you don't wanna do that to your little brother, then step bigger. We're going up this hill and we're staying in the thick part under the trees the whole time. No walking out in the open. And we're looking for a pond. We gotta clean you up. We gotta clean up that wrist. Your whole wrist is cut up. Looks like you were trying to commit suicide. I don't know what you did to get that wrist so cut up. But I got a good idea what you did to get your knuckles so cut open. You must have been something to see. Punching out cops on all sides. Just beating the living shit out of every one of 'em who was comin' for us. When I saw you coming back to the cop car where I was, I thought you were a monster. The way you were walking. You were stumbling and I thought you were drunk. You were covered in blood. And then when I could see your face—I was terrified. You looked fucked up. I wish I had a camera. You don't know how different you looked. The only people who'll ever know how fucked up you looked are the ones who saw you coming at 'em. Shit. Sorry. I bet you were amazing. Going after cop after cop, looking for the keys to the car where I was. You're lucky you didn't get shot. Or Maced or Tased or clubbed. Maybe you did. You must have been amazing. Big steps now. Good. Shhh. Hold on a second. Listen. Listen. Wait. Listen. It's nothing. You're lucky you didn't get Maced or Tased, huh? Although, how do I know? Huh? When we get to a pond or something like that, I'm gonna hafta undress you and give you a good going over. I need to make sure you don't have some sort of gunshot or stab or—what kind of marks do Tasers leave? Probably a couple of little burn marks like a little electric Dracula has been after you. Are you having trouble breathing? I'll slow down a little and you can try to catch your breath. But we're not stopping. Shhh. What was that? I thought I heard a dog. If we get caught by a bunch of dogs, that would just be too much, wouldn't it? Keep walking. It's starting to get light. Everything is going all black and white. It's a step up from everything being pitch-black. There's no moon anywhere, so I guess you're the kind of werewolf that changes in the dark. Maybe some werewolves are shy. That sounds like you. How long does it last? When are you gonna come back to me, Robert? I can't tell if you can't talk because of the change, or because you're hurt. Or because of what you had to do. You didn't kill anybody, did you, Robert? I don't care if you did, but if you did they'll keep looking for us forever. But if you didn't, then they probably just have to make a good show of it and then they can blame the cops who let you go. They probably won't admit to being beat by just one kid. They'll probably throw in the whole pack of your friends to excuse their mistake. I'll probably get into the story. They'll probably put me in the fight to explain how we could overpower 'em. They'll say they were dealing with you and I snuck up behind them and started swinging a baseball bat. They'll never admit I was sitting in the backseat of a car waiting for you. Hoping you would come back. I mean, I knew you were gonna come back for me. Just like when you ran away. But I want you to do me one more favor. I want you to come back to me one more time. Come on, Robert. Please? Don't die on me. Don't be hurt bad. Keep walking. And don't stay like this. There's no point in changing if you can't change back. Come on. Come on. Wait. Shhh. There's someone following us. Like a dog or something. I can hear it every once in a while. Hold on.

87

Timothy tries to kill the dog that's followed them.

—All right, Robert. You sit there. With your back against these rocks. I'm gonna take this stick and when that dog comes through that clearing, I'm going to kill it.

    —Wait.

    —What? Are you all right?

    —Wait.

    —I'm waiting. What? What do you want me to do?

    —Put down the stick.

    —No. You wouldn't. The dog is coming. And I'm not leaving you here.

    —Wait. Let me talk.

    —The dog is coming. It's right there.

    —Put down the stick!

    —Why?

    —I know that dog.

88

The dog licks Bobert clean.

—That's gross.

    —You wouldn't say that if you were a dog.

    —I'm just glad that almost none of it's your blood.

    —Just around the wrist.

    —Are you gonna be all right?

    —Now that my dog is here.

    —What's his name?

    —He doesn't have one. Or if he does, he hasn't told me yet.

    —You didn't name him?

    —He has his own name. He doesn't need one that I make up.

    —You think they left him behind when the old lady called the cops on them and they had to scramble.

    —I don't know. Why don't you ask him?

    —Oh, he talks now, too?

    —If you listen right.

    —What are we gonna do?

    —I'm gonna sleep.

    —Don't you think they're looking for us? Don't you think we should keep walking?

    —Let's vote. I vote sleep.

    —I vote we keep walking. Just one more day.

—What about you, dog? Haha. He's lying down. He votes sleep, too.

—You think we'll be all right?

—I dunno. But sleeping through the day and walking at night got us this far.

—Where are we going?

—These coordinates. 34° 2′ 29″, 102° 38′ 41″

—Yeah, but where is that at?

—I dunno. I guess we keep walking until we find a little town that will have a little library where we can look it up.

—I'm hungry.

—I really can't do anything about that, Tim.

—I know.

—Tomorrow.

—That's how they're gonna catch us.

—Maybe.

—We're not fully self-sufficient. We need food. We need a library.

—We could eat the dog.

—We can't eat your only friend.

—What about you? You still like me, don't you?

—I'm pissed that you won't keep walking.

—If you eat the dog while I'm asleep, you'll double the power of your vote.

—Maybe tomorrow. If we haven't been caught.

—All right. If we haven't been caught by tomorrow, we eat the dog.

—Fuck you.

—What?

—I'm glad you came and got me.

—Me, too.

—I didn't know if this was real until you did.

—Me, too.

—I was scared. I thought I was gonna go to jail and you were gonna disappear for good.

—If we disappear, we're gonna disappear together.

89

The smell of bacon and eggs and coffee wakes up Timothy.

—What's going on?

　—Tim, this is Susan.

　—Hi, Tim.

　—Are these your friends, Robert?

　—He calls you Robert? That's cool.

　—How do you feel, baby?

　—This is Tanya. That's Anquille. And I don't know all the others. Susan and Tanya and Anquille will have to introduce us.

　—We all start to blend in together as you get to know us.

　—You drink coffee, baby?

　—Yeah. And I eat the shit out of eggs and bacon.

　—He's kinda got a mouth on him, doesn't he?

　—I tried to get him to cut it out, but it's what distinguishes him.

　—He sounds a little like Angel.

　—No. He's nothing like that.

　—All right. All right. You like going by Timothy, or Tim?

　—Tim, I guess.

　—All right. It's nice to meet you, Tim. I'm Tanya.

　—How come *he* gets to say what he likes going by? I like going by Robert.

—But Bobert is what distinguishes you.

—Hi, Tanya.

—I want you to meet somebody special, Tim. This is Malcolm.

—No shit. I didn't recognize him.

—Yeah. He got a little fucked up by Angel.

—I thought if two werewolves fought each other, they both died.

—Some of us think Angel wasn't really werewolf.

—And some of us think we need to change that rule.

—The jury's still out.

—Is Malcolm still our leader? I mean, if you'll take me. Robert said y'all would let me into the pack.

—What exactly did Bobert tell you, Tim?

—*Robert* wouldn't tell me hardly anything.

—You gonna stick with "Robert" for your brother?

—Yeah. It's what he likes.

—All right, baby, Robert it is.

—You didn't answer Tim's question, Tanya. Is Malcolm the leader?

—I take care of Malcolm. He needs help eating. In return he whispers to me what he thinks we should do, and I share it with the group. I'm the only one who understands him.

—And he told you to send me that postcard?

—He told us to come here and get you.

—Why'd you tell 'em that, Malcolm? Why'd you come back for me? Mumble. Mumble. Mumble. Mumble. Mumble.

—He says you're one of us, Bobert. He says you belong.

—That's so cool. Come 'ere. Let me get a welcome home kiss.

90

Bobert asks himself a few questions.

Do you think she can really understand Malcolm?

Can you comprehend how serious it is that she came to get you? To save you?

You know what you did hurt people, right? What you did was wrong.

Should you find some way to send Tim back to Mom? It's not just Mom.

Do you think you could even get Tim to go?

Take your time, think back through your whole life. Nobody ever came to save you before, did they? Not like this.

This is it, isn't it?

91

As they pack up camp and head out, Timothy has second thoughts.

—Where are we going?

—We found a little place behind a NO TRESPASSING sign. There's no one there. Someone owns it, or some corporation, but nobody uses it.

—How far away is it?

—Why? You don't like being out in nature with your friends, Tim?

—I do. I'm just tired.

—Well, you'll be able to rest a little when we get there. But not too much. There's a lot to do.

—But why do I get to come with you? Is it 'cause of my brother?

—What do you mean?

—What if I'm not one of you?

—The story in the paper of what happened in the old lady's house makes it sound like you're one of us. The sheriff and the old lady say that the two of you stole a shotgun and overpowered the detective and went wild.

—Robert went wild. I was locked in the cop's car.

—I see. Well, you hang around us long enough and you'll change, too. And we'll do it right. We'll put you in a safe room and we'll get everyone to write down everything they can remember about what you were like before. And what led up to your change. And what you want it to be like when you come out of it. And then we'll sit down and read it to you. And at the end, they'll tell you all the rules of what it takes to be a werewolf. But first we have to get a move on. We started some crops, and some of us are gonna start families, and we need somebody to go out hunting for us. How does that sound?

—That's what I want. That's exactly what I want.

92

Rules for Werewolves

If two werewolves fight each other they both die, because every werewolf is the exact same strength as every other werewolf and werewolves can only fight to the death.

You don't have to get bit to become a werewolf, but it helps.

You become a werewolf by prolonged contact with other werewolves.

An actual physical change is required. It's not a state of mind.

A werewolf can't own anything because you have to be able to drop everything and run.

Eventually everyone will be a werewolf.

You don't have to have sex with a werewolf to become a werewolf, but it helps.

Never look at a werewolf during her first change.

If a werewolf is seen in a halfway state, she could get stuck or have trouble going back and forth.

If everything goes fine for the first change, the werewolf can decide when and where and how much she changes.

She can run faster. Eat less. Sleep lighter. Fuck longer. Like a wolf.

Money is bad for werewolves, especially coins.

In the same way you become a werewolf by staying in contact with other werewolves, you become normal by staying in contact with others who think they're normal.

A lot of the violence in this world comes from people who think they're normal resisting the change and trying to act a way that they aren't.

There is no first werewolf. It began with two people who each made the other feel this way.

When it comes to questions of violence, it's the person who's getting hit who gets to decide what's too much.

I think big cities are natural, the same way that an anthill or a coral reef is natural.

Werewolves live off nature. They look at your home and they see a nest full of eggs. Werewolves look at an unlocked car and they see a fruit tree. A grocery store is like a big woolly mammoth carcass lying on its side.

Sleep when you're so tired you collapse. Eat when you're so hungry you attack. Die when you're dead.

Every system has rules that conflict. Werewolves are the result of conflicting systems.

Keep writing down rules as long as you live.

The backyard is a wilderness. That shed in the garden is a cave. There are ten thousand hidden places in the city where no one ever looks.

Every werewolf is related for now.

We're new, so this is all new. All the rules are new. And we're still finding stuff out. We're like the scientists of whatever this is. And this is just what we have so far.

In the same way the moon changes, so do the rules.

If you feel trapped, run away. Running away is a form of attacking a trap. Run until you find other werewolves.

ACKNOWLEDGMENTS

Thank you to Carrie Fountain. To Emily Forland. To Mark Krotov and everyone at Melville House. To Corrine Hayoun. To C. C. Hirsch and Olivier Sultan. To Peter Stopschinski. To Madge Darlington, Thomas Graves, Lana Lesley, Sarah Richardson, Shawn Sides, and all the Rudes. To James Magnuson and Suzan Zeder. To Bryson Brooks. To Naomi Shihab Nye. To Steve Moore, Jake Silverstein, and Steven J. Dietz. To Adam Greenfield and Tim Sanford. To Michael and Rachel Feferman. To Anita and Freddie Lynn. To Julia Bathke. To Jenny Larson, Katie Pearl, and Salvage Vanguard who helped develop Part One of this novel. And to my students.

ABOUT THE AUTHOR

Kirk Lynn is one of six coproducing artistic directors of Rude Mechs theater collective. He is the head of the Playwriting and Directing Area in the Department of Theatre and Dance at the University of Texas at Austin, and received his MFA from the Michener Center for Writers. Lynn lives in Austin, Texas, with his wife, the poet Carrie Fountain, and their children.